BLUE FLOWER RED THORNS

A Vincent Malone Novel

TED CLIFTON

Blue Flower Red Thorns (A Vincent Malone Novel)
Ted Clifton
ISBN 978-1-77342-066-0

Produced by IndieBookLauncher.com
www.IndieBookLauncher.com
Editing: Nassau Hedron
Cover Design: Saul Bottcher
Interior Design and Typesetting: Saul Bottcher

The body text of this book is set in Adobe Caslon.

Also Available
EPUB edition, ISBN 978-1-77342-064-6
Kindle edition, ISBN 978-1-77342-065-3

CONTENTS

Prologue

The drive from Denver to Durango was six or seven hours, depending on breaks. But it seemed to take forever. Rick Flores was not one for being trapped in a car. His parents had taken him on a couple of long road trips to Disneyland and Yellowstone, and he'd been carsick most of the time. After that, he'd vowed never to torture his own kids, if he ever had any, with family vacations that only turned into unpleasant memories.

He'd been raised in Santa Fe by two of the nicest people who ever lived—even he would admit that. But it might have been better if they hadn't been so nice. Rick loved his parents, and they did their best to give him everything they could to help him be a success and to be happy, but he was embarrassed by them all the same. They were Mexican immigrants, and most comfortable around people from a similar background. Rick wanted to be an American, just like any other American from any background, without all the family baggage. His conflicted feelings on the topic weren't too noticeable as long as he was in Santa Fe. But going anywhere else highlighted them, which made him feel like a misfit. He'd feel ashamed of his parents, and then would hate himself for being such a lousy son.

"Look, Rick, if you don't want the goddamned job, that's okay with me. I recommended you because I thought you said you wanted something better than what you have now. So, I'm the bad guy, because I recommended you for a better job and gave them your number? Terrible, terrible me for causing you so much pain." Joe Small was loud and used a lot of foul language, but he was Rick's only friend.

"Joe, calm down, man. I appreciate that you recommended me. And yes, I want a more responsible job. But, Durango—I don't know about that. It reminds me too much of Santa Fe, you know—small, touristy town. I came to Denver to get away from Santa Fe, and I like it here."

"Well, then, fuckin' stay. Just stop bitchin' about your job if you're not going to do something about it."

The two men worked at Mountain Growers Inc., a marijuana-grow operation in Denver, with more than twenty thousand square feet full of plants. They were managers, supervising several dozen other employees who grew and harvested the crop twenty-four hours a day. Joe got the job because of his degree in horticulture from Metro State, where they'd met. He'd helped Rick get a job after he graduated with a degree in business management. The pay was good, even if it always felt odd to Rick to be paid in cash. But most things about the legal marijuana business were a little odd. Still, he could put up with a little odd, given the money people were making. Even so, the job was mindless work. Each day seemed to involve telling the same people how to do the same job they did the day before. It was like everyone who worked there woke up in a new world every day. He wanted more.

"I talked to that guy, Ken Simpson," he told Joe. "He said they wanted to get going immediately, and if I wanted the job, it was mine, but I had to decide by tomorrow. Something about him made me nervous." What he thought, without saying it out loud, was that this whole thing seemed too good to be true. Suddenly people nobody'd heard of wanted to hire him at top dollar to do a job he had very limited experience with. That didn't make sense.

"Well, hell," Joe grumbled, "I don't know anything about him. He and some other asshole came around talking to everybody about opening a grow facility in Durango, saying they were hiring. The guards ran them off, but I got his card. I called him and told him about you, thought it would be great to get that kind of experience. Go down there and get the thing started, and I bet you can come back here and double the money you're making now. Nobody in this industry has any experience, except shit they can't talk about. What makes you nervous about the guy?"

"It's stupid." Rick frowned. "He reminded me of a TV hoodlum, maybe from the sixties or seventies. A Broderick Crawford kind of tough guy."

Joe looked at Rick like he was nuts. "Who the fuck is Broderick Crawford?"

"Just an actor, played a lot of bad guys. He mumbles when he talks."

"Oh, now I get it. You won't work for a guy who mumbles, right?"

Rick gave up. He decided he was being stupid. He should take the job, and if it didn't work out, he would just come back to Denver. He could always get a job, and at least he would have taken a risk, for once. He knew he was usually way too cautious.

In spite of his concerns, he called Simpson, aka "Mumbles," and told him he would take the job. Simpson gave him directions to the building in Durango and told him the company would reserve a room for him at the Traveler's Inn for a week from that day. That seemed awfully fast. He told Simpson that he had to give proper notice to his employer.

"You want the damn job or not?" the man mumbled.

It put him on edge again, but he'd made up his mind he wasn't going to let his nerves get to him. He gave a week's notice. His boss was pissed, but told him if it didn't work out, he should come back. Rick was a good, reliable worker—and sober.

Rick had a lease on his apartment, which he didn't want to give up in case things went south, so he paid a month in advance and told the landlord he was going to be gone for a while. There was a lot of demand for apartments in the area, so if he decided to stay in Durango, he was pretty sure he could sublet.

The first part of the drive had been a little bland, but for the last few hours he'd passed through some impressive mountains covered in vast forests. He had an urge to take one of the side roads and explore the beautiful scenery, but he stayed on task and on the highway. By the time he reached Pagosa

Springs, he was getting tired of being cooped up in the car. The great thing about traveling off the interstates was that the highway usually passed right through the towns along the way. That was the case with Pagosa Springs. Spotting a parking spot in front of the Peak Deli made up his mind for him—time for lunch. The small town was surrounded by the San Juan Mountains, with woods stretching in every direction. For no particular reason, he felt safe here. Maybe he should just stay. *Stupid thought*, he chastised himself. He needed a job, and working at Peak Deli wouldn't be a good career move. He enjoyed his pastrami sandwich stacked high with seasoned meat, and got back on the road.

The beautiful drive reminded him that he hadn't seen much of Colorado since he'd moved to Denver four years before. He'd tried skiing one very forgettable afternoon, quickly gave up all hope of becoming a Super G champ, and hadn't ventured out of Denver since. Living downtown, he felt very urban chic. He spent most of his free time enjoying the restaurants and bars in his neighborhood. He would mostly go out alone, and usually ended the evening the same way. He had a few dates, but his quiet, reserved manner wasn't exactly that of a chick magnet. Once in a while he'd spend time with Joe, but the guy was a drinker and usually more trouble than he was worth. He knew if he was ever going to find a girl, he'd have to be a bit more assertive. But it didn't come naturally.

Some of his most enjoyable days were spent visiting one of the many museums in Denver. It was his regular outing on Sundays, with the Denver Museum of Nature and Science being his particular favorite. He'd even signed up to be a volunteer, but hadn't heard anything. He would spend hours visiting exhibits, all of which he'd already seen, often many times. He took comfort in the building, the exhibits, and the people. Everything combined to make it feel like a welcoming place. He'd even met a girl there once, and they'd enjoyed a great time together, laughing as they walked through almost the entire massive museum. She'd given him her number but he'd never called, afraid she would reject him. Carol Lawson. He still had her number.

He entered Durango at long last, and it surprised him a little. It was more urban than he'd expected, with more traffic than he wanted. But it was not Santa Fe. The buildings had some Spanish influence, but were more western-looking, and rugged. It had a comfortable, outdoorsy atmosphere, with a lot of bars and restaurants catering to tourists—a resort town much like Santa Fe, but with a Colorado uniqueness. Following the directions, he'd been given, he quickly arrived at the Traveler's Inn. It wasn't luxurious, but it seemed nice enough, and it was busy, with a full parking lot—always a good sign. He checked in and found there was an envelope waiting for him. Once he was in his clean, pleasant room, he opened it.

Cash. He counted it, and it came to ten thousand dollars. He'd heard of large cash bonuses given to employees in this new and confusing industry after a successful year, or to mark a major milestone, but a large bonus before he even started? *Man, something's not right.*

He called Simpson, but was sent straight to voice mail. He

left a message saying he was in town, and that he wasn't sure what the money was for. His voice sounded weak and whiny in his own ears. It crossed his mind that maybe he should just take the cash and run. *Nope—stupid, stupid, stupid.* The next logical step was to go to the grow facility and see if someone was there who could explain things.

Just a short distance from downtown, the touristy charm of western mining-town buildings and lots of foot traffic gave way to an industrial section that wouldn't have been out of place in many of the less-than-desirable neighborhoods in Denver. The directions Simpson had given him didn't seem very accurate, so he entered the address into an app on his phone. A short time later, he was parked in front of a nondescript building. It had just one sign, which read, "For Rent." He could feel his desire to take the job waning rapidly.

He tried the front door, but it was locked. He walked around the side and spotted another, next to a loading dock. It was unlocked.

"Hello, anyone here?" Rick cleared his throat and tried again. "Hello, this is Rick Flores, anyone around?"

"How the hell did you get in here?" The gruff voice came from a very large man with an ugly scar across his face and a menacing look in his eyes.

"The side door was unlocked. My name is Rick Flor—"

"I don't give a fuck who you are. Get the hell out of here now, before I decide to hurt you. And I mean right fucking now, asshole!"

Rick's heart rate was definitely racing as he slammed the

car door and immediately pulled away. *What the hell was that all about?* He knew some people in the marijuana business were still paranoid about the feds, and even about local officials who sometimes decided for themselves what was legal and what wasn't. But that guy was nothing but a thug.

He went back to the Traveler's Inn. Once in his room, he hooked the chain lock and drew the drapes. After a few minutes of thinking, he decided to get the hell out of Dodge—or Durango. He'd go back to Denver. This was just too bizarre and threatening. He wasn't sure what to do with the money now, but decided to turn it over to the Denver police once he got back. He wasn't familiar with Durango, and wasn't sure if he could trust the police. And all he wanted was to go home.

He was packing his stuff into his car when two oversize Durango police officers approached him.

"Goin' somewhere, asshole?"

The cop's grin wasn't friendly. Even for someone used to dealing with police, which Rick wasn't, this wouldn't be a good start.

"I'm—I'm just going back to Denver. Is there something wrong?"

With a swiftness he hadn't expected from such a large man, the second cop shoved Rick up against his car and began a search. He pulled out the envelope with money.

"Well, looky here. We got our guy red-handed."

"I don't know anything about that money. It was left at the front desk for me by my new boss, but I don't know what for." Even to him, it sounded stupid.

"Right. Just a little gift." The cop pulled out a card and pretended to read Rick his rights. "You're under arrest, asshole, for grand theft and conspiracy to defraud. If I were you—and I'm so glad I'm not, you little prick—I would call a good attorney, fast."

"No. This can't be right." *Stupid, stupid! Man, I knew this mystery job was too good to be true. Shit!*

1

Home Again Maybe

Santa Fe, New Mexico

Vincent Malone pulled into the Albuquerque airport with a load of passengers from the Blue Door Inn, ahead of schedule. It was a minor victory, but Vincent was of the view that, as difficult as life could be, every little win should be counted, so he cheered silently to himself while he maneuvered the van to the curb. The Albuquerque airport was called a "Sunport." Vincent wondered for the umpteenth time just what in hell that meant. He was convinced there were groups of people who sat in dark rooms all day long, dreaming up this kind of nonsense just to mess with the rest of the world.

"Careful, Mrs. Johnson. Watch your step."

"Oh, thank you, Vincent. Be sure and tell Cindy and Jerry we had a wonderful time at the Inn. They're great hosts. We'll be back, real soon."

Vincent helped the departing guests carry their luggage to check-in, said his goodbyes, and quickly got back onto Interstate 25, headed north toward Santa Fe. It had been months now since he'd escaped his crumbling life in Denver and, while passing through Santa Fe, taken on the unlikely role of driving a van for a new bed-and-breakfast.

That was how he marked the end of more than thirty years in Denver working as a private legal investigator, helping attorneys find facts and evidence—and occasionally helping them lose either or both. He'd fallen into the dubious life of a PI after falling even further, from a respectable, blossoming career as a young Dallas lawyer into a big pile of shit. From that aromatic pile, he dragged himself to Denver, minus one attractive wife, one law license, and just about everything else. After some on-the-job training, he discovered he was actually a very good investigator, and settled into a routine of working, drinking, and then working some more. His ultimate downfall had come by way of his health, as a victim of gout.

Vincent never played well with others, so his investigation business had been a one-man band, by design. After he developed gout, the flare-ups began to leave him bedridden, with no backup plan. His clients soon lost patience and said *adios*—no clients, no money, no future. His plan had been to pull up stakes from Denver, which was expensive, and head for cheaper housing in Phoenix. If he could find a know-nothing job for a few years, just to make ends meet, he would reach Social Security retirement age, and be done.

But he'd only gotten as far as Santa Fe. The driver job at the Inn was definitely know-nothing, but he was quickly thrown into the middle of a murder mystery involving the first guests there. He'd found himself suddenly energized, and most surprisingly, he developed an unexpected friendship with the Blue Door Inn owners, Jerry and Cindy Oliver.

He soon felt like he belonged in Santa Fe—if not forever, then at least for a while. Vincent was cynical enough for a small army, but he pushed back against his natural tendencies only to see the bad side, and tried to relax. Life got better, though his curmudgeonly ways were only intermittently dormant, rather than dead and done with.

Arriving at the outskirts of Santa Fe, his face seemed to soften. He decided to take a slight detour to drop in at the Crown Bar downtown, not far from the famous Plaza. Back in his drinking days, it would have been part of a daily routine, but his drinking was more or less under control now. This visit was more about love than liquor. Nancy McAllen owned the bar. Her late husband had bought it as a retirement investment, although he also simply loved spending time in bars. He'd been a cop. One night he opened the wrong door, and died. Maybe partly as therapy, and partly out of financial need, Nancy took on the bar and made it into a landmark in Santa Fe, a favorite watering hole for local law enforcement. She'd spent years in mourning, but finally was becoming more comfortable with herself and the tragedy she'd gone through. And although she was in her early fifties, she still got admiring stares from male patrons.

She and Vincent were in the throes of trying to figure out whether they might be compatible. Given some of Vincent's qualities, it was like being attracted to a thorny bush—you really had to be careful you didn't get hurt. But there was no doubt she already cared about him.

"Hey there, Mister Malone. How are you this fine day?"

Nancy was glad to see him, and gave him her best smile.

"Well, aren't you cheerful? What makes this such a fine day?" He had to work at being anything other than grumpy, but he was getting better at it.

"Three reasons. First of all, you're our twenty-second customer today, so you get a free beer. Second, I need to be cheerful to offset your gloominess, otherwise the universe will be out of balance. I forgot the third reason."

Vincent actually laughed. "Free beer ought to cheer up anyone. I'll tell you what—if you have time, I'll buy *you* a free beer."

It wasn't a match made in heaven. But they were trying, and that counted for a lot.

"Back from your Albuquerque run?"

"Yeah. The last guests were all such nice people. I'm not sure how they found out about the Inn, but Cindy and Jerry were a great hit. The guests couldn't stop saying nice things about them, and about how they were already planning on coming back."

"Is Jerry still doing most of the cooking, or is Mary doing more now?"

"Well, actually, that's a problem. Jerry can do some things, but they've started offering a light lunch. It's a convenience for some guests who don't want to go all the way into Santa Fe for lunch, and then again for dinner. So, Mary's been fixing that, plus helping with breakfast. And she's starting to have trouble keeping up with her cleaning."

"Well, that fits right into what I wanted to ask. Do you

think they'd consider hiring someone to help with the cleaning? A cousin of mine—actually, I think she's my late husband's cousin, although the whole relative thing gets mixed up unless I sit down with paper and pencil and draw a family tree, and anyway, that's not important—she has a niece who's visiting her from Houston. She asked me if I could give her a job, because she thinks she needs to do something other than be on her phone all the time. She had some boy problems in Houston, and her mother shipped her out here, under threat of being disowned. The cousin here says she's a sweet girl, though, and thinks the whole problem may be the domineering mother. The point is, I can't hire her at the bar, because she's only twenty. So, I was thinking maybe the Olivers could use her help, as a maid or whatever."

"Sure. They might. I'll ask. What's her name?"

"Mariana Garcia. And not that it matters, but she's absolutely beautiful."

"Hey, good looks helped me get my job." Vincent often hid his sense of humor well, but it was always lurking around his rough edges—especially around Nancy. It was nice that he could chat so easily with her. She made him feel good, and he enjoyed her company. He was still shocked that he could find someone at his age. He'd thought he was done with relationships, apart from, maybe, health care providers.

He said goodbye, and headed to the Inn, outside Santa Fe in a forested, hilly area dotted with mostly high-end homes. The Blue Door Inn was enchanting. Set down a small, narrow lane, a newcomer's first impression could be almost magical. Jerry and Cindy had invested a lot in the property, and it showed. And while it wasn't Vincent's business, it still felt like home to him, even if his personal space was a single small room. He was proud of where he worked.

Entering the kitchen, Vincent found Jerry staring at his laptop, reading a recipe. "What are you makin'?"

"Blueberry-walnut banana bread." Jerry looked concerned. "The thing is, we have no guests right now, so I'm thinkin' about experimenting a little and tossin' in some chocolate chips—what do ya think?"

"I'd say, toss away. Saw Nancy just a little while ago. One of her many cousins has a niece visiting from Houston who needs a job to keep her busy. Nancy said she could do cleaning or whatever you need. Her name is Mariana Garcia. Would you be interested?"

"Hell, yes, we'd be interested. We've got that Dutch artist and her entourage coming in a few weeks, and as of right now, Mary's barely talking to me because I keep asking her to do more. When can she start?"

"I'll call Nancy and let her know. Do you want her to come by and interview, or what?"

"Nah. Nancy's recommendation is enough for me. Just a minute, let me ask Cindy."

"Ask Cindy what?" Cindy asked, coming in just then. Jerry told her about Nancy's cousin's niece.

"Oh, by the way, Nancy said she's gorgeous," Vincent put in. "Not sure if that's good or bad." Vincent was being honest. Hard workers were often not the most glamorous of people.

Cindy gave Vincent a look he couldn't quite interpret. "I agree with Jerry," she said. "We need somebody, and I'm fine with relying on Nancy's recommendation. Tell her she has the job, and see if she can show up starting tomorrow."

"What's the deal with the Dutch artist?"

Cindy took over and began to beam. "This could be a huge deal for us. I met Anna Marks at one of the women's groups I've been going to, and she asked me if we could have them as guests, and host a showing here at the Inn. Anna owns the Howard Marks Gallery on Canyon Road, and according to a few people I've talked to, it's one of the most successful galleries in town. I don't know anything about art, so I didn't have a clue about what a big deal this art show was. This guy at the paper—I swear he's the biggest gossip in town, and I always blank on his name—he said that this was on an international scale. Apparently, this young woman from the Netherlands is quickly becoming a huge deal in the art world. Anna has booked every room with us for more than a week, and she's scheduled a small private reception here, with a special showing of a few pieces. What shocked me was that apparently rumors are flying that if all of the paintings in the show sell, it could bring in over ten million dollars."

"What's the artist's name? Have we heard of her?" Vincent asked.

"Her name's Ilse De Vries, but unless you follow contemporary art, you wouldn't know her name. She's in her mid-twenties, and something of a wild child, according to the newspaper guy. He said she'd had affairs with lots of famous people, mostly movie stars—of both sexes. And she's had some bad press about her drug use."

"I wonder if she's interested in mature, sophisticated, older gentlemen?" Vincent managed to say it with a straight face.

Cindy laughed. "Well, before you get your hopes up, you should know she's traveling with her mother. On kind of a troubling note, the guy at the paper told me in complete confidence—which probably just means he can't publish it—that the Marks gallery could be in financial trouble. He said if this show isn't a huge success, they might be at serious risk of going bankrupt."

"Ouch. Does that mean we should get our money up front?" Jerry asked. So far, they'd only been stiffed once by a guest. But Jerry worried about money incessantly, even though he and Cindy were reasonably wealthy, living off the proceeds from the sale of a software business he'd built up over many years. Vincent once asked him why he seemed to worry about money so much, given they were loaded. He'd said it was an old habit he found hard to break.

"I already told Anna we have to have half the cost up front," she said, "especially since they're renting the entire Inn. That was before I heard about their finances. But even so, I'd say we're okay. As long as we have half the fee, that'll cover all our costs, easily. And, who knows? Mister Gossip may be saying similar things about us. He doesn't seem to be the most reliable person."

"I'll call Nancy and let her know about the niece having a job if she wants it. Sounds like we could use the help. How many guests will there be?" Vincent asked.

"Nine altogether. Only three are in the artist's group—Ilse, her mother, and her manager. But Anna wants six of her best customers to stay with us, too. I think she chose us because she lives in the area and it's convenient to have them close, but not have to deal with putting them up as houseguests." Cindy thought a moment. "I think our biggest challenge will be the reception—that could go as high as forty people, which is pushing our limit for space, and it's way beyond our capacity for preparing and serving food. I'm thinking it might be best to get that part catered. I've met a couple of caterers in town, and several of them have offered generous discounts to get us to try them."

Jerry didn't look happy. "I'm not sure about having events catered. Does that say that we can't handle our own business?"

"I think what it says, *is that you're smart*," she replied.

Vincent gave Jerry a look that warned him not to bite off more than he could chew. Jerry and Cindy continued their event planning while Vincent stepped into the dining room to call Nancy. He returned a few moments later. "Got hold of Nancy, who talked to her cousin, and Mariana Garcia will be here tomorrow. And Nancy said she used to work for a catering company, but it was as a driver."

"Everybody's a comedian." Jerry shook his head as he headed into the kitchen.

Vincent grinned at Cindy, then went outside to admire the gazebo and the beautiful gardens while he smoked one of his two nasty cigarettes of the day.

Smoking is almost as addictive as obsessively making notes, even mental ones, at the end of each day. You're not an investigator anymore, Malone! I keep doing it, anyway.

There's a real comfort to my life right now, and that has me very nervous. Bad shit always seems to sneak up on me when I least expect it. If I'm already in the shit, then I don't waste too much time worrying that more will come along—the bad stuff has already found me. But, when things are going well? I sure as hell don't deserve Nancy, which means that trying to have her will probably result in some kind of train wreck. That's the law in Vincent's world.

2

Ollie Ollie Oxen Free

Amsterdam, North Holland, The Netherlands
Some Months in the Past

The sun was sneaking in through the shaded window with the promise of a bright, beautiful day. Ilse had been up for hours, working at her computer. She was in touch with people all over the world via Facebook and Instagram, and a few special admirers by email. If she could be said to have friends—and that was a big "if"—it was this faceless crowd of adoring fans who reached out to her every day, fawning over her and praising her. She never tired of it. Many of them were art lovers, but most were celebrity worshippers. Being famous, even in a small circle, gave Ilse power. And she adored power.

She stared out the window of her room in an upscale boutique hotel. Behind her, she could hear the shower running, while in the square below she could see a fountain, which later in the day would attract kids, all running and laughing. She was always comfortable in her city. Unlike many major metropolitan areas of the world where conflict was common, Amsterdam seemed at peace with itself.

By contrast, she was tired of all of the conflict in her life.

She regretted her fling the previous night with her American gallery owner, Anna Marks. Anna was ancient by Ilse's standards, and tiresome. She wasn't sure why she'd even slept with her—just a lark, more or less. But poor, sad Anna now claimed to be in love with her, which made Ilse want to puke. She had done more stupid things than she could possibly remember, but most of them while she was drunk or high—or both. She forgave herself those things since, in a way, it wasn't really she who'd done them. Not the same person who woke up in the morning, anyway. But this nonsense with Anna was just her being controlling, having some fun when there was nothing better to do. She'd gained very little, and now she had to pay the price of dealing with Anna. It was going to be difficult—mostly for Anna.

She still needed Anna for a few more months. Her out-of-control life had recently begun to cost more than she could afford. Even being the hottest new artist on the contemporary art scene didn't mean unlimited money rolling in, and she'd spent a lot in a short time. Her evil witch of a mother and her poor, long-suffering manager constantly scolded her, but she ignored them. She knew her manager, Dirk Jensen, meant well. However, he'd earned a place on her shit list because he agreed too often with her mother. And her mother, the useless lump, had lived off men for most of her life, including Ilse's father—husband number two in a sequence of four. But years had passed, and men weren't interested anymore, so she sponged off her disrespectful daughter, instead. Ilse had asked her repeatedly to leave, but Bente Smit had nowhere to go.

In her place, a normal person would at least shut up and stop criticizing the gravy train—but not Bente.

Now Ilse needed money, pronto, and Anna was the answer. The showing she was setting up in Santa Fe, New Mexico, could generate as much as three or four million for Ilse if everything went as planned. That would fill up the money hole, and give her plenty of cash to do whatever she wanted. The Howard Marks gallery hadn't been the biggest one to approach Ilse about representing her in the United States, but they'd made the most generous offer on commission splits. Dirk had been opposed to doing business with the Marks gallery because of a recent scandal over forged work, but Anna convinced Ilse that the gallery had reached an out-of-court settlement to end the harassment of a lawsuit, and all that was completely over now. According to Anna, the gallery hadn't done anything wrong—it was the victim. Between that and the substantially smaller commissions Anna was willing take, Ilse signed the contract for the show. The biggest event would be in Santa Fe, presumably because Anna lived there, but that didn't really matter. Most international buyers were comfortable traveling to Santa Fe for shows like this. The city was one of the biggest art markets in the world. After that, there would be smaller shows in New York, Dallas, and Los Angeles. Ilse was confident that Anna would hit her sales targets, which meant she had to find a way to put up with her for a while. Not that it had required having sex with her—Ilse had seduced her to gain a greater sense of control. She liked controlling people.

"Good morning, sweetheart."

God, Anna was already clinging. She was a tall woman with a no-nonsense, short haircut, shot through with touches of gray. She was pretty, but in a plain way, with a slender figure. Her age was showing, and she'd reached the point where she was trying a little less to hide it. Her striking, intense blue eyes still conveyed a keen intelligence, but around them a few crows' feet had begun to show.

"Anna, I don't want to be mean, but I'm not your sweetheart. Look, it was fun, okay? But I'm not looking for a relationship. It was an impulsive thing, that's all. Plus, we've got way too much going on with the business. We don't want that to get all confused with personal stuff."

Ilse was young and emotionally unstable, but she was beautiful, with a gorgeous body she put to good use, both for pleasure and to get things she wanted. At the moment she was dressed in nothing but a loose T-shirt, showing herself off. She was a little shorter than Anna, but to Ilse, it felt like she was taller—like she dominated.

Anna just stared. "I'm sorry, did I do something wrong?" Her face was forming itself into a pout—not attractive.

"Please, let's approach this like adults. I think it would be a big mistake for us to start a personal relationship at this point—at least, wait until the show is over. This is too important to both of us, financially and professionally—we can't take our focus off the show. Let's be friends for now. Then, maybe after the show is a huge success, we can take some time and see if there's anything else. What do you think?" Ilse didn't really care what Anna thought. She just wanted to pacify the older woman until she had her money. After that, she'd be only too happy never to see the pitiful old hag ever again.

"Yeah, I guess you're right," Anna agreed, if a little glumly. "This is really important. We shouldn't let our personal feelings get in the way. You're so smart for someone so young—and so beautiful." Anna was in love, and confused about her sexuality as well. She'd never been with a woman before. At that very moment it dawned on her that she actually wanted to leave, to get out of the little hotel room. She was afraid, and didn't know why. "I think I'll just get my things together and head back to my hotel. Might be best if I got an early flight and started getting everything ready for the show."

"Sounds smart." Ilse turned back to her computer and forgot about Anna completely.

Anna knew her feelings for Ilse were wrong. She also knew Ilse was an evil little brat. What she didn't know was why she was so attracted to the little monster. She had taken a cab back to her modest hotel, and once in her room she'd begun to cry, and found it hard to stop. She crawled into bed and slept for several hours, woke at dusk and took a shower. Feeling better, she called the airlines and managed to move her scheduled flight to New York City to the afternoon of the next day. Once everything was set, she went back to bed and slept until morning.

As soon as she woke, she ordered room-service breakfast

and made her first call.

"Howard Marks Galleries. Trent Taylor here."

"Trent, this is Anna. Change of plans. Headed back to New York this afternoon, won't get in until late. Staying at the Belvedere. Meet me in the morning for breakfast at the café in the hotel, say around nine. I want an update on our finances and what it's going to take to put on this De Vries exhibition. Okay?"

"Sure Anna, I'll be there. Everything okay? You sound a little down."

"Fine. I'm just tired. Ilse's a handful, but I've got it under control. We've got to do this show right, no mistakes. I'll see you tomorrow."

If Anna had listened to Trent four years before, they wouldn't have been dealing with this mess. The financial side of the business had always been her weakness, but its current trauma had been the result of too much confidence in her instincts regarding art. Anna had grown up in the business, with a domineering father who didn't tolerate mistakes. She'd been under his thumb for most of her life. So, after he suddenly died of a heart attack, she went a little wild. Her father's rules, expectations and demands had always felt like huge weights she had to bear. With all that gone, she wanted to prove her worth, and maybe even prove she knew more than he ever had. The opposite happened. She knew the business as well as anyone, but she was taken in by some very clever people.

It was no mugging. It was the most sophisticated type of crime there is—art forgery. She was the victim, fleeced by expert criminals. But what hurt the most was the publicity. Patrons who had bought the forgeries sued. Ultimately, she'd been able to settle the suits with out-of-court agreements that stated the Howard Marks Gallery did no wrong. But it had been extremely costly. Paying out that kind of money was the most humiliating thing Anna ever had to do, and it was soul-crushing to put at risk the business her father had spent his entire life building. She had to make a lot of money off this show, or she might as well be dead.

Anna called the gallery in Santa Fe, but no one answered—not surprising, considering the time difference. She left a message. "Clive. Change of plans. Taking an early flight to New York this afternoon. Will meet with Trent in the morning and then I'm headed back to Santa Fe. Won't arrive until very late tomorrow night. Want to meet with you the next morning, early. I want to know every detail of the De Vries exhibit—and I want details, Clive, not your usual bullshit. I know we're getting a lot of blowback because of the lawsuit, but you have to pull every trick you know to get people to this show. It has to be a success, or you can kiss your cushy-ass job goodbye."

She hung up. Clive Walton was the artistic director for her galleries. She'd hired him after the forgeries. He had a well-deserved reputation for recognizing new talent, and even more importantly, a huge following of art patrons. She was overpaying him, but having him on board was essential to calm the hubbub after the forgery nightmare. Still, he was probably the prissiest and most annoying man she had ever met, and if he didn't have all the details she needed and everything teed up properly when she got to Santa Fe, she just might fire the little twit.

Anna spent much of the day thinking about what she really wanted. She hated the pressure of running a business her father had built to suit himself. He'd loved to travel, so having several galleries in different locations around the country was ideal for him, but not for her. She hated travel, and just wanted to stay at home. And while Anna loved artists, they changed once they had some financial success—every one of them seemed to turn into a whore, in it only for the money.

When Anna had first gotten her feet wet in the industry, she'd worked with up-and-coming artists and put on small, intimate shows that targeted patrons of the arts, not financial investors who frequented the more famous artists' larger exhibits. She knew that money drove the industry, and recognized the hypocrisy in criticizing the influence money had while she lived a lavish lifestyle, but none of that changed the bottom line; the money detracted from the art. The art became secondary, as if it was nothing more than one more valuable commodity mined out of the earth, rather than the creative output of brilliant human beings. She wanted to get back to the part of the art world that loved the work more than the money.

But, she wondered, was there any point in thinking about the future? Was it already too late? The terrible weight of dealing with the diagnosis that she hated even to think about, plus the enormous need for money was crushing her. She knew she could not go on much longer, especially alone. Still, even with that immense burden, she was not ready to give up. She was going to fight to her last breath.

Of course, she could only do that with money—lots of money. She promised herself this would be the last big show. She would sell or close all the galleries except the one in Santa Fe. She would rebrand it under a different name, and focus on emerging artists—maybe even sell the million-dollar house and live a simpler life. She didn't want to be anything close to poor, but she was tired of worrying every minute of every day about money.

Already beginning to feel better about herself, she had made a profound decision that would change her life. She was determined to carry it out. All she needed to make it happen was one more big success. The De Vries exclusive exhibit at the Howard Marks Galleries had to be a huge hit. Nothing else mattered, and she would do whatever she had to do to make it happen—and if that little brat Ilse wouldn't cooperate, Anna would strangle her. She smiled, but it had something of an ugly sneer in it.

3

Worry Me Sometimes

Santa Fe, New Mexico

On some days, Vincent had duties at the Inn that required him to get up early and get with it. On most days it didn't matter too much when he got going. But, being a proud man and totally denying his age and need for more sleep, he would always try to be the first one up. No one seemed to notice—but he did, and that's what mattered. Today was not one of those days. Today he felt older than he wanted to admit. He woke up sore and achy, with a slight congestion, and rolled over for an additional thirty minutes of sleep before he got up to head for the kitchen. He hoped everyone else overslept, too. Pushing open the kitchen door, he confronted the entire household of Jerry and Cindy along with Hector and Mary. They were sitting around the large kitchen table, with looks of doom on their faces. It was obvious Mary had been crying.

Just because I'm a little late? That's not the end of the world. "What's going on? Something wrong?"

"Vincent, can I talk to you a minute?" Jerry was getting ready to steer Vincent out of the kitchen.

"It's okay. Everyone can stay." Hector sighed and looked

down at his shoes. "He will know soon, anyway. Our son was arrested in Durango. He called this morning and said he needs help. We don't know what to do."

Vincent frowned. "Arrested for what?"

"He said it was some kind of theft, and something to do with conspiracy. I really did not understand all of what he was saying. But I could tell he's scared. Is there something you can do?" Hector was a proud man, and asking for help did not come easily to him.

"I can sure try." Vincent gave Hector and Mary a reassuring smile. "I thought your son was in Denver. Was he just visiting Durango?"

"We thought he was still in Denver, too. He told me on the phone that he'd taken a new job in Durango, and he had not said anything to us because he was not sure it was going to work out. He said he was arrested when he arrived in Durango, and that he thinks there is something wrong with the new people he was going to work for." Hector usually never talked this much. He looked worn out from the effort.

"It's probably a little early to get much done, but I'll make some calls and see what I can find out. I'm going to call Peter Tucker and see if he has any connections in Colorado. If not, I know some people in Denver who can make an appearance in Durango quickly. Or they will know a Durango attorney. Okay?"

"Mister Vincent, we don't have a lot of money. We can't afford a big-time attorney like Mister Tucker."

"Sure, I understand. Tucker doesn't need any more money,

so if he can help, it won't cost anything. Anyone else I talk to, I'll make sure it's very reasonable. This would be just to get something done today—find out what the status is, and how we can get your son out of jail. We just need someone local to get us information. It won't cost much, and don't worry about it." Vincent wasn't sure whether he should say not to worry—he sure didn't have a bank account full of money. But worrying now was not going to help. Plus, he had a lot of dirt on attorneys in Denver if they didn't play nice.

"Hello, good morning. Should I just come in?" Someone had entered the front door.

Cindy jumped up. "Must be our new employee." She headed toward the front hall. "Good morning, you must be Mariana."

"Yes, ma'am." Mariana was obviously a little shy. She also was beautiful. She gave Cindy a nervous little smile.

"We're so glad you're going to help us. We're a new business, just getting started. That means we really don't know what we're doing, yet," Cindy chuckled. "Let's go into the conference room and we can go over employment forms, your pay and your schedule. Will that be okay?" Mariana nodded slightly, and seemed to relax a little.

"Hey, you must be the gorgeous new employee hired to replace me. My name is Vincent. Nice to meet you." Vincent extended his hand and, after Mariana's slight hesitation, shook hands with her. If she'd been a turtle, she would have withdrawn into her shell after quickly taking her hand back. She gave Vincent a wary look.

"Vincent, please, try to be on your best behavior. Sorry, Mariana. Vincent is our resident comedian and sometimes van driver. You are not replacing him, although maybe we should consider it."

Mariana seemed to pick up on the good vibes. She smiled warmly at Cindy and just a little at Vincent.

"Sorry," Vincent apologized. "Mariana, you are going to love it here, even if Cindy is a tyrant to work for. See ya later, and welcome aboard." He headed to his room to make calls.

"Everyone else here is much nicer than Vincent." Cindy winked at Mariana who rewarded her with a small giggle. Cindy liked her already.

"Give me a call back if you can find out anything." Vincent disconnected. He had given Peter Tucker the information he had, along with the Flores' son's name. Tucker said he knew a firm in Telluride, and thought they also had an office in Durango, and they owed him, "big-time." He would call and see what he could find out, and call back. Tucker was in his early seventies, and had more or less gone into the woodwork after a long career as a gun-for-hire defense attorney with a long list of clients associated with organized crime.

In his past, Tucker was referred to by New York tabloids as the "mob fixer." His whole career was driven by money, and only money. After some bad press associated with his ability to get the worst people on the planet released from legal jeopardy by using every dirty trick in the book, he was smeared as being complicit in deaths caused by the bad guys he helped spring loose. He was wealthy beyond belief by that point, and feeling some remorse for a life based on no values other than accumulated wealth. He bought a mansion in Tulsa, Oklahoma, and hid from his notoriety until his nephew was accused of murder in Santa Fe. He swooped in to try to make amends for his past ways. That was how he became acquainted with Vincent, and they became kindred spirits of a sort. He had since moved to Albuquerque and was taking on a few cases to keep from withering into dust before his time was up.

Vincent's phone vibrated. "Yeah."

"Got hold of the desk sergeant. Not much help there. But Rick Flores is still being held with a charge of grand theft and conspiracy. He did tell me there was an arraignment hearing later this morning. Called my contact in Telluride. He said they'd have someone at the hearing, and call me afterward. So, for now, probably best to just wait. Even if I could get over there, which I can't that quickly, not much I can do until we know what is going on."

"I agree. We wait. Thanks."

Cindy introduced Mariana to Mary, and talked about how they should go over what Mariana would be doing. They seemed to bond immediately. No doubt Mary was glad to have some activity to take her mind off her problems, and she made

Mariana feel very comfortable. They went off together to go over the Inn's layout and the various responsibilities Mariana would have.

"Well, that could not have gone better. Mariana is a lovely young woman who is very polite, and she and Mary hit it off immediately. I think we may have a winner here—need to thank Nancy for recommending her." Cindy was feeling better about the day, even though she still was concerned about Rick Flores' problems.

"That's great," Jerry agreed. "Maybe Mary will start talking to me again. What do you think about that stuff with their son?"

"Don't know. We haven't met him, but if he's anything like his parents, I just can't imagine him doing anything illegal."

"Yeah, I know. Hector told me his job in Denver was working for a grow facility where they harvested marijuana. Hard to realize that's legal in Colorado, but illegal in New Mexico or Arizona. Seems odd. You can go to jail in Santa Fe for doing something that is a smart career path in Denver."

"I know. It just seems crazy." Cindy was not against things changing as society changed. It was just the strangeness of having one set of laws for one state while the neighboring state had another.

"Malone."

"Vincent, it's Tucker. Got some information. Bond hasn't

been set yet. The grand theft probably is not that unusual of a charge, but the conspiracy to commit fraud is. And apparently that charge is based on a sworn statement by the guy who hired Rick. That's caused the judge to want a hearing on the bond amount. The guy who hired Rick—his name is Simpson—stated that Rick must have known he was going to do this from the beginning, and set him up. What has been stolen, or is missing, is a semi-trailer loaded with marijuana plants and a bunch of very expensive equipment to build out a grow operation in Durango. Simpson said it was worth over $250,000. He does not think Rick actually stole the truck. He thinks he was paid by someone for the information. And tying that all together was an envelope Rick had on him with $10,000 in it when he was arrested, which he said was left at the hotel front desk for him, and came from Simpson. Simpson told the cops he didn't leave any money for Rick. Bottom line is, not much we can do until the bond hearing, which will be in two days. I've hired the Telluride firm to co-counsel with me, so I plan on being there for the bond hearing. Tell Hector and Mary not to worry about money. I'm sure Hector would be upset if he thought it was charity—just tell him there's no cost at this point. Do you want to be there?"

"I do. I looked earlier, couldn't find any direct flights. The cheapest and best connection is from Albuquerque through Phoenix. Driving, it's about four hours from Santa Fe, so I think that's what I'll do. Want to ride along?"

"Nah. I also looked at flight schedules, and while it will take a little bit longer with the layover in Phoenix, I think I'd rather fly than be stuck in the car with you for four hours. Once I get a ticket, I'll call and let you know when I'll be there, and you can pick me up. How's that?"

"I'm sure my feelings are hurt in some way, but I'll get over it." Vincent was grinning.

"I'm working off an assumption that the incredibly nice Hector and Mary Flores would not have a son who would actually commit these crimes, right?"

"Nice parents don't always mean nice kids. But it would be shocking to me if those two could raise someone who would even be rude, much less involved in conspiracy to commit fraud." Vincent paused a minute. "This is really strange. I've been having an odd feeling that this whole mess has happened before. Can't put my finger on it, but something feels really familiar."

"It's the Santa Fe air. That *deja vu* feeling happens to everybody. Doesn't mean shit."

"Yeah, maybe." Vincent was thinking. "That name seems familiar." There was a moment of silence. "I got it! Ken Simpson, right?"

"Ken Simpson, right. Didn't I tell you his name?"

"You just said his last name. I know that sonofabitch. This is not good. I need to get up to Durango, fast."

4

Travelin' Man

"How 'bout a road trip?" Vincent's nature was to be direct, even over the phone—an approach often ill-advised while dealing with women, including Nancy.

"Where to?" she asked.

"Durango."

"When?"

"Oh, 'bout an hour."

"Vincent, you're just a bad child. You can't ask a woman to go on a trip to another state—with all the implications that carries—and say you're leaving in an hour." Nancy's tone sounded annoyed, but he knew her a little by now, and was confident it was a put-on.

At least, he hoped so. "Yeah, guess that's not enough time." He told her what was going on, saying he thought he'd better go to Durango right away, because he'd had dealings with one of the people involved, and it hadn't been even close to a good experience.

"Give me fair warning and ask in a conciliatory, polite manner, and I might, just might, go on a road trip with you at some point in the future," she said. "But even if I decided to ignore your manners, I couldn't go today. Got a health department hearing. It's some stupid violation I've already fixed, but I have to show up and show them the proper respect if I want to avoid a penalty. Call me when you find out anything. And be careful, Vincent. I know you're a tough guy, but you don't have to keep proving it."

Vincent would have dropped to the floor in shock if Nancy had said yes on such short notice. But inviting her was a way to establish something without actually establishing something. He smiled, thinking he'd been clever this time— usually, he wasn't. He'd already loaded his Mustang and gone over his plans with Jerry. He hoped to be back the day after next. Jerry asked him to call right away if he learned anything. With a sly wink, he also gave Vincent a very nice advance on his salary. "Don't worry about your expenses. The Inn will take care of everything. Don't tell Hector or Mary, though. This is just between us."

"That's good of you Jerry." Vincent shook his hand. "By the way, the Taj Mahal was booked, so I'm staying at the same place Rick was—Traveler's Inn. And it's cheap." Vincent grinned and felt a real comfort with his new friend.

If it'd been a straight shot from Santa Fe to Durango, the trip would probably have taken about half the time, but there were mountains to deal with. Although it was going to take longer, the scenery was magnificent. He headed out on Highway 84 through Espanola to Abiquiu, where Georgia O'Keeffe use to live and work, to Chama and then into Colorado. From Pagosa Springs it was a more or less direct line west into Durango. Vincent, being primarily a city creature, had never seen so many trees in his life. He definitely wanted to do this same trip again at a more leisurely pace, with Nancy.

Entering Durango wasn't quite like venturing onto an old West movie set, but it wasn't far off, either. Much of the downtown area was obviously devoted to the tourist trade, and had been designed to evoke a past age. He found the Traveler's without any trouble at the south end of downtown. He'd made a reservation, so checking in was quick and easy. Next stop was the attorney's office.

Tucker had made arrangements with the Maxwell Franks Law Firm to co-counsel with him on the matter, but never said why they owed him "big-time." Their main office was in Telluride, another resort town, but they had a satellite office in Durango with a local attorney, Chet Morgan. That was where Vincent was headed. *Tucker's a big-time gunslinger,* Vincent thought. *Why would he have dealings with a small resort-town firm?* He shrugged it off. There was a lot about Tucker he still didn't know, and Tucker didn't always share details about his past.

According to his phone's mapping app, the law office was only a few blocks from where he was now—ah, the joys of a small town. The Maxwell Franks Law Firm was in an ornate, three-story building. Based on the directory, it seemed to occupy the entire top floor. He took the stairs to stretch his legs after the long drive, and found himself in a small reception area with a young, male receptionist, or maybe a law clerk pulling double duty.

"May I help you, sir?"

"Hello, my name is Vincent Malone, here to see Mister Morgan."

"I'm sorry sir—was he expecting you?"

"I don't have an appointment. I'm working with Peter Tucker on a case, and wanted to stop in and introduce myself. Only take a minute."

"Of course. The problem is, Mister Morgan has already left for the day. Would you like to make an appointment for tomorrow?"

The man's manner seemed odd to Vincent—like he was lying. Why would he lie?

"Sure, that'd be great. Say, first thing in the morning?"

"Well, Mister Morgan has court most of the day tomorrow. It looks like his first free time would be about four tomorrow afternoon."

The clerk smiled, but he didn't actually seem friendly, and the odd feeling Vincent got from him persisted. Faced with this little boy's bland refusal, he could be polite and friendly, and bow and scrape, and maybe someone would be kind enough to give him a minute of their valuable time. Or he could be himself.

"I don't know what kinda fuckin' game you're playing, but I will not play along." The receptionist suddenly looked alarmed, maybe even afraid. "You call him, or go into the back and find him, and you tell Morgan to call me. If he doesn't have the time to handle this matter, then he *and* you *and* this law firm can fuck off. Got it?"

Vincent scribbled his number on a pad and gave it to the gaping clerk. On his way back downstairs, he questioned what he'd done, but pushed his doubts away. He knew from experience it was generally best to establish yourself right off as an unreasonable asshole, so nobody made the mistake of thinking you were a tolerant guy who would allow them the option of treating you like shit. His phone vibrated before he could reach his car.

"Malone," Vincent said, his tone too loud and angry, intentionally.

"Mister Malone, my clerk got that all messed up. Sorry about that. I'm in the office, if you have a minute."

Vincent bit back the urge to lay into the voice on the phone. It wasn't in his nature to play games. He tended to address things bluntly, head-on, so it wasn't easy to hold back. But he thought about Mary and Hector, and forced himself to bite his tongue.

"Sure, I'll be up."

When he got back upstairs, the clerk was gone. A very short man, who weighed maybe two-eighty, was waiting. He looked very nervous—something was still amiss. Vincent needed to call Tucker and get a better handle on this law firm, because he was not impressed so far.

"Morgan?" Vincent extended his hand.

Morgan stepped forward and shook it, he led Vincent into his opulent office. If wealth could always be equated with competence, Vincent would have had a lot more confidence in the firm.

"Once again, let me apologize. We weren't expecting you today. This is a little awkward for me, because my boss was going to call Mister Tucker. But I guess he hasn't yet."

"Who's your boss?" Definitely something wrong.

"Well, Mister Franks Junior, of course. I don't believe he actually knows Mister Tucker—our dealings with Mister Tucker in the past were with his dad, Mister Franks Senior. Anyway, we agreed to be co-counsel on this matter with Mister Flores, but it turns out we have a conflict of interest. So, we're going to have to withdraw." Morgan stopped there. Apparently, that was supposed to be the end of the story. Good-bye.

"What's your conflict?"

"I'm not at liberty to tell you that, Mister Malone. It might be best if Mister Tucker called Mister Franks Junior and talked to him."

"You know we're going to find out, so why don't you stop playing games, and just tell me what the fuck's going on?"

"Mister Malone, we don't use that kind of language in this office, and I don't appreciate your aggressive attitude."

Vincent couldn't help himself, he laughed, then kept laughing as he got up and left. Outside he called Tucker, who said he'd call the young Franks and then call back. It didn't take long.

"Malone."

"Looks like the young Franks is a real jerk. Something's changed since I talked to him—my guess is money. He said they only belatedly realized that one of their clients has had some dealings with Simpson's company, and that they'd have to withdraw as co-counsel. I'll find out what this is about, and I will definitely hold a grudge. But for now, we need a new local attorney. Can you find someone while you're there?"

"Sure. Everything about my exchange with that Franks firm seemed off. They're hiding something. I have no idea how it might affect Flores, but we need to be careful. I have a feeling there's a lot more going on here than we know." Vincent's bullshit meter had been in the red through the whole encounter.

"Find someone to co-counsel, and let's try and get the kid out on bail. Then we can focus on these assholes."

"You got it."

Vincent had spent years dealing with attorneys and their clients. He knew one place he could be sure to get the information he needed; a bar. And if you wanted a tough, no-nonsense criminal lawyer who would fight to the death for clients, you wanted the local biker bar. It took only a brief stop at a restaurant and bar that catered to tourists, and twenty bucks, to find out where he should go—Mel's Roadhouse, a few miles south of town on Highway 160. Once he got there, he could see he was in the right place by the number of Harleys parked out front.

The place was dark, and it took a few moments for his eyes to adjust so he could avoid colliding with anyone, so he paused near the door. He headed to the bar once his eyes focused. The bartender was huge and buff, and had what appeared to be battle scars on his face and hands. Life hadn't been kind to him, but he looked like he probably gave as good as he got.

"What do ya want, pal?"

"Tecate."

The bartender moved with surprising speed for someone his size, and Vincent updated his impression of the man—he would be a lot to handle if you made him mad. He took out a twenty and a ten and put them on the bar. Bartenders can see money from a hell of a distance, even in bad light.

"Nice tip?"

"I'm looking for an aggressive, smart lawyer to handle a local matter. Thought you might know someone." Vincent gave the man his best smile, which friends had sometimes uncharitably compared with a sneer.

The bartender nodded. "Yeah, I might. For that price, he'd be second-tier, though." A successful bartender was usually skilled at assessing how much you'd pay for whatever it was you needed.

Vincent laid down another twenty.

"George Younger is the only lawyer in this part of the world if you need someone to go to war for you. Most of the locals work in a herd, like they all belong to the same social club. Prosecutors and defense lawyers in this town will pretend to go at it in court, then go drinking together after hours. George doesn't give a shit about other lawyers, or anyone else—he just gets shit done. If I had my dick in the dirt, he's the asshole I'd call."

"You, sir, perform a very valuable service to your community. Thank you." Feeling relieved, and uncharacteristically generous as a result, Vincent dropped an extra ten. He got

Younger's phone number and headed out. It wasn't exactly business hours, but for any criminal lawyer worth his salt, that wouldn't matter. He called.

"Yeah."

"Mister Younger, my name's Vincent Malone, and I'm looking to hire an attorney who knows his asshole from his elbow. That you?"

"That's kind of a low bar to set—must not be a very hard case. Will I get paid, or are you going to try to screw me?"

"You'll get paid. You'll be local co-counsel for Peter Tucker."

There was a moment of hesitation. "Thought that bastard was dead."

"He was—for a while. Now he's back. Old, but just as fuckin' mean as ever."

"You drink beer, Malone?"

"I do." Vincent liked this guy already.

"Meet me at Steamworks Brewery Company on Eighth, just off Main Street, in about thirty minutes."

"I'll be there. How will I know you?"

Younger chuckled. "Look for a big, ugly guy. How about you?"

"Look for a big, ugly guy."

Vincent headed to the Steamworks Brewery. He considered stopping by the Traveler's, but there was no point. He'd be a little early, but that was okay. He liked the hybrid restaurant and brewery the moment he got inside. It was designed to be rustic, and looked like it had an extensive selection of beers, some brewed on site—and, from what he could see, some wonderfully unhealthy bar food that he really shouldn't sample, but undoubtedly would. He settled in at a table, quizzed the waiter about the various beers, and ended up with a Backside Stout, which came highly recommended. In just a few minutes, the waiter had brought him a tall, frosty glass. He took a sip and smiled.

"Great recommendation, that is wonderful. Thanks." Vincent relaxed and reflected on his day. He still had more questions than answers, and he had a bad feeling that Rick Flores might have stumbled into real trouble.

"Hard to tell because you're sitting down, but you look like a big, ugly guy. Vincent?"

Vincent stood and shook the firm grip of a man who was about his size. They might easily have turned it into a contest, but why would you do that? "Hey, you're not so ugly. Great choice of bar. This place is fantastic."

"Yep, this is my favorite. Plus, I only live a few blocks from here."

The waiter came and greeted Younger like a regular. He ordered a Steam Engine Lager, and Vincent made a mental note to give it a try. Then Younger got down to business. "So, what brings you to the fair city of Durango?"

Vincent told George the whole story, even digressing a little to provide some of his personal background. Some people you can trust immediately, and George Younger was one.

"I knew your name was familiar. I had a case in Denver once, and you were recommended to me if I needed an investigator. Turned out I didn't. My client skipped bail and disappeared."

They discussed various connections and people they had worked with in Denver.

"Do you know anything about the Maxwell Franks Law Firm?"

"Sure. Big-shot attorneys out of Telluride. They also have a small office here. They don't travel in my circles—or, more accurately, I don't travel in theirs. Mostly corporate law, with a small criminal practice to help clients who get in trouble. I heard that at one time, when the father ran it, they were considered one of the best firms in the country. But now that Junior's in charge, their reputation's gone to shit. I've never met the man, but I've been told more than once that Franks Junior thinks he's some kind of gift to humanity. He's also very dangerous."

"Dangerous? How?"

"At least three people who were directly connected with that guy in Telluride and Durango have died under mysterious circumstances. None of the murders has been solved. The bar talk from the bikers is that Franks is really just a thug in a suit."

Hit a home run with Younger. Just the kind of no-bullshit lawyer we needed. He also told me there's absolutely no reason for someone to build out a large marijuana grow operation in Durango. Some weed is sold there, but it would be a lot cheaper just to ship it from Denver. The real estate would be less expensive in Durango, but the water and electricity would be a lot more expensive than in Denver, and it takes a lot of both. Sounds like young Flores was somehow scammed, but usually a scam victim doesn't end up with ten grand in cash.

5

Good Times, Bad Times

Vincent got a text message from Tucker asking to pick him up from a private flight early in the morning, so he drove out to the small municipal airport at what felt like the crack of dawn.

"You open the vault and rent an entire plane?"

"You know what, Mister Wiseass, I think I probably saved a few bucks. Plus, I got here in record time. I called the FBO at the Albuquerque airport and asked about short-term rentals, and the guy said they had at least one plane going to Durango almost every morning, and the pilots would usually take a passenger or two for a token payment. They're not supposed to have passengers who pay, but a nice contribution to offset fuel costs is welcome. And having a little company on the flight is a bonus."

"I apologize for ever questioning your frugalness."

"So, what do you know?"

Vincent covered what had happened since he'd arrived on the way into town, giving high marks to George Younger. The bond hearing was scheduled for that afternoon. Younger would try to see Flores in the morning to make sure he knew someone would be at the hearing. Then they would meet up with Younger for lunch to discuss what he'd learned. He also gave Tucker more details about his uncomfortable encounter with the Franks Law Firm.

"What's your best guess on what's going on?" Tucker asked.

"First, nothing really fits well, so anything I say could be way off. I think Flores was set up as a fall guy for something. The only thing we know at this point is that a truck with lots of stuff inside is missing. Maybe he was supposed to be blamed for the missing truck, but that doesn't hold much water. Was he supposed to have hijacked it by himself? How would he have done that? So, I think the idea is that someone else did it, and they paid him ten thousand dollars for the information they needed on the truck—where it was supposed to be, and what was in it, and all that. It seems like a lot of money just for information, though. So maybe he was supposed to be framed for something else, something that didn't end up actually happening. I don't know. He had ten grand on him. If the money was just part of a frame so there would be some evidence, that's a lot of dough to throw away. That would suggest a big crime, bigger than the truck, but we have no idea what. All the cops have is the complaint by Simpson claiming that a truck is missing, and the money Rick had on him. I don't think they actually have any evidence of a crime being committed at all, much less something they can use to hold Rick."

"Call Younger and see if we can get in to see Flores. This feels all wrong, like someone is pulling strings, for some reason. Find out who the judge is, and the DA, too. Get me some names so I can check with some people." Tucker seemed energized and ready for action.

Vincent got Younger on the phone. "Hey George, this is Vincent. In the car with Peter Tucker. He'd like to see Flores before the hearing, if possible. How do you think we should proceed?"

"I tried to see him this morning, and the normally friendly jail clerk told me no one was seeing Flores before the hearing, on orders from the DA. So, I guess the only approach is to go through the DA, guy named Bill Jefferson. He and I have butted heads before, but he always seemed like a straight shooter."

"Okay. Could we meet you at your office?"

"Sure. I'm a one-man show, so it's nothing elaborate."

Younger was in a nondescript building mostly otherwise occupied by real estate agents, with a central reception area—not fancy, but functional. His office was an exception—it took up most of the top floor. The receptionist said Mister Younger had just arrived and that they should go on up.

"Come in, guys. Just straightening up a little. I'm a slob by nature. Used to have some partners until we disagreed. Should move into something smaller, but too damn lazy. Don't know how, but it seems I end up making messes in every office." He steered them to a conference room. "Have a seat."

After quick introductions and handshakes, Tucker pulled a document out of his briefcase. "This is a pretty standard co-counsel agreement. Look it over, and if it's agreeable, we can sign. Once it's signed, we can bind our deal with this retainer."

Tucker handed Younger a check.

George looked at it and raised his eyebrows. "Who do I kill to earn this?"

"If you don't accumulate enough hours, just hold onto the balance," Tucker said. "Maybe I'll need your assistance in the future." The man knew that one way to command loyalty was to pay for it.

"Thanks." George looked at Vincent and smiled.

"I made a couple of calls and got good reports on Bill Jefferson. Just as you said, a straight shooter," Tucker said. "Why would they hold Flores when they have such limited evidence that a crime's even been committed?"

"Somebody pulled some strings. My experience with the police department here hasn't always been positive. They have a very political perspective on how they deal with offenders. If you're on their good list, they follow the book. But if you're on their shit list, they turn into the Gestapo. Of course, a lot of my clients are on the shit list—bikers, old hippies, street people, anybody who's not part of the establishment. Flores has been identified to them as a drug guy, and even though it's weed and it's legal, he's still a drug guy, in their eyes. So, it's the shit list for him."

"Vincent told me you didn't think it made sense to put a large marijuana grow operation in Durango because of limited demand and high cost. Any idea why they would have told Flores they were going to do that?" At this point, Tucker was gathering info and collecting possible explanations. He didn't expect a precise answer.

"Just because it doesn't make good economic sense doesn't

mean someone might not do it. People do stupid stuff all the time. That guy Simpson is known in these parts as a hustler, but as far as I know, he's not into anything illegal. He's connected with the Franks Law Firm in some manner, apparently a good friend of Franks Junior. I've heard from some locals, after a few drinks, that Franks Junior has lots of things going on in Denver—things he wouldn't want his mother to know about. Not sure what that really means. Could be it's just bar talk." George shrugged his huge shoulders, signed the co-counsel agreement and handed it to Tucker, who also signed. They made copies, and agreed to head to the courthouse to wait for the hearing.

It was only a short trip, so Vincent and Tucker decided to walk. Younger said he would meet them in a little while. The air was cool, with a slight breeze, making the world seem fresh and clean, and they had a pleasant, mostly silent, walk.

"Thought you were going to storm the jail doors earlier to see Flores," Vincent said, finally. "Change your mind?"

"Yeah. I think this has nothing to do with anyone specifically targeting Flores—he was just arbitrarily selected to take the tumble. For what, who knows? But the goal is to get Rick out of jail, and that's best done in court. I think we can get him released, since I doubt they've actually charged him. And if they *have* charged him, then we should be able to get him out on his own recognizance. If the judge had the reputation of being in someone's pocket, I might take a different approach, but that doesn't seem to be the case. So, it's probably best to simply play it straight and by the book."

They entered the courthouse, passing through the metal

detectors. The judicial offices were on the third floor. Tucker had Vincent wait while he went in to see if he could talk to the judge's clerk. He was back in only a few minutes. "Very nice lady. Apologized for the jail officer refusing to let Flores meet with his attorney. She said she'd pass that information along to the judge. She also said we could see Flores now. He's here. She made the call, and they're expecting us."

"You didn't have to threaten her." Vincent was grinning.

"My guess is that if I'd threatened her, I might have been at some physical risk."

They followed the clerk's directions and were soon in a small, windowless, cinderblock room with Rick Flores. They introduced themselves.

At the mention of his parents, Flores almost lost his composure. "I didn't do anything, and I have no idea what this is about. Can you get me out?" He spoke quickly, very tightly wound.

Tucker did his best to calm him, and assured him that the worst would likely be over soon. He asked Flores about everything that happened, including how he came to have the money, and details of the arrest. The interview went on for some time, and eventually there was a light tap on the door.

"Sorry to interrupt, but we need to take him back to the courtroom holding area. His case will be called soon." The officer could not have been more polite.

Rick was still anxious, but a little calmer than at first.

"We'll see you in just a little bit. Stay strong." Tucker wasn't used to dealing with this kind of client. The majority of his cases had involved career criminals, people who were guilty of something bad, even if not the particular crime they were charged with. He had taken their money and headed on down the road. This was different.

"Shouldn't George be here by now?" Vincent asked.

"Keep your pants on. A lot of criminal lawyers have busy practices, always running from courthouse to courthouse. He'll probably show up at the last minute."

Court was already in session when they entered, and the judge was running through "housekeeping" duties for the moment. It was clear he had been dealing with various matters for the entire morning. The time set for the hearing was, as always, an estimate, and several defendants were scheduled for the same slot. As a result, there was a small crowd of attorneys present, besides a group of defendants in jail garb behind a glass barrier. Tucker approached the court clerk, the same one he'd talked to before, and they exchanged whispers. She pulled a file from the stack and handed it to the judge.

"Maybe you're right, Vincent," Tucker said when he got back. "Younger should be here by now. Nothing we can do about it, though. We have the co-counsel agreement in place, and that gives us standing with the court, so we're fine for the moment. We're going to have to go ahead without him, and ask about it later."

"Case number CV-21806548-90, Rick Flores." The judge opened the file and, after a short look through it, looked up at the assistant district attorney. The DA, Jefferson, wasn't present. "Can you explain what this is about? It appears that Mister

Flores hasn't been charged with anything, and you are requesting his bail be denied. How do you square those two sets of facts, Mister Adams?"

"Actually, I can't, your honor. We were told that Mister Flores would be charged before his hearing today, but that hasn't happened."

The judge stared at Adams like he expected him to say more. When Adams didn't, the judge referred to a note. "Mister Tucker, you're representing Mister Flores?"

"Yes, your honor. But, sir, I seem to be doing a lousy job. My client's been held in jail for almost two days, though he hasn't been charged with anything. He's had his property taken from him, and he's been handled in a rough and aggressive manner by police. He was never read his rights in a proper fashion, nor told the reason for his arrest. And when I asked, and my local co-counsel asked, to see our client, we were told that he was being held incommunicado until the DA said otherwise. So, I must be doing one lousy job if I can't protect my client from this kind of obvious abuse. My client doesn't have a criminal record, he's been an upstanding citizen for many years, and he's helping to support his parents in Santa Fe, yet he's being treated like a major crime figure in some old-time movie—lock him up and throw away the key. He should be released immediately."

The judge turned back to Adams. "Mister Adams, I'm not sure I agree with all of Mister Tucker's hyperbole, but I definitely agree with the substance of what he's said. The state does not have the right to hold someone indefinitely without charging them. Do you know what is going on here?"

Adams looked queasy. "I—I have to say, I don't know what is going on, your honor. I'm sorry."

"You're going to be a lot sorrier soon, if this isn't put right. I'm holding you personally responsible for making sure that Mister Flores is released from jail within the hour. And I mean *on the street* within the hour—not released six hours from now because of some procedural nonsense at the jail. We will take a short break so you can make those arrangements."

The judge rose, the bailiff declared court adjourned, and everyone groaned—more waiting. Once Rick was taken away, Vincent and Tucker went outside to wait. In less than forty minutes, Rick was back in his street clothes, and looking a lot happier.

"Thanks, Mister Tucker." He clearly meant it.

"Did they give you the money back?" Vincent inquired.

"I wasn't sure what to do, but it's not my money. I told that guy Adams, I didn't want it. He seemed annoyed, but he got a form and filled it out, and I signed it. I wrote on the form that I did not know why the money was left for me at the hotel. Was that wrong?"

Tucker thought about it. "No. I should have thought of it beforehand, but I think that was exactly the right way to handle the money. I don't think this is over, Rick. But for right now, you're not charged with anything. So, you're free to go and do what you want."

"What I want is to go back to Denver, and see if I can get my old job back—forget any of this ever happened."

"Then that's what you should do. We'll exchange contact information and maybe Vincent can come up and visit you in a few days, and go over everything that happened, in detail. If anything changes, you need to call me immediately, or Vincent, if you can't get me for some reason. If you're arrested again, you don't say anything until I'm there—nothing, absolutely nothing, no matter what the police say to you. This is really odd, but I think there is some chance it will just go away."

Vincent added his two cents. "If that Simpson guy shows up again in Denver, and you feel even a little threatened, call the police immediately. Don't even think about it, just call and tell them he's harassing you. Don't talk to him, got it?"

"Got it. Thanks to both of you. Sorry to be so much trouble." Rick shook their hands and left.

"Guess we head back to Santa Fe. Can I get a lift?"

"Sure. That's very weird that George Younger didn't show." Vincent was frowning.

"Yeah. Should we try and contact him?"

Vincent scrolled to the number and called, but it went to voice mail. He left his name and number, and said they were headed back to Santa Fe at the moment, but he wanted to talk with him about the hearing. "I don't like this." He sounded unsettled. "But Younger is more than capable of taking care of himself. I'm sure I'll hear from him soon."

"Let's make sure Rick Flores gets out of town okay," Tucker said. "This whole mess is screwy." He shuddered, though it wasn't cold.

6

Enemies and Friends

"We've got to get our act together on this show. Anna was all calm and nice when we first talked about it, but lately she's on my case about everything, asking about every little detail—it's driving me nuts!" Cindy was normally calm, but this morning she needed to vent.

"I know," Jerry said. "I've heard her. Look, everything *is* together. We've got the caterer for the reception, all the rooms are cleaned within an inch of their lives, and we've arranged for extra chairs and tables. I don't know what she's so damn nervous about. We will not put up with her attitude. If we have to, we will just end it." He also was getting frustrated with Anna. "Maybe it's time to tell her to calm down, or she can hold her damned show somewhere else."

"Someone going to kill Anna?" Vincent walked in on the conversation, and jumped in with his usual bad humor.

"Welcome home, Vincent." Cindy was all smiles, completely ignoring his comment. "That was so wonderful that you and Mister Tucker were able to get Rick out of jail. Mary and Hector can't wait to thank you."

"Yep," Jerry chimed in. "Really good job. Got your note

about Mister Tucker being in one of the rooms—no charge. Glad you're both back. What do you think happens next?"

"Don't know for sure, but my guess would be literally nothing. The Durango police have really screwed the pooch on this one, and I'd bet they never want to hear about it again. Just to make sure we've got everything covered, I'll run up to Denver in a few days and arrange a session with a stenographer for Rick to tell his full story while it's fresh in his mind. Then we'll have his statement in our back pocket, in case something does pop up."

"Well, we've got those art-show guests arriving next week, and a reception here for about forty people, so it'd be great if you could be around for that. Anna's nervous about everything and making herself a real pain, but we agreed to do it, so we need to have everyone's help to make it a success." Jerry wanted to pull it off, more for Cindy than for the customer.

Vincent nodded. "Sure, I'll be here. Rick's statement can wait. What's the problem with the arrangements for the show and reception?"

That was when Cindy jumped in. "Nothing. There is not *one actual thing* that she's complaining about, but she acts as if one tiny mistake will bring the world to an end. She wanted an absolute guarantee from me that the caterers have done this type of reception before, and that they won't get anything wrong. I gave her the only sensible answer to that question, which is that I can't absolutely guarantee anything, other than they're the best in town and that I'd watch them and do everything I could to make sure there are no screw-ups. She came unglued and said something to the effect that I must not know what I am doing. I'll tell you, Vincent, at that point I was very close to telling her to forget the whole damn thing, and she could go to hell."

Vincent and Jerry were both quiet for a moment. Neither wanted to step in front of the charging Cindy train.

"Cindy you're doing a wonderful job," Jerry finally said, when she seemed to lose steam. "Don't let this Anna woman get to you. Let's just do the best we can and then, after it's over, we'll forget about her. Remember, we have a nearly full house for the next three weeks after the art show. All the promotions and advertising you've been doing are paying off, which means we don't need Anna Marks's approval."

"Wow, three weeks of full bookings," Vincent said, glad to see things shift to a happier topic. "Congratulations, you guys. That's great."

"Clive, you and I have never really bonded, which may be because every time I turn my back on you, I expect to be stabbed."

Anna was in a foul frame of mind already, and just seeing the fidgety Clive Walton had worsened her mood. Clive smiled without joy. "Anna, my dear, I can walk out of here right now, and your make-or-break show would collapse into an ugly pile of crap. So, why don't you try to be nice, at least until the show's over? And then maybe we can discuss how we break up our little arrangement."

Anna stared at Clive with malice. "I agree. You get a nice bonus off the sales at this show, and I get some money to change my life. After that, we need to stop tormenting one another. I'll make the effort—if you will—to ensure that this little gathering is a financial success. You have to keep your people engaged in the art, and buying. We need to sell every piece here in Santa Fe, and at top dollar. That'll ensure the other shows will be successful, too. I want no surprises. And I want you and my financial advisor to stop being all lovey-dovey in public—my god, Clive, the man is married."

Clive's whole being took on a new persona when he was angry, and he was angry now, although he didn't raise his voice. "Anna, I think you should concentrate on controlling your own weaknesses—not mine. And although it's none of your busi-ness—and why he has not told you, I don't know—Francis *is* divorced. I'll keep my buyers in line, and they'll buy what I tell them to. You just keep your little bitch from saying anything stupid to these people. They don't want to spend millions on a bunch of paintings and then find out that the artist is just a potty-mouthed little tart."

There was a pause. Neither seemed to have won a deci-sive victory. But it was time to concentrate on the matter at hand, and leave personal vendettas for later. Anna began, "Fair enough. She can be a problem. I've talked to her mother, who's assured me that Ilse will be on her best behavior. The success of this show is critical for her, too. I think the biggest risk is the show at the Blue Door Inn. I almost regret arranging for Ilse and her mother to stay there, and to have the reception there, as well. They're a new bed-and-breakfast, and the owners don't seem to have a lot of experience. But, it's too late to make changes. I need you involved, making sure everything goes right at that reception. If we get through that without some kind of fuckup, I think we'll be okay."

"Mother, I don't care what you think I should do. You and Dirk should do as we planned. Fly to Albuquerque, and you will be picked up and taken to Santa Fe. I need a little break before this show. I'm going to Denver to visit a friend. I'll either rent a car and drive to Santa Fe, or I'll fly, but I need a day or two to compose myself."

"Ilse, please, don't do this. You know Anna's going to blow a gasket if you're alone in Denver when the show's already scheduled."

"Fuck Anna. And what you mean is that I won't be watched. Well, I'm tired of being watched, so you just do what I say. I'll be in Denver for a couple of days, and I'll get to Santa Fe in plenty of time for the show. All this financial pressure, and bullshit about me being something I'm not, just so people can make money off my art—it's making me sick. Don't you get it? If I don't get away from everything for a few days, there's no way I'll be able to deal with these awful people, including Anna. Believe me, then you'd see some bad behavior. And from now on, I decide who handles my work, not you and Dirk."

Bente Smit's response to all emotional threats was to cry,

so she did. The tactic had worked for years on most men, and even on her daughter until the girl reached her late teens, at which point Ilse stopped giving a damn. Now she told her mother she wasn't going to sit around and watch her cry. She stormed out of the room.

The next day, Ilse left Amsterdam for New York. It was a grueling flight, but being alone, and upgrading to business class, made it almost enjoyable. She knew she was on the verge of a nervous breakdown. She hadn't been able to paint for months. She had never had a dry spell like this. The money problems, her constant battles with her mother, the absence of anyone she could trust—it all had her on edge, emotionally spent and ready to lash out at anyone. Before, she'd painted with flourish, a free spirit who saw the whole painting from the beginning. But now that vision was gone, and she was scared she wouldn't be able to get it back. Something told her this show could be her last for a while, which alarmed her, but was also somehow soothing. She really needed the money. But being out of the public eye for a while afterward would be good for her.

There was one person she absolutely trusted. When she was eighteen, and emerging as an up-and-coming artist, she won a scholarship to attend a prestigious art school in Boston as part of a special program for young artists from around the world. They chose only twelve artists every year. For three months they were involved in great programs about art, but also about money management, how to manage your art career, and how to maintain your sanity once you were discovered. It was there she met Bobby Hawkins. She almost giggled now when she thought about the first time she'd seen him—it had literally been love at first sight.

Now she was going to see him in Denver. In Boston, all that time ago, if he'd asked her to marry him, she would have. Hell, if he'd asked her to give up her art career and bake cookies for him, she would have. But he hadn't. He encouraged her to push as hard as she could to reach new heights with her art. He said she was the best he had ever seen. He said all the right things, except "I love you." It was after that emotional period she became the self-absorbed, self-destructive creature she was. She reached new heights in her art, and new lows in her life.

She followed his career in graphic art from afar. He'd become a leader in computer-generated graphics for video games, achieving wealth and, in the narrowly focused gaming world, a measure of fame. He lived in Denver, and had his own company. He'd been married, but wasn't anymore. When she'd reached out to him a few months before, he seemed friendly, but hadn't given her any reason to think that they were anything but old acquaintances. She'd talked to him a couple of times, and he'd even invited her to drop by Denver if she ever had the chance. It wasn't much of an offer, but she decided to treat it as an opening. So, here she was, off to Denver. She needed someone to talk to, and he was her choice.

"In Denver? Well, that's—that's great, Ilse. Where are

you now?"

"I'm at the airport. I know I should have called before, but everything has been so hectic lately. I have this big show in Santa Fe next week, and I was going to be in your part of the world, so I changed my flight a little, and ended up here. An impulsive sort of thing—you know me." She was having trouble making sense. She paused. He was quiet.

"Ilse, is there something wrong?"

"My whole life is wrong. I really need a friend." She started to cry. She hated the resemblance to her mother, but she couldn't stop.

"I'll come and get you." He told her how long it would take, where she should be for him to pick her up, and what kind of car he'd be driving.

"Thanks, Bobby." Her own voice sounded pitiful to her.

"I can't wait to see you, Ilse. I think about you just about every day."

She gathered her luggage, and waited at the curb where Bobby told her, excited and nervous. Before long, she saw a car matching the description he'd given her, parking a few spaces away. When Bobby jumped out, all the feelings she'd had so many years before crashed over her like a wave. They embraced, and she started to cry again. She felt suddenly weak. Bobby helped her to the car and got her luggage. "Welcome to Denver."

All she could do was smile.

7

Mine All Mine

Francis Mitchell had been Howard Marks's financial advisor from the very beginning of his art gallery business. He'd helped Marks accumulate a substantial fortune, and in the process had managed to amass a tidy sum, himself. Since Howard's death, though, under the management of his daughter—who, in Francis's opinion, was frequently out of her depth—much of that wealth had disappeared. He was often angry with Anna Marks for more than her refusal to manage the business the way he thought it should be done, which was the same way her father had managed it. A lot of the anger was her constant criticism of him, both personally and of his handling of the family's wealth. She would make one stupid decision after another, and when something inevitably went wrong, blame him, even if he'd specifically, sometimes pointedly, advised her not to do the very thing that caused the problem.

Mitchell had experienced his own crisis when his alcoholic wife decided to divorce him and marry one of her bar buddies, with their future in drinking to be financed by alimony. While married, they had lived in Fresno, California, where her family and parents owned a large amount of land and were considered wealthy, although Mitchell knew they weren't. They were part of the upper crust there, but it was an illusion.

His wife had never done anything other than live off someone's else's money and drink. She'd treated him like a possession, and one she was neither proud of or really wanted, at that. He'd let her walk all over him because he was weak. When she asked for a divorce, over the phone and obviously drunk, he readily agreed, thankful to be rid of her. During much of their unhappy marriage, he'd spent considerable time in Santa Fe working with his top client, the Howard Marks Gallery. He'd purchased a small house in Santa Fe, which he considered his true home. His wife sought—and got—half of everything they'd owned, but he didn't really care, so long as he got to keep the small adobe house. The divorce happened after Howard Marks died, and he'd certainly never shared the facts about it with Anna or anyone else at the gallery. It was none of their business.

Francis spent most of his time in Santa Fe after the divorce, and started to investigate the local food scene. The number of great restaurants was unheard of for a town of such a small size. Tiny Santa Fe was frequently listed as one of the top cities in the country for great dining, and Francis became a regular at some of the best restaurants. It was his love of food that created a close bond between him and Clive Walton, another gallery staffer whom he'd barely known.

One evening, when they were both working late, Francis casually mentioned he was going to head out because he had a reservation at La Boca. Clive jumped up and screamed like a child, "I want to come, is that okay?" His enthusiasm made Francis smile. They had a great evening discussing food in general and Santa Fe restaurants in particular. Soon they developed a routine of dining together two, sometimes three, times a week. They became friends, each surprised by how interesting he found the other to be.

It was after months of these dinners that Clive made his first move. Francis was shocked, but didn't withdraw, and they became intimate. Francis was confused by what was happening, but he was happy, too—happy like he'd never been before. He fell in love with the flamboyant Clive Walton.

Clive moved into the tiny adobe house with Francis. It was a lovefest, but a secret one, augmented by a bond of antagonism toward Anna Marks. Francis also told Clive that Howard Marks, in his will, had left twenty percent ownership in the gallery to him, something he'd hidden even from his wife, which was probably illegal. But he didn't care. It was going to be his retirement fund, if he could only figure out how to get at it. Very few people knew about Francis' ownership other than Howard's attorney and of course, Anna. Anna had screamed bloody murder at Francis when she found out, threatening him with legal action, and even death, if he ever tried to collect his share or mentioned it again.

Francis had gone to Howard's attorney, who assured him the inheritance was legal and enforceable—he owned twenty percent of the business, and there was nothing Anna could do about it. The problem was that, as in any small corporation, all power is in the hands of the majority shareholder, and that was

Anna, and she could prevent him from ever profiting from his share unless she sold the gallery. She could take all the gallery's profits out as her salary or pay it to herself in bonuses, and never pay a dividend on the shares she and Francis owned. So, while the inheritance was real, unless Anna went along with the idea, he'd never get anything from it unless she sold the business—or died.

"She's where?" Anna yelled into her phone. "That's insane. She needs to be here, as agreed. When did you last talk to her? What! That's two days ago. You'd better find her, and I mean now!" Livid, she disconnected.

Trent Taylor spoke up from across the room. "Something wrong?"

Anna looked at him like she wanted to kill him. "Of course, there's something wrong, you moron." She paced. "That was Ilse's mother. She hasn't talked to the evil brat in days. Ilse went to Denver for god knows what reason, and now she's not answering her phone. Her mother and her idiot manager will be in Albuquerque tomorrow without her. So, yes, something is definitely fucking wrong!"

Taylor hesitated to say anything more, but after a minute or two, Anna seemed to calm down. "What'll we do if she doesn't show up?" he asked.

"The show happens, with or without her. All I can hope for is that if she's not here, she's dead. A dead Ilse would boost prices through the roof. I'm sick of this whole business, constantly kissing up to these people. Trent, don't say anything to anybody, especially Clive, but this show goes ahead as planned, with or without the artist."

⎯⬦⎯

"Morning, Tucker."

"It *is* a good morning. How're you today, Vincent?" Tucker was dressed and had brought out his small suitcase, ready for Vincent to drive him to Albuquerque.

"Just got off the phone with George Younger, up in Durango. After we left him, he was attacked. Two guys he didn't know surprised him and knocked him unconscious. He said they didn't take anything and didn't say anything. He thinks it might have to do with the Flores case."

"Is he okay?"

"Yeah, I guess so. Said he was taken to the hospital and apparently blacked out while he was there. The doctors thought there might have been some brain damage, and did all sorts of tests and kept him medicated for quite a while. That's why he didn't get in touch sooner—half the time, he was out of it. But he says everything checked out okay in the end, no problems."

Tucker looked thoughtful. "Why does he think it has to do with the Flores case?"

"Mostly because he doesn't have anything else really contentious going on. Of course, it could be something else, like an old case where somebody held a grudge, or maybe they really were going to rob him, and just got scared off. But he says they seemed like hired thugs. Most of the people he deals with handle their own dirty work, and most of them would have taken his wallet, just to make it look like a robbery. The guys who attacked him seemed to be delivering a message. It wasn't personal."

Tucker frowned. "Sorry he got hurt. I'm not sure there's anything we can do about it from our end. What d'you think?"

"Nah. Risks of the trade. And he's okay. He did say that he'd poked around a little, and gotten some info from some of his lowlife buddies. Seems Ken Simpson's disappeared. His trucking company office in Telluride is closed up, and no one's seen him in days. According to George, word on the street is that he's back in Denver. He also dug up some interesting legal filings. Apparently, Simpson and Franks Junior had a lot of business connections to certain companies in common. George says that within the last few days, Franks has dissolved most of those companies or removed Simpson as an officer. So, some kind of breakup is going on between the happy couple. George thinks the situation with Rick Flores attracted too much attention, and caused some kind of rift."

"Well, maybe that's good for Rick. If they are fighting amongst themselves, then they're not focused on him."

"That's probably right. One last bit of news from Younger; the feds and the attorney general are interested in Simpson, which in turn could touch Franks. Younger heard it's about violations in his trucking business, and insurance fraud."

Tucker was a murder defense attorney—other crimes,

especially lesser ones, didn't interest him much. "It may not be absolutely necessary, but I still think you should go to Denver and have Rick Flores give a sworn statement about what happened. He may be at risk just because there's so much law enforcement going after Simpson. If they find out about what happened to him in Durango, I bet they'll want to talk to him."

"Yeah, I agree. Once this art show's over, I'm going to Denver. Should be just a few days."

With business matters settled, they chatted a while about politics and the weather. They'd become friends and enjoyed each other's company. After more coffee and a muffin for Vincent, Tucker said his goodbyes to everyone at the Inn, and they headed to Albuquerque.

"Jack Hill asked me if you would do some work for him," Tucker said once they were on the road. "I told him I thought you'd probably be okay with it, but that I wasn't a hundred percent sure. I think he has something specific in mind."

"I have to say, Hill makes me nervous. You know I'm not some kind of righteous bastard, and I prefer to work with hard-hitting, take-no-prisoners attorneys." Vincent made a gesture indicating he meant Tucker and others like him. "Hill's different, though. He's sneaky. He's not the kind of direct, in-your-face person I work best with. He's always working the angles—which I don't like. I don't think I can count on him being straight with me."

"A fair point—that's Hill to a 'T.' Most of what he does is behind the scenes, not in the courtroom. I'm not sure what he wants you to do for him, but he can be a great contact if you're going to stay in New Mexico. I wouldn't burn that bridge."

"Yeah, I know. What are you doing for him?"

"Not much. I've advised young lawyers in his office on a couple of criminal cases—more like a coach than anything else, never appeared in court. He seems to think I'm some kind of criminal defense guru who can remake any young lawyer into F. Lee Bailey. Not going to happen. I can advise them and critique their performances, but neither of the two I worked with had the fire in the belly you need to be a good criminal lawyer. Hill wants to take corporate lawyers and turn them into asshole defense attorneys, but that just doesn't work. It's a whole different breed. The take-no-shit defense attorney he wants in his office wouldn't work for him in the first place—he's way too establishment for that. But with all that said, I like Jack. I think he's actually an honest man, most of the time. I also think he's a very powerful person in this part of the world, so you either work with him or you very delicately tiptoe around him and hope you don't offend."

Vincent spent some time thinking about what Tucker said. "Tell him I can be bought, and my price is reasonable. I've worked with a lot worse than Jack Hill—no reason to get picky this late in life. If it gets uncomfortable, I'll move to Phoenix as planned, and find a job sweeping floors."

"You'd have a hard time finding a job sweeping floors. You're too abrasive. Janitors need to be at least halfway pleasant."

8

Love Is In The Air

Vincent and Nancy had decided to meet for a late lunch after his trip to Albuquerque. He'd talked to her several times, but hadn't seen her since he'd gotten back from Durango. They'd arranged to meet at the Coyote Rooftop Cantina, not far from her place, and one of several rooftop bars in Santa Fe. Although the winters could pose challenges, they did a good business year-round.

Vincent was enjoying a beer, glancing at the menu, when Nancy showed up. They hugged, and he wanted to hold on to her, but settled for a kiss on the cheek. Nancy settled in and ordered iced tea.

"Sounds like everything worked out in Durango," she said. "I'm glad for Hector and Mary. They must have been really worried."

"Yeah. Rick was awfully lucky to get out of a mess that serious without any real problems. Or at least, we don't see any right now." Vincent wasn't sure if he was picking up something or not, but he felt a little tension. "Everything okay?"

"Oh, sure." Nancy smiled, but she didn't look happy. "I'm sorry. Guess I'm a little distracted. It's just money. The bar is doing great, but there was some equipment I needed to replace, so I've been working on my financials to get ready to see the banker and ask for a loan, and it's depressing. I really do great business, but it's so hard to make a profit. Anyway, you really don't want to hear this stuff."

"Sure, I do." He didn't want to seem happy that she was having problems with her business, but he couldn't help feeling relieved that they had nothing to do with him.

"You know I put in long hours, and I almost never take time off. I have a lot of money invested on top of my time, but what I actually get to keep as salary and return on my investment is shockingly small. I could make more money just working as a manager for some of the restaurants in town, and invest in something else, and get a decent return. And it wouldn't be so draining on me. I'm not sure why, but suddenly this morning, when I was looking at the numbers, I found my-self wondering if I should borrow more money, or whether it would be better to just sell out and do something else." She looked like she was on the verge of tears. She'd bought the bar with her late husband, so it had to mean a lot to her. And he knew she did put in very long hours, and probably had no one to vent to about her struggles.

"You know, I don't know the restaurant business, and I'm definitely not a financial kind of guy, but it sounds like this involves more than just money."

Nancy got up and left without a word. Judging by the path she took, he figured she headed to the restroom. Had he said something wrong? Vincent knew he could be abrupt—he wasn't a subtle man. If he'd upset Nancy, he surely didn't intend to, but he felt immediately nervous, worried that he'd screwed up for the millionth time in his life. At one time he would have been able to blame his drinking for his poor choices, but he didn't drink enough at a sitting anymore for that excuse to hold water. He waited and worried. Eventually, she came back.

"Vincent, I'm sorry." She paused. Vincent wisely kept his mouth shut. "You're right. It has to do with my life, my husband, my age, you, not having children, feeling like I'm alone—*everything*. What you said was sensible, and right. But for some reason, it made me cry. I hate it when women cry for no reason, or over tiny things, so I went to the powder room. I'm not a baby, and I'm not weak, but for some reason, right now I feel isolated, alone. And it seems like it's not going to change. I guess I'm scared, and don't know what to do about it."

Vincent had spent a lifetime saying and doing the wrong thing, inviting pain in the process. But today, for once, he had the good sense to be quiet. He reached out and took Nancy's hand. Once she seemed more in control, he offered his thoughts. "There is no one more important to me than you. I'm alone, too. And scared, just like you. I want us to be more than friends. And I want you to rely on me for whatever you need. I want to be a part of your life—the good, and the bad. I'm not much, but no one could care for you more than I do."

The tears came again, but she stayed. Vincent stood up and pulled her into a hug, holding on without worrying about what the other patrons might think. Most of them smiled, anyway. And a few had tears of their own.

Cindy came into the kitchen. "Just got a call from Trent Taylor, the business manager for the Marks Gallery. He's a lot easier to deal with than Anna. He gave me the itinerary for the guests arriving tomorrow—minus the artist herself, though. He said she'd be here later, no details. We'll need to coordinate with Vincent to have them picked up at the airport in Albuquerque. Also, he said he wants to come by in the morning, before the guests get here, and walk through arrangements for the reception. Not sure if it means that Anna won't be part of it, but I'm fine with that."

"Perfect," Jerry said. "Maybe she has bigger fish to fry. It'll be nice if irritating you isn't her number one priority, anymore. As far as I know, everything's set and ready to go. If anything, I think everyone's eager to get this over with. It's been more trouble than it's worth." He was still annoyed that Anna had upset Cindy as much as she had.

"One good thing that'll come from this," Cindy said, "is the contact with the caterer. Carla Hitchens is the owner, and she's supposed to be one of the best in Santa Fe. She's also been a chef at several well-known restaurants located here. I've been working with her on the tapas-based menu for the reception, and it sounds delicious. She assures me that if someone's hungry enough for a full meal, there'll be plenty for them, while others can treat it as just appetizers. We've also been talking about having a light dinner catered here on a regular basis when we have a full slate of guests. Her prices are so reasonable, I think we could toss it in as a bonus to our guests. So, maybe a Thursday evening dinner here, on the house. She would have her people set it up as a buffet, so we wouldn't need to hire servers. I think it would be a real plus."

"I like that. Maybe we can do that the week after the art people leave."

"Sure. I think we've got twelve guests that Thursday, so we can give it a try. I'll put together some announcements about it, and email them to the guests who're going to be with us that day. Free food—who could complain?" Cindy seemed a lot more relaxed now that she would be getting a break from Anna.

"Any idea why the star of the show is on a different schedule?" Jerry was mostly just making conversation—he didn't care that much.

"None. I asked Taylor when we should expect her. He hemmed and hawed and ended up saying he didn't know. I bet that's why Anna is busy with something else rather than bugging us. Not having her star attraction at the opening could be a real problem."

"This is just a wild guess, but I bet Anna's driven her nuts with this show, just like she was doing to you. And she decided that the fewest days dealing with Anna, the better."

"Yeah, could be. I know it's silly, but I actually feel kind of sorry for Anna. I get the impression that she's not normally like this. For some reason, she's acting like this one show is life or death for her."

"Bobby, why don't you come down to Santa Fe for the show? You can stay where we are staying. How 'bout it?"

"I'd love to, Ilse, but we have the rollout of our new game going on. This is a huge deal for my company. I don't think it'd look right if I wasn't around."

Ilse pouted, but she knew he was right. "You're right, of course. But I don't like it."

"Didn't you say there was a show in LA a couple weeks after this one? How about we plan that I go to that one—okay?" He was trying to please her, as best he could. He still had a lot of questions about this budding relationship.

"Yeah, I guess that makes sense."

"Haven't you been ignoring a lot of calls? Is that a good idea?"

Ilse almost snapped at him. She really didn't like to be questioned about anything. "No, it's not a good idea. Mostly it's my mother, or the very annoying Santa Fe gallery owner. I'll call them both in a little bit, and tell them I'm not dead, and make sure they know that I'll be in Santa Fe in time for the big show. It's really strange. When we used to talk about having success selling our art, it was like a dream. Now there are plenty of buyers, and it's awful. I don't want to suck up to buyers, or goddamned hangers-on like Anna. They drive me nuts, acting like they're just as important as the people who do the work—two-faced, money-hungry leeches. But I get my money through them, and I want the money as much as they do." She laughed at herself. "Sounds like I'm the horrible one."

"Hey, you're the *temperamental artist*. You have a right to be a little difficult."

They laughed, and decided to stay in bed and let the outside world do without them a little bit longer. Ilse would have liked nothing better than to stay with Bobby and never deal with her mother or Anna and her ilk ever again. But she knew that before she could even think about that, she needed to deal with this show, and sell as many paintings as possible. She wanted to be left alone, but she also wanted plenty of money in her bank account.

Bobby, meanwhile, knowing it was totally irrational, had decided to go to Santa Fe with Ilse, after all. All he had to do now was to call in his most trustworthy manager and ask her to pinch-hit for him. Of course, that meant he'd also have to explain his inexplicable behavior somehow, without once admitting he was in love.

Vincent drove to the Inn, feeling a little melancholy. He was in love, and it scared the hell out of him. At the same time, he felt even more afraid for Nancy—his track record with women wasn't very good. If he was her chance for a better life, that was a bad sign. He thought about ways he might improve. But somehow, he just kept coming back to the same bottom line; he was just too flawed for anyone to rely on. He'd been alone, apart from a few short-term girlfriends here and there, for a long time now. It was his comfort zone. It wasn't in his nature to be particularly empathetic. He'd survived emotionally by worrying about one person, and just one—himself. Now he was thinking about Nancy and her feelings more than his own. And it made him nervous.

"Vincent, glad I caught you," Jerry greeted him. "Here's the schedule for tomorrow for picking up the guests. It's the art-show people, but without the artist—she's somewhere else. We're not sure what that means, but her mother and business manager are coming in tomorrow. Any conflicts?"

"No, no problem, Jerry. I'll be there, and bring 'em back alive. Need anything else while I'm in Albuquerque?"

"No. I think we're all set. The reception will be on Friday. Hey, you should ask Nancy if she wants to come. I have no idea what this art looks like, but my guess is it'll be a little unusual. So far, everyone we've had contact with for this shindig is a little strange. But, on the plus side, the food will be from Hitchens Catering, and according to Cindy, they're by far the best in Santa Fe—worth the price of admission all by themselves. Nancy might even know Carla Hitchens."

"Thanks, I'll ask her. I have no idea what she might think about an avant-garde art show, but I know she'll want to see what the caterer's serving. Cindy doing a little better now?"

"Yeah. Looks like the artist is missing, so Anna has more important matters to worry about than harassing Cindy. So, we're back to being happy."

"Best way to be. Best way to be." Vincent headed down

the hallway to his room.

Jerry watched him go, thinking he seemed sad.

Responsibility. Relationships. Connections. For me, at least, all that shit has meant mostly one thing—pain. Why am I doing this? I'm old enough to know better. Was never able to connect with anyone after my big downfall, losing everything, including my beautiful wife. You can't be hurt again if you never get into another relationship. Everything since then has been casual. I could walk away from each person—I never let them matter much to me. But this is different. And not good. I need a good murder case to get my mind off of this stuff. Murder and mayhem! That's where I belong—not in an intimate conversation with someone I love.

9

Mothers, Managers and Artists

Vincent stood at the airport gate holding the small sign Cindy had made that said, "Guests of Blue Door Inn," waiting for his passengers. Cindy was always planning ahead and organizing things, even when it wasn't strictly necessary—the thought made him smile. Luckily, he didn't have to wait long. The passengers began deplaning.

The flight had come in from New York, so it hadn't been a short trip. But by appearances, many of the passengers had been traveling all night from somewhere else before boarding that flight. None of them looked happy to be in Albuquerque. Soon, two of the least pleased among them approached Vincent.

"We are Bente Smit and Jensen, your guests." The man's speech pattern seemed German or angry or disgusted or all three. Whatever it was, beneath his words lay a definite sense of superiority in dealing with a lowly van driver. Of course, with Vincent and his huge size, even a king might tread lightly. Not Jensen, though. "Here are our claim checks. We will find a restaurant to have some refreshments before we travel. Once you gather our things and are ready to depart, find us." He and

Smit headed toward a coffee shop.

Vincent considered just leaving with their luggage, but decided he owed Jerry and Cindy better than that—and maybe there would an opportunity later to punch Jensen in his smug face—so he went to pick up the luggage, and there was a lot of it. It took him two trips, with a cart, between baggage claim and the van to get everything loaded. As it turned out, it was a good thing he was only picking up the two passengers for now. The van was packed almost full. He headed back up to the coffee shop to retrieve the human part of his load. As he approached, he could see they were having a heated conversation. Other customers were staring, but they were speaking in something other than English, so whatever they were saying—although loud—was still private. Vincent hurried over before the staff could decide to call security.

"The van is loaded and ready to go, sir."

Jensen glared at Vincent for interrupting, but the woman smiled. She seemed to appreciate the interruption. There was no conversation on the drive to Santa Fe. Vincent tried a few pleasantries, like, "How was your trip?" and, "Is this your first time in the U.S.?" He got mostly grunts, so he drove the rest of the way in silence.

When they arrived at the Inn, Bente Smit seemed to respond to Cindy's cheerfulness, and went with her to see her room. Jensen remained unfriendly. Once he had his key and his luggage was taken to his room, he shut the door abruptly, saying he didn't want to be disturbed.

"My goodness. Vincent, did you do something to that

man on the drive?" Jerry was smiling.

"No. Probably should have. He and the lady are not happy with one another. I get that something isn't going well in their world. But that guy is a pain in the butt." Van driver or not, there was no reason for him to take shit from a self-important twit like Jensen.

"Well, sorry if they were rude. Maybe it was just the long flight, although that's no excuse. Glad we don't have any other guests yet for them to afflict with their grumpiness."

Cindy came into the kitchen. "Here's the story. Bente Smit is Ilse De Vries's mother. As we've already heard, Ilse made separate travel plans. At this point, they haven't heard from her, for several days. Jensen thinks the whole event should be canceled, but Smit says Ilse would never miss this show. The threat of canceling has Anna upset, and she's threatening to sue everyone. She and Jensen had a big argument yesterday about who would pay the expenses if it's canceled. These are large paintings, so having them shipped here is very expensive, and then there are all the other costs directly to do with the show. And, reputations are on the line. There are already buyers in town for the event, so it'll be devastating to Ilse *and* Anna if the show doesn't happen. So, at the moment, no one's happy, plus Bente is worried about her daughter. Ilse's prone to acting up, so it's not unusual. But even so, her mother's very upset that they haven't heard from her."

Jerry spoke up. "We did have our inspection by the gallery's business manager while you were gone. He said everything looked great to him—gave us a thumbs-up. He was even polite."

"Yeah." Cindy smiled. "He said the menu and setting up the tent in the back all sounded perfect. Very nice man. Not sure how he fits with this crowd."

Their new guests stayed behind closed doors most of the day, only asking for tea and sandwiches, which Cindy had taken to their rooms. The Inn didn't actually offer room service, but it didn't seem worth arguing about.

The afternoon was busy for everyone, what with the tent, rental chairs, and tables being delivered and set up. The paintings would be delivered the next day—the day of the reception. Everything seemed to be in place, and preparations were beginning to create an air of excitement. But, still—no artist.

The remaining guests, mostly buyers, checked in. They behaved well and were very complimentary about the Inn. It was nice to have guests who weren't perpetually dissatisfied.

That evening, Taylor, the business manager, came by to pick up Smit and Jensen to take them to Santa Fe for dinner—however, there was no sign of Anna. There was an obvious tension in the air, and Vincent decided to retire early.

Cindy and Jerry had way too much wine, enjoyed some lovemaking, and forgot about the Inn. They were happy, and that was what mattered.

The day began in a heavy, damp fog. Vincent stood outside having coffee, admiring the dense mist and the way it made everything seem alien. He loved this kind of weather, shrouding the whole wooded area in mystery. Jerry walked up beside him, holding his own cup of joe.

"Better hope this clears off soon, or Cindy will be in a panic."

"Yeah. Mother Nature better not mess with this reception, or your lovely wife will be on the warpath."

Jerry chuckled. "Funny. You know, we don't have to run this place at all. But we decided we'd be happier if we had things to do. Now, I'm not so sure."

"Dealing with people, in almost any way, is going to have its challenges. But it does seem like you guys have had more than your share, so far."

They both smiled, and headed inside to the kitchen, which was filled with wonderful aromas. Mary and Mariana were both working diligently, getting organized to start baking new breakfast goodies.

"What's that amazing smell?" Vincent was always hungry.

"Heating up some leftover banana-blueberry muffins, just for you, Mister Vincent."

Mary smiled at him. He just might have been her greatest admirer, other than Hector. If Vincent had been the marrying kind, Mary's name would've been at the top of his list—good cooks really are a gift from God.

Cindy entered the room. "Just watched the weather. Suppose to clear up by mid-morning and be a beautiful day. So, the plan is still to use the outdoor serving area for drinks. We'll need to set up the bar in the gazebo and wipe down all the chairs and tables in the tent." General Cindy was in charge. It was her event, and she wanted it to go off without a hitch as much as Anna did.

Jerry gave her a happy salute and headed out back to dry off the furniture. After taking a warm muffin, Vincent joined him. Soon Hector arrived to help, and in short order everything was ready at the gazebo. The tent had been erected by the rental people and now, with the white chairs, small tables, and bar, it looked very festive. The atmosphere boosted almost everyone's mood.

"Oh, it's so beautiful. We should have weddings here." Cindy looked like she might actually cry. The men slumped around her, exhausted, not seeming to see what she saw.

Soon delivery people arrived with the three paintings to be exhibited at the reception. The works were large and well crated, and took time to unpack and place on special stands. They dominated the large dining area, which had been cleared of most furniture.

Bente Smit came in just then. It didn't look like her mood had improved. "Cindy, dear. My daughter or Anna should be here to help set the paintings up. I don't understand where they are. I've tried to call them both, and have not been able to get them. I'm so sorry this is all left up to you. But your place looks so lovely." She paced in front of the paintings a little, then stood back and looked. "I have never really understood my daughter's art." She laughed, more from nerves than humor. "I once asked her if a certain painting was finished. It was a stupid question, since it was at a showing, and she nearly took my head off—said I didn't understand anything about art." Bente shook her head. "She was right. I have no idea what's good or bad. But I'm not a buyer, so I guess it doesn't really matter if I get it or not."

Cindy felt sorry for her, but could see how she could be very annoying to any daughter, much less a world-famous one. "Well, I'm sure your daughter and Anna will be here soon. If we've put anything in the wrong spot, it'll be easy to move. Have you heard from Ilse at all?" She wasn't being nosy—it was her caring side showing through.

"No. I'm very worried. She often has spells where she avoids me. Says I'm too smothering, or something like that. But just before her biggest show? That does not seem like Ilse at all. She may be young, and she can be irresponsible, but she knows this is not just art. It is also a business, and I can't believe she would deliberately avoid being here. I'm so worried, I'm thinking about calling the police."

Cindy hesitated. "I know this is going to sound weird, but our van driver—Vincent, you met him—he used to be a lawyer, and he knows all kinds of stuff about police and things. Would you like to talk to him and see what he thinks you should do?" She was pretty sure Vincent wasn't going to like that she had butted into this family matter and dragged him in along with her, but she could see that Bente was close to a breakdown, and she wanted to help.

"Oh, thanks, Cindy. But I don't think so. Dirk has already told me the police wouldn't do anything. She's a grown woman, and if she doesn't want to talk to her mother, that's not a matter for the police." Bente chuckled, in a sad way. "It's not so much that she's avoiding *me*, it's that she's not here getting this show ready. That's the part that's out of character for Ilse."

"I must admit I'm surprised that Anna hasn't been down here at least a couple of times this morning. When we were planning everything, she wanted to be involved in every little detail. But suddenly, she's just disappeared." Cindy realized she sounded like she was gossiping—which, of course, she was.

"She and Ilse are having a major feud, and I know that both of them are upset about it. I don't know if it's just business or something more, though. My daughter told me that Anna has serious financial problems, and that this will be her last show with Anna's gallery, so there is a lot of tension between them." Bente looked like she wanted to say more, but didn't.

For about the hundredth time, Cindy regretted ever getting involved with these people. Every single one of them seemed to be at least a little off-center. Then the front door opened.

"Hello, is anyone here?"

"*Ilse!*" Bente raced toward the entry.

"Ah, mother, good. Get someone to help Bobby with the damn luggage, will you? What kind of place is this? Isn't there anyone to help us get checked in?"

"Where have you been? I've been calling for days! And now you just pop in and start to be so fucking annoying. *You* get someone to help with your damn luggage." Bente started to cry and ran down the hallway.

"Nice to see you too, mother," Ilse said, to no one. Then she noticed Cindy. "Do you work here? I need some help with my things and I need to get checked in. *Now*, if you don't mind?"

Cindy almost screamed. Welcome to artistic hell.

10

Bad Receptions

Cindy helped Ilse and her guest register, and showed them to one of the casitas. They'd originally slotted Ilse into the room next to her mother, but under the circumstances it seemed best to put them some distance apart. Plus, the boyfriend was a surprise, and the two-bedroom casita helped to sidestep awkward questions. Vincent and Bobby managed the luggage in two trips. For his trouble, Vincent got a very generous tip.

"Thanks for your help. I think she's a little nervous, but she shouldn't be so rude. I'm sure she'll be better after a little rest. Could you have someone bring us some tea, and maybe some sandwiches? We barely stopped on the way down from Denver, and a little food might help calm some nerves." Bobby smiled.

Vincent smiled back. Guy seemed okay. "Sure. I'll have Mary put together a tray for you, and I'll bring it around in just a few minutes."

"More room service?" Jerry wasn't happy. "Better not let Cindy hear that. I think she's ready to kick the whole damn bunch out into the parking lot, the mother included." He paused, then slowly broke a smile. "No problem. I'll have Mary put something together. I'll take it to them—you don't have to do that."

Vincent pulled the twenty out of his pocket. "This was the tip for carrying the bags. I think he could be even more generous for food."

"Vincent—are you telling me that you can be bought off with mere tips?" Jerry threw his arms up in mock disbelief, and they chuckled.

Mary worked her magic, putting together an impressive tray of sandwiches and baked goods, with tea and coffee. Vincent put the tray on a cart and headed back to the casita. Bobby was delighted, and seemed to cheer up a little more. He pushed another twenty into Vincent's hand, and thanked him profusely. As Vincent left, he marveled at the extra forty dollars he'd made in a matter of minutes, thanks to nothing more than hunger. He thought it might look strange if he started following Bobby around. But he was definitely going to stay close.

The next unwelcome visitor was Clive Walton, who hemmed and hawed over the placement of the paintings, eyeing each one for an extended period, and asked Hector to make many minor adjustments to the position of each. Finally, he nodded several times and declared them perfect.

Cindy came in just as the process was wrapping up. "Mister Walton, is everything okay with Anna? We haven't heard from her in several days. She was so anxious about getting everything right for the reception, and now she's just disappeared." She shrugged.

"Well, she's been busy. To tell you the truth, I haven't seen her today, either. That's unusual, but she can be a little weird sometimes."

Cindy thought Clive was venturing onto dangerous ground. "You need to let her know that Ilse is here. She arrived just a while ago, and she's in her room, resting."

"Well halle-fuckin'-lujah! The princess has decided to grace *her own show* with *her* presence. Aren't we all honored? I'll let the queen know." Clive made a disgusted face and left.

Hector, who'd been standing in the back, remarked, "That little guy has a lot of anger in him."

"You aren't wrong, Hector," Cindy said. "So far, all these art people seem to have a screw loose." She smiled, and together they laughed a little.

Just then they heard Mary yell from the kitchen, and ran to see what happened. They found her hugging a handsome young man with all her might.

Hector laughed. "Why didn't you tell us you were coming home?" Hector shook his son's hand, beaming with pride.

"Sorry, Dad. It was a last-minute thing, and I thought I'd just surprise you. Hey, this is a great place. Mom has told me so much about it, I couldn't wait to see." Rick was talking to his parents, but his gaze mostly settled on Mariana.

Hector noticed. "Rick, I want you to meet Cindy Oliver. Miss Cindy and her husband own the Blue Door Inn."

Rick crossed to Cindy and shook her hand. "My parents say you are the most wonderful person in the world. It's a great honor to meet you."

Cindy dropped his hand and gave him a hug, smiling. "Well, you're a very handsome young man, Rick, and maybe a little bit of a tease. We're very glad you are visiting. We were all worried about you and the situation in Durango." She paused, then glanced from Rick to Mariana. "Your parents are very important to us, and we're lucky to have them here. Let me introduce you to our newest employee." She took his arm and walked him over to a blushing Mariana. "Rick Flores, I'd like to introduce Mariana Garcia."

Rick barely seemed to hear Cindy while he took Mariana's hand. "It's very nice to meet you."

"It's nice to meet you, too. Your mother has said many nice things about you."

"Okay," Cindy said, breaking the spell. "We still have a few things to do before our guests arrive. Sorry, Rick, but we have a reception here this afternoon with a large, and very demanding group, so we need to get back to work."

"Sure. Can I help?"

"Kitchen work or bar setup?"

"I didn't inherit my mother's skills in the kitchen. Maybe I shouldn't say too much about setting up a bar, but it might be something I could do." He grinned.

"Great. The bar's outside in the gazebo. My husband—his name is Jerry—he's out in back there somewhere, along with Vincent, who I think you've already met. Find Jerry and introduce yourself, and he can get you started."

"Perfect." Rick squeezed Mariana's hand and went outside.

Mary came over and gave Mariana a hug. "Don't worry, Mariana. Rick's a nice boy. And if he doesn't behave like one, you just tell me, and I'll fix it, immediately."

They giggled like little girls.

"Where the hell is everybody? Hello! Is this place open or not?"

"Sounds like Anna's back," Cindy said with a sigh. "I'll handle it." She headed toward the small lobby.

"Oh, there you are." Anna seemed relieved. "Cindy, everything looks wonderful. I'm so sorry I haven't been around to help. The paintings look great, and I saw the tent before I came in—it's just perfect. Thank you so much."

Cindy had been all ready to lay into Anna, even to toss her annoying behind out of the Inn, if necessary. Now she wasn't sure what to say. "Uh. Thanks. Clive helped with arranging the paintings. We have them covered now, as Clive said to. The caterers will be here in just a few minutes to get set up. Everything will be ready on time." Inwardly, Cindy was half apologizing for all the things she'd been ready to say, but hadn't.

"Clive tells me our favorite bad penny has turned up—that's good. The reception will be a lot better if we don't have to explain why the star's missing. Thanks again, Cindy. I'll be back in an hour or so, along with our guests. See ya then."

Cindy was beginning to feel like a ping-pong ball bouncing back and forth between the various players and their ever-changing emotions. She shook her head and went back to the kitchen. Everyone else had returned to their various tasks. She could see Vincent and Rick in the back yard.

"While you're here in Santa Fe, we should get that statement done. How long are you going to be home?" Vincent wasn't trying to be nosy—he just wanted to get the job done.

"I quit my job in Denver, so I guess I've moved back permanently. Can't live long with my parents. We love each other, but they don't need me underfoot. Not sure what I'm going to do, exactly. Maybe look for a job in Albuquerque." Rick looked thoughtful, but didn't say anything further.

"Does moving back have anything to do with Simpson and the Durango mess?"

"Not really. Well, maybe. It definitely spooked me. And I know this is going to sound pathetic, but it made me realize how much my parents mean to me. I guess I had to be gone for a while to get that straight in my head. But I want to live closer. Not in the same house, but close."

Rick seemed reluctant to say more, and Vincent wondered if there might be more to his new love of being a homebody than just parental appreciation. He had always been good at picking up on fear, and fear was what he sensed in Rick. "Well, good. Still, let me set something up with a stenographer here in Santa Fe, and we'll get what Tucker wants. Okay?"

"Sure, I still want to do that—just in case something else happens."

There went Vincent's antennae again. He would have bet his entire generous tip from Bobby that "something" had already happened, and Rick was running from it. Why wouldn't he say so? More fear, probably. He had come home to hide out or get help, or both. Vincent wasn't likely to figure out what it was right now. But eventually, he'd know.

The arrival of the caterers set in motion a whirlwind of activity. They were like a well-drilled invading army, with delicious food in place of ordnance. Soon the new people had all the ovens working, and had arranged the first serving of appetizers, inside and out at the tent. A skilled bartender took over the bar with practiced efficiency.

Cindy realized immediately that her best course was simply to stand back and let the caterers do their thing. She'd been told that they were the best and so far, that seemed to be true.

Right on time, Anna arrived with two vans and a small bus full of buyers. The group of buyers were upbeat and in a party mood. Unnoticed by the growing crowd, Clive and Francis Mitchell were huddling in a corner, discussing something in private. Within thirty minutes of when the event was scheduled to begin, all guests seemed present. Bente Smit and Dirk Jensen mingled with the buyers, some of whom they seemed to know. There was a festive buzz as everyone enjoyed the company, the good food, and the generous drinks. Cindy smiled.

The early evening weather was perfect, with a pleasant, mild breeze allowing the large doors to be left open so there was no barrier between inside and outside. The servers were efficient. And, based on samples Cindy snagged, the food was great.

As if the event had been scripted, just as anticipation over the paintings reached its peak, Ilse and Bobby made a grand entrance. The small crowd broke into applause when they caught sight of her. She was clearly more relaxed and better rested than when she'd first arrived, wearing a stylish ensemble suitable for the Parisian catwalk.

"Thank you," she said to everyone and no one. "Thank you all so much for coming. Isn't this place beautiful?" There was another round of applause. "Anna and her people have done a fantastic job. I owe her my deepest gratitude. Now, please enjoy yourselves and we'll unveil the paintings in just a few minutes." She smiled in a mischievous way. "Oh, and yes, they will be for sale."

The crowd gave a good-natured laugh at that. Not everyone was happy, though. Cindy noticed that Anna had gone into the kitchen when Ilse mentioned her name. It seemed an odd time to leave, but her thoughts were interrupted when Clive came up to her.

"I'll do the unveiling in about twenty minutes. After that, we'll have a viewing period for about thirty more minutes, and then comes the bidding, which I'll conduct. While I'm doing it, I don't want the waiters in the room. But before that, they should serve as much liquor as people want. Once the bidding's over, and the lucky buyers have been congratulated, we'll close down after about fifteen more minutes, and clear everyone out." He was doing his best to be all business, but it seemed obvious to her that he was upset about something.

"Okay, that'll work just fine," Cindy said. "We'll get all the food out now, so there'll be nothing after the unveiling, except the booze. And nothing during bidding. Good luck!"

She wasn't sure who was more nervous, Clive or her. She badly wanted it to be over, but first, she had things to do. She returned to the kitchen and found Anna sitting alone at the small kitchen table, drinking. Cindy wasn't sure what to say to her.

"Can I get you anything, Anna?"

Anna gave her a look that seemed threatening—and maybe a little bit crazy. "Maybe a fuckin' gun! You should keep one handy, Cindy darlin'. Couple more belts of this vodka, and I'll go out there and blow out the brains of our wonderful, talented little bitch of an artist. Might take out her new fuckin' boyfriend, while I'm at it."

Cindy looked around to see at least ten people who heard that outburst. "Unless you want this sale to fall apart, I would think it might be best if you went out back and didn't say anything more." Cindy had lowered her voice to a whisper.

Anna glared. It seemed clear it was fortunate for Cindy that Anna didn't have the gun she'd been fantasizing about. But the moment passed. "You know, Cindy darlin', I think you're right. I'll kill her *after* the sale." She tipped her glass as if in a toast, and went out the back door.

Cindy looked around at the collected group. "Tension and booze. Probably not a good combination."

She smiled, and not happily. Why did all her guests want to kill someone? *Come visit the famous Blue Door Inn, B&B and psycho ward.* If she'd been alone, she might have cried.

11

Haters and Lovers

There were audible gasps as the first painting was unveiled. Before the crowd could collect themselves, the second painting was exposed, eliciting more appreciative noises, and a quick round of applause. Clive Walton could feel the room's excitement, and immediately went to the final work, stopping with his hand on the drape that covered it.

"Ready?"

People laughed and cheered and yelled, "Do it!" Clive knew they had a hit. Of course, he'd seen the paintings, and thought they were Ilse's best work by far. Like many people, he thought she was a spoiled brat who should be locked in her room most of the time, but she was also the most gifted contemporary artist he'd seen in years—maybe decades. Shapes and colors jumped off the canvas and seemed to demand attention with images that were comfortable and disturbing at the same time. She was a vast talent wasted on a petulant woman-child.

"The best for last." He pulled away the cover, and the crowd broke into applause. The buyers they'd assembled for the reception were some of the most knowledgeable—and influential—around, and he could tell they were impressed. Anna's money problems would be over soon. This kind of enthusiasm meant big checks.

"We will start the bidding in approximately thirty minutes. Thank you."

The crowd turned their attention to Ilse, congratulating her on her work. Everyone was excited, and for once even Ilse looked pleased. But she wouldn't let go of Bobby, clinging to him like a life preserver while the sea of admirers engulfed her with words of praise.

Soon everyone was talking and drinking. Small groups formed, with people guessing who would bid on what, and how much, and remarking on what a special moment this was—a star being born.

⎯◯⎯

Ilse and Bobby went out back to take a break from the attention.

"Well, looks like you're a hit." Anna's drunken, bitter voice came from behind them. They turned to her. "You'll be rich and famous, and you still won't know shit."

"I don't know what your problem is," Ilse retorted, holding onto Bobby for security, but clearly livid. "You'll get your money. Isn't that what you wanted?"

"Have you told your new boyfriend about all of your sexual exploits? I'm sure he'd love to hear the details."

Ilse charged at Anna. Her target, being drunk, toppled

over easily, falling to the ground and hitting her head. Ilse, now on top of her, beat at her with her fists. Bobby grabbed her and pulled her away.

Vincent saw the encounter from a distance, but couldn't hear what was said. He ran over and tried to take care of Anna, but she cursed him with as much venom as she did Ilse.

"You evil little bitch," she howled at the artist. "You think you can treat me this way and then just walk away, all rich and happy? Think again, you piece of shit. I can keep *all* the money until *all* the events are over. And then I can do an audit to determine how much you owe me for the expenses we agreed to share. And then, maybe a few months later, I might release *some* of the money to you."

"You can't do that! I never agreed to sharing the expenses—that shit comes out of your commission."

"Little Miss Know-It-All didn't read the fine print, did she? Too bad, princess. I can keep the money until I decide everything's accounted for—you can let your new boyfriend support you and mom for a while until I decide how much you get. And there's nothing you can do about it."

Ilse broke loose from Bobby and got close enough to Anna, even with Vincent blocking her path, to kick her hard in the knee. Anna went down again. There was more shouting and name-calling. Bobby dragged Ilse back to the house. Anna pushed Vincent away, and headed toward the parking lot.

"Now for the final—and, I would suggest, most impressive—painting of the night. Let's open the bid at five hundred thousand."

Clive was energized by the prices the paintings were commanding. These three alone were going to top two million dollars, and they still had twenty-five more to sell in the three other venues. Everybody was going to get rich—except him and Francis, of course. He pushed the thought aside so he could deal with the auction, although his temper rose a little. Just as he was wrapping up, he saw Ilse and her new boyfriend come in from the back yard. He had the distinct impression something was wrong.

"Sold to Mister McDougal, for one point two million."

The crowd applauded and cheered, and celebratory drinks made the rounds.

"I saw Ilse come in and then go out to her room," Clive told Francis, once he could get free. "What the hell happened?"

Francis looked nervous. "I'm not completely sure. That van driver told me Anna and Ilse had a little exchange, and that Anna got in her car and left."

"Shit." Clive paused with an angry scowl. "Those two morons are going to screw up everything. At the moment, Anna would blow up the whole world just to get back at Ilse—this is not about business, it's about sex. We've got to stop her before she ruins this for everybody."

"My god, Vincent, did you hear how much those paintings sold for?" Jerry was dumbfounded. He thought the art was horrible.

"Strange world. And strange people. In here, millions were being spent on confusing paintings of nothing in particular, while in the back yard the artist and the gallery owner were in a fight." He shook his head.

Jerry stared. "A fight? You mean, like a real fight?"

"Yep. Hitting, kicking, name-calling. Reminded me of my bar-crawling days, when I wasn't exactly frequenting high society."

"Where are they now?"

"Ilse and Bobby came back in, but I didn't see them afterward. So, I guess they went through the main building to their casita. Anna took off in her car. Almost ran down one of the caterer guys."

"Oh, man. Does Cindy know?"

"I don't think so. I was the only one who saw the fight, other than Bobby. I think everyone else was at the auction."

"Did you hear what they were fighting about?"

"No. I saw them arguing, and then all of a sudden, they were on the ground. I ran over and helped Bobby pull them apart." Vincent looked around. "Have you seen Nancy?"

"Yeah, just a few minutes ago. She was in the small conference room, talking with Rick."

"Okay, thanks."

Vincent went off in that direction. Nancy hadn't gotten there until after the bidding had started. They'd waved at each other from opposite sides of the crowd, and then he lost her.

He poked his head into the conference room. From behind him, Nancy whispered, "Looking for somebody?"

Vincent actually jumped. "Hey! There you are. What did you think about the art auction?" He was glad to see her, and wanted to give her a hug, but held off.

"Truthfully, I was amazed that someone would pay that much for any piece of art that wasn't a Rembrandt. Definitely not something I'd spend big bucks on."

They laughed together.

"Yeah? So, what would you spend big bucks on?"

"You know, and this may surprise you, I don't think I would spend big bucks on much of anything. Some of my happiest days were when I was first married and we lived in a tiny one-bedroom apartment. We had no money, but it was glorious, anyway. I think money can make people lose their minds—do stupid stuff."

Vincent smiled, taking the moment to just look at her. "Greed is a bad thing," he said, finally. "But money isn't. I don't want millions, but having enough, whatever that means, is okay with me. Do you mind if I kiss you?"

"No, I don't mind at all."

"A fight?" Cindy gasped. "I can't believe that. A real fight, or just yelling?"

"Vincent said it was a real fight. A hitting, falling-to-the-ground catfight."

Cindy shook her head. "I don't know if I can deal with much more, Jerry. These people are nuts."

"Well the show's tomorrow, and our guests are scheduled to leave the morning after, so we're just about done with them. I'm sure you can manage to avoid ever seeing Anna again, so just suck it up for one more day, and we'll welcome some old retiree guests next week who, I'm betting, don't want to kill anyone." He was smiling. It could be funny if you looked at it from the right angle.

"Okay mister, that's the plan. But you have to promise me that once they leave, we sit down with a bottle of wine and re-evaluate this whole B&B thing. I wanted to keep myself busy, but dealing with wackos isn't my idea of fun."

Jerry was standing by the window. "Come over here. This'll make you feel better."

Cindy got up and went to where Jerry was standing and pointing outward. Sitting in the gazebo in the back yard were Rick and Mariana. Even at that distance, you could see the love in the air.

"They seem made for each other, don't they?" she said. "How does stuff like that just happen?"

"My first guess is that you had something to do with it."

Cindy feigned shock. "Not me. I didn't even know he was coming. And I'd never met him, so how would I know that they would make a perfect match?" She winked at Jerry, then headed to the kitchen.

Soon the guests began to leave. Within half an hour they were gone, and the Inn was suddenly quiet. Without planning it that way, everyone ended up in the kitchen. Cindy and Jerry passed out glasses of wine.

"Congratulations to everyone. It was a very successful event," Jerry said. "It was our first, and I think it turned out just great. We need to get everything back to some kind of order, obviously, so we can serve our guests in the morning. But just ignore the back yard. We can deal with that tomorrow."

Clive and Francis had supervised the repackaging of the paintings and followed the van to deliver them back to the gallery, so the dining room was vacant. Everyone chipped in, bringing back the table and the chairs, and putting everything back to normal.

"We have plenty of leftovers," Cindy said. "Help yourself to anything you want." She felt better about the world now that the guests were gone.

But the break didn't last long.

"Hi. Can we maybe get something to eat?" It was Bobby. "I know you don't serve dinner, but if there's something left over? We're going to stay in our room and not go out this evening."

"Sure. We'll put together something and bring it to your room. I'm sure you're tired." Cindy didn't ask about the fight. Mary prepared three trays, just in case the other guests wanted something, too.

Vincent and Nancy grabbed a plate of leftovers and went out back. They sat down and nibbled for a while, neither saying anything for a while.

"I think we're a little old to be playing games, don't you?" Nancy said at last. "I like you, but I don't want to get hurt. I know you only planned to stop in Santa Fe for a little while, but it seems like maybe you belong here. What are you thinking you'll do now?"

"Yep, no reason to play games," he agreed. "Back in the day, I married a beautiful woman I was madly in love with. But I ignored her to be with a bunch of drunks. After that, I never trusted my emotions again. Maybe, in an odd way, I decided that part of my punishment for screwing things up so badly was that I'd always be alone. That was my plan for the future—no matter where I was, I expected to be alone. Now I want to be with you. It surprises me, but it's real." He paused and took a deep breath. "I wasn't sure I was going to say this to you, because I don't want to be rejected. But, I love you." He was immediately nervous. He didn't want to be hurt, either.

"Maybe you should take me home, and we can discuss this further." She was smiling. She grabbed Vincent's hand, and they left.

12

Openings and Closings

Vincent's phone vibrated. He put down his cup and answered it.

"Yeah?"

"Vincent? Jerry. Not sure where you are, and of course, it's none of my business." Jerry waited, but Vincent didn't say anything, so he continued. "De Vries and her group want to go to the gallery around noon. They have a car, but they want to go in the van. Will you be able to take them?"

"Sure. No problem. I'll be back at the Inn in about thirty minutes. And you're right, it's none of your business, but I guess in a way it is—I stayed at Nancy's. See ya in a bit."

Vincent was up early, enjoying a great cup of coffee at Nancy's tiny kitchen table. Her small house was located downtown, and had a comfortable feel the moment he walked in, like he'd been there before. For the moment, Nancy was still asleep. He decided to leave her a note and head back to the Inn, but once he got outside, he remembered he didn't have his car. He wasn't sure about getting a cab this early. But he was getting his phone out to make the call when Nancy came out. She looked wonderful, and even better when she held up her keys and smiled.

"Saw your note. I don't need my car today. I can walk to work."

On impulse, Vincent hugged her—and hung on. He didn't usually show his emotions very openly, apart from occasional outbursts of anger, but he was in love. "Thanks for a wonderful night. Need to haul Ilse and company around this morning, but I'll get your car back to you a little later. Will you be here?"

"I'll be at the bar. Come by, and we can talk."

"Good talk or bad talk?" He was starting to sound needy, and he didn't like it.

"Good talk. I'm not going to run away, Vincent. Relax. Let's just enjoy ourselves and see what happens."

He kissed her on her cheek. "I can do that."

As he was driving to the Inn, he noticed he was smiling—not a normal expression for him. He parked next to the van, and checked to make sure it was clean inside, then went in through the back door to the kitchen.

"Good morning, Mister Vincent." Mary's voice had an unusual lilt to it that suggested she knew his secret.

He wasn't sure he liked being on display, but decided it was part of belonging in a place. The thought made him smile. "Good morning to you, Mary. What's that wonderful aroma?"

"Applewood smoked bacon, green chili omelet with avocado sauce, and a sopaipilla from my special recipe—with spicy honey. There'll be plenty if you want some."

"Yes, I do. I really, really do." He headed to his room to prepare for the day.

Vincent was nobody's gourmet, but he sure enjoyed good food. The omelet was something special, but the sopaipilla with spicy honey was out of this world. He thought about having a third one, but decided it would be too much, even for him. "Mary you're the best cook I've ever known. How did you learn how to do all this?"

"There were eight kids in my family, and my mother was the best cook in the world. She made wonderful meals every day with very little money. Her mom taught her, and then she taught me. The boys would go outside and play ball or something—the world has not changed much."

Vincent heard an edge in Mary's voice, and decided not to ask for more details. "Well, thanks to your mom, and thanks to you. That was a great late-morning breakfast. Guess I'll go find our guests and see if they're ready."

Mary nodded and smiled. "Mister Vincent, if you ever need someone to drive the van and you aren't available, Rick would be happy to help. No cost, he just wants to help."

Vincent almost made some wiseass remark about Rick being after his job, but decided Mary might not get that he was only joking. "Sure, that would be great. I'll talk to him about it. See ya."

As he entered the dining room, he saw Bobby standing out by the gazebo, talking on his phone. He wondered whether he should wait until he got off the phone to ask him when he thought they'd be ready, or just go to Ilse's room and ask her, and decided to wait a bit. It wasn't long before Bobby pocketed his phone. "Hey Bobby. Morning." He walked out and shook his hand. Bobby seemed like a good guy, but experience told him first impressions could be very wrong. "Soon as you and the group are ready, we can go. I'll pull the van around to the front."

"Great, great. I think we're ready. I'll go get them."

No one said much while the group gathered and then boarded the van. Ilse wore large sunglasses and seemed distant. Bente and Dirk sat together, while Bobby and Ilse went to the far seat in back. Vincent was fine with having little or no conversation as he drove. But the tension in the air was palpable, and he soon felt on edge.

The Howard Marks Gallery occupied a prime location on Canyon Road, and was one of the larger galleries in the area. Vincent pulled up in front and helped his passengers out. Looking into the gallery, he could see a lot of activity, even though it was still hours before the official opening. He gave Bobby one of the Blue Door Inn cards with his number on the back.

"I won't be far, so if anyone needs a ride back to the Inn, just give me a call, and I'll be here. If it's all right, I thought I might come back once everything gets started, and see what a big-time art show looks like. Think that'd be okay?"

"Oh, sure." Bobby nodded. "There are seven paintings for sale today. This time it's not the auction format. Each piece is negotiated separately, with Clive and Anna handling the sales. In fact, could be they've all been spoken for—the gallery people haven't done a very good job of keeping Ilse informed, and she's a little pissed. But, anyway, you should come back and look around, as our guest."

"Great, okay. I'll see ya later."

It was a short drive to the Crown Bar. Vincent was a little nervous—anytime a woman said they "should talk," it never seemed to end well. It was probably nothing, but he was still on edge when he entered. He spotted Nancy behind the bar, and waved. She indicated he should take a seat at one of the tables in the restaurant part, and soon joined him. Seeing her wonderful smile made his nervousness go away almost immediately.

She squeezed his hand and sat down. "Want something to eat?"

"Mary forced me to eat an omelet and some sopapillas, so I probably should skip at least one opportunity to stuff my face."

She signaled a waiter for some chips and salsa, and two iced teas. "Let me start. I know your instincts are to run. I also know we have something that could be special. No reason to beat around the bush. I think you should move in with me. Let's find out if this is real, or just a fling."

"What will your neighbors say?"

"They'll say, 'It's about time she had a man in that house.'" Nancy gave Vincent a big smile. "I know we should probably go slow and test the waters and all that shit. But I thought about it last night, and I think we need to jump in with both feet. If it's a disaster, we'll find out quickly, and get it over with. And if not, well, we'll try to make each other happy and more complete."

"I can tell you all the reasons you shouldn't do this," Vincent said. "But I wouldn't want you to listen to me. If you're willing to give this a try, so am I." He reached over, took her hand, and squeezed it gently.

"Another thing we need to get straight, though," she said, "I don't want to marry you. For us to make this work, we both need to keep some independence. Agreed?"

Vincent smiled, even if her words hurt him some. He realized he *did* want to marry her. He'd just have to work on that. "Agreed."

He headed back to the art gallery, thinking about what just happened. On one hand, he had the feeling he'd just negotiated a business transaction rather than dealing with something romantic. On the other hand, he couldn't stop grinning an idiot grin that told him otherwise. As he got close to the gallery, he could see a crowd out front. He found a parking spot down the street. Walking back, he thought it seemed odd that so many people would be out front and not inside.

"What's going on?"

One of the sidewalk crowd responded. "Not sure. The police are inside, and they asked us to wait here while they searched the building. Maybe some kind of theft, or something?"

Vincent saw the police chief inside. He moved to the door and tried to open it, but it was locked. He managed to catch the chief's attention. An officer came over and let him in.

"Hello, Vincent." Chief Stanton didn't look pleased about whatever was going on. "You have something to do with this place?"

"A little. The artist, Ilse De Vries, and her group are staying at the Inn. I brought them here earlier, and was coming back to check on them. What's going on?"

He took Vincent aside. "Not sure. Do you know anything about an argument between the artist and Anna Marks yesterday at the Inn?"

"Sure. I was there. I was off some distance when they started arguing, so I didn't hear what they said. But it turned into an actual fight pretty quickly. Ilse rushed Anna and knocked her to the ground. I ran over and pulled them apart, with help from Ilse's boyfriend. Has something happened to Anna?"

The chief gave Vincent the familiar cop look, the one that said, *I'm going to tell you something, but you can't tell anyone else.* "Her body was found this morning in her car. She was strangled."

Vincent's investigator's mind immediately considered different scenarios. He concluded he needed more information. "Where was the car?"

"Parked on the street, not far from here—Cathedral Park on East Palace. She was in the back seat. Covered by a tarp."

"Not exactly a remote hiding spot. That's in the middle of a high-traffic tourist attraction."

The chief nodded. "Yeah, obviously, it was going to be found sometime today. At first, we assumed that was where the murder took place. But we're starting to get some forensics back, and we think it happened someplace else, and then the car was driven there. No idea why."

"What's all this action about?" Vincent indicated the art gallery.

"Once we identified the body, this is where we headed. We're questioning everyone right now who had any connection with her. After the fight at the Inn, what happened?"

"Well, Anna was a wee bit drunk. She yelled some things at Ilse, and ran off to the parking lot. Got in her car before anyone could stop her, and blasted out of there—almost ran down one of the caterers. I think she lives around there, although I don't know that for sure. But I assumed that she was headed home. I think we all did."

"Did anyone at the Inn hear from her after that?"

"Not that I know of. I'm sure that if she'd called Jerry or Cindy, the owners out there, they'd have told me about it this morning. I know Ilse and her group hadn't heard anything, because they were nervous about how Anna might act today at the big opening."

"I've been told this show could bring in as much as twenty million. Is that true?" The chief sounded dubious.

Vincent nodded. "I don't know for sure how much these other paintings would have sold for, but at the reception at the Inn yesterday three paintings sold for a total of over two million."

The chief still seemed skeptical. "I know I should have a better understanding of a major business segment of this town, but I just find that hard to believe. Most of what I saw in here I wouldn't pay much of anything for, much less millions."

"Yeah, well, I'm not exactly an expert on art, either. But I saw it with my own eyes yesterday—this stuff was bringing in amazing sums. There were buyers there from all over the world. This is a big business, and there's no doubt in my mind that Anna's death is tied directly to all that money."

"Money and sex—it's always one or the other. Or both. You can hang around if you want. I have investigators questioning everyone, but we should be releasing people pretty quick. We're going to close the gallery, though, despite some guy—a Mister Walton—raising hell about it. It's my understanding that the financial side of everything was finished, anyway, and it was just the reception that was left. Anyway, even if I've got that wrong, Walton can object all he wants, but we're still closing it down so we can do our forensics. We also have security video to review. If we get really lucky, we might learn something important—maybe even who did it."

The chief headed off to attend to the full plate the murder had handed him. Vincent looked around, but didn't see any of his passengers. He had a lot of confidence in the chief. They hadn't known each other all that long, but they'd quickly developed a mutual respect for each other's abilities. Once again it seemed that one of the prime suspects in a murder was a Blue Door Inn guest. Poor Cindy was going to be in tears—again.

13

Crime and Punishment

The police cleared the front area with practiced precision. There was some grumbling from the crowd, but mostly it seemed about not knowing what was going on. The police issued and reissued their standard response, "We'll let you know something when we know something."

Soon the only people left were in a large room that had been meant for the reception. Clive still looked angry, going back and forth between saying, far too loudly, how awful the police had been in handling the matter and whispering secretively to his friend Francis about something that was clearly not only private, but also very important.

Bobby and Ilse sat quietly at a small table in a corner. He held her hand to give her some reassurance, but she looked dazed. Her mother and Dirk, who seemed more interested in Bente than in managing Ilse's business, stood against a wall opposite them. Something must have happened between the mother and daughter, Vincent figured.

Another man, whom Vincent didn't know, moved about like he was important, but didn't talk to anyone. Vincent had heard the name Trent Taylor, and thought it might be him.

For his part, Vincent kept to himself. Soon Bobby approached him.

"Saw you talking to the police chief. Do you know what they're going to do?"

Vincent wasn't sure he should offer his opinion to anyone. "No. I know the chief, but he didn't tell me anything we don't already know."

Bobby looked troubled. "Ilse should have a New Mexico attorney. Jerry told me you used to be a lawyer, and that you've done investigative work for lawyers, too. Any chance you know someone we could call?"

There was a brief pause while Vincent debated with himself about what to say. "Why do you think Ilse needs an attorney?"

Bobby looked briefly annoyed. "They haven't accused her of murder, if that's what you mean. It's to do with the paintings and the money. I know someone's dead, and I don't mean to be disrespectful, but I didn't even know Anna—my concern has to be for Ilse. She has a huge amount of money floating around, as well as some very valuable paintings, and we're not even sure who has the authority to do what. Anna being dead has created legal issues that need to be dealt with sooner rather than later. Ilse can bring in her attorneys from New York, but I told her it might make more sense if she had someone local. Do you think that's wrong?"

"Nope, you're right," Vincent agreed. "Ilse needs to get some legal help to make sure she protects her assets. The best lawyer in the state is probably Jack Hill, at Johnson, Johnson and Hill." He took out his phone, looked up Hill's number, and gave it to Bobby. "I've worked for someone associated with that firm, and Hill's asked me to do some investigative work, so I've looked into them a bit. I've been told that Hill is the best—not just by New Mexico standards, but on a national level."

"I know that name. Is that the same firm as the one in Denver?"

"Yeah, they have an office in Denver." Vincent dearly wanted to ask Bobby about Ilse's alibi for the night before, but it wouldn't have been appropriate. He sure as hell was curious as to whether she had one, though. At that moment, the chief came out and had a brief conversation with each group, then made a general announcement.

"There'll be follow-up questions for each of you. We have your contact information, and we ask that you do not leave the area without notifying us first. We'll move as quickly as we can to solve this, but during that period the gallery will be sealed as a possible crime scene. Everyone should have my card. If anything occurs to you that you think we should know, please give me a call. For now, everyone is free to go. Thank you."

Vincent went over to Bobby and Ilse to tell them he would get the van and that he'd be out front in just a few minutes. The trip to the Inn was uncomfortably quiet, and at the moment they arrived, everyone headed to their rooms.

Jerry found Vincent in the back yard, smoking one of his few daily cigarettes. "My god, we just heard. Anna was murdered?"

Vincent filled Jerry in on what he knew, which wasn't

much. "I suppose this could have been some kind of random killing, and had nothing to do with the art show. But my gut says that's not the case."

"So, you think it is something to do with the gallery, which means the murderer is someone we've met. Maybe even one of our guests?" Jerry was looking a little pale.

Vincent's phone vibrated before he could respond. "Malone." He listened. "Sure, I can do that." He put his phone back in his coat.

"Something important?" Jerry couldn't help being a little nosy.

"That was Tucker. Looks like Ilse hired Jack Hill to help her with some financial matters regarding the art gallery. Tucker wants me to do a little research for them." Vincent remained silent after that, for a little too long.

"Something wrong?"

"Jerry, you and Cindy have been incredibly generous to me, and I sure don't want to cause any problems. But I think it's going to be hard for me to continue being the van driver. Also, I'm thinkin' about movin' in with Nancy. We haven't settled everything yet, so please give me a few days to be sure what's going to happen. I just don't want to put you and Cindy in a bind. I'll still help any time I can, at no cost. But I think I'm going to be a little busy doing investigations again."

"Hell, Vincent, that's great. Don't worry about us, we'll manage." He gave Vincent a grin. "Movin' in with Nancy—*how about you!*"

Vincent ignored the grin, and the comment. "What about

offering my job to Rick? He told me he quit his job in Denver. I think he'd be great."

⎯◯⎯

"Did you kill her?" Bobby didn't know how else to ask.

Ilse looked shocked. "What kind of an insane question is that? Of course I didn't kill her!"

"You left the room and took my car. Where did you go?"

"I'm not going to be interrogated by you! Fuck you! Get out!" Now she was yelling and crying, completely out of control. She picked up a glass and threw it at him.

The glass hit him in the shoulder and broke, scattering glass across the floor. "Damn it, Ilse, calm down. I'm trying to help you." He stood, staring at her, then began cleaning up the pieces.

Ilse ran into the bathroom, slammed the door, and locked it.

Bobby didn't know if he would lie for Ilse. He cared about her, maybe even loved her, but lying to the police, and possibly covering up a crime, weren't ideas he was comfortable with. He knew from overhearing a couple of gossiping cops talking about Ilse's alibi; that she had told them she'd been in the casita with him all night. They hadn't asked him to confirm that story yet, but they would. He knew she was scared, and that her actions pointed toward her having killed Anna. And he was having trouble dealing with what it said about her—the kind of person she was. Could she really kill someone? He knew she was volatile, but something that extreme was hard to believe.

He decided to go to the kitchen and get a cup of coffee, since it looked like Ilse wasn't coming out of the bathroom anytime soon. On the way back to their rooms with his coffee, he spotted Vincent. "Got a minute?"

"Sure, what's up?"

"Could we go out back?"

Vincent shrugged, then headed to the gazebo. It had been a cool morning, but as the middle of the afternoon approached the temperature was rising quickly. "How's Ilse after this morning's events?"

"Not good. I've got a problem, Vincent, and not sure if I should be talking to you at all. But I need some advice."

"We don't know each other very well, but if this has anything to do with the murder, or the financial matters at the art gallery, you should only talk to a lawyer. If you say something to me, that isn't a privileged communication. And if I'm asked about it, I have to tell the truth."

Now Bobby seemed even more unsure what to do, but with some difficulty he made up his mind to forge ahead. "Okay, I understand. Ilse called the Albuquerque attorney, and she's supposed to meet with him tomorrow. My problem is that I don't know that Ilse will tell him the truth."

Vincent thought that was an odd thing for Bobby to say; and wondered why he would say it, but decided to just convey legal-like advice. "You need to tell her to tell her attorney the truth—never lie to your own lawyer. If she killed Anna, tell the attorney. It'll be her best chance of coming up with a defense. If she didn't kill her, but she knows something she didn't tell the police, she needs to tell that to her attorney, too."

Bobby looked unhappy. "Could you talk to her?"

Vincent sighed. "I don't think I should. You should know I've been hired by the Hill firm to do investigative work on this case. But even so, I'm still not the person she should talk to. She needs to call her attorney and go see him, probably right now."

"Well, she had a bit of a fit and locked herself in the bathroom. She needs someone to talk to, and I'm not sure I know what to say. This is really not my thing. Can you come to the room and just tell her the same stuff you're telling me? I'm worried sick about this, and if I go to her mother, Ilse will be livid."

In the casita, Vincent knocked gently on the bathroom door.

"Ilse? This is Vincent Malone. I work here at the Inn. Bobby's very concerned about you, and asked if I'd come and talk to you. I know a lot about the police and how these matters work, so maybe we could talk some, and decide what you should do next. Is that okay?"

There was no response. He knocked again, but no sound came from inside the bathroom. Vincent went back into the yard, where Bobby had decided to stay, thinking it might make it easier for Ilse to consider coming out. "Are you sure she's in there?" Vincent asked him.

Bobby looked stressed. "I don't know—I don't have any way *to* know. She was in there when I left. Jeez, what should we do?"

Vincent decided he'd had enough of this game. He went back to the bathroom door and used a small tool from his wallet to pick the lock. Inside, Ilse lay on the floor, unconscious, and she didn't look well. After a brief search, he found an empty medication bottle. He took out his phone and called 911. "Need an ambulance at the Blue Door Inn." He gave them the address and said the person in distress appeared to have taken some pills and was unconscious. He gave them the name of the drug and described, as best he could, her breathing and overall appearance. The dispatcher assured him an ambulance was on the way.

Vincent told Bobby what happened and asked him to get Ilse's mother. He called Jerry to tell him what was going on, asking him to be on the lookout for the ambulance. He went back into the bathroom and covered Ilse with a blanket from the bed. He could see she was breathing, but it seemed shallower than before. His instinct was to do something, but he knew doing something wrong could be worse than doing nothing at all. Hearing voices, he went back into the back yard.

"Please, everyone shut up!" he hissed to Ilse's mother and manager, both of whom had begun yelling the moment he appeared. "She's unconscious, and we shouldn't do anything until the ambulance gets here." He sure as hell hoped he was doing the right thing, but he was pretty damned certain that having her mother stand over her and scream while she lay unconscious wasn't going to help. They heard the siren.

With professional detachment, the emergency responders quickly took over. The medics communicated with the hospital and followed orders to start an IV. After checking various critical signs and relaying the information to the hospital, they put Ilse on a gurney. They had a brief conversation with the waiting group, then took Ilse and the pill bottle and headed to the hospital.

"You bastard, what did you do to her?" Bente Smit was crying, pointing a shaky finger at Bobby. Dirk strained to hold her back.

Bobby fumed right back at her. "If anyone did anything to her, it was you. Why can't you just leave her alone?"

"Everybody shut the hell up, right now!" Vincent hated drama for drama's sake. He glared at everyone until they were quiet. "Bobby, you take your car to the hospital. You two," he nodded toward Bente and Dirk, "can come with me."

He gave Bobby directions. Bente and Dirk headed out to the van without comment, though it was clear they thought they'd been treated badly. Vincent decided that before he could leave, he needed to give Jerry and Cindy an update. He found them in the kitchen, obviously worried.

"What's going on, can we help; we've stayed out of the way, but we will do whatever is needed." Jerry was holding Cindy's hand and they both seemed very upset.

"We're headed to the hospital. I'm taking the mother and that manager guy with me in the van. Bobby went in his car. Everyone's pretty upset, and they've been saying some stupid things to one another. Last I saw, Ilse was still unconscious. Didn't look encouraging. But there is nothing anyone can do now but wait and see what happens."

"Do you think she's really in danger?" Cindy was tearing up some.

"Yes. I'm not sure what the stuff was that she took, but it was definitely powerful and fast. She hadn't been in the bathroom all that long, so it's a bad sign that she was already unconscious when I got there."

"Do you want us to go with you to the hospital?" Jerry asked, looking pale.

"No. I don't think that is necessary. I'll call you as soon as I know something. The only reason I'm going to stay is to make sure her loved ones don't kill one another."

14

No Visitors Allowed

Vincent had barely settled into the van when Dirk spoke up.

"Is there more than one hospital in this town?"

"Yes. They took her to Saint Vincent's." If it hadn't been such a serious situation, he would have thrown in several wiseass remarks, but he kept those to himself.

"How long to get there?" Dirk didn't look pleased.

"Fifteen minutes or so."

Bente hadn't said anything, but her glare at the back of Vincent's head seemed to suggest she thought he was somehow at fault. Maybe he could make it in ten if he ran a few red lights.

The hospital was an imposing facility, filled to the brim with bustling medical professionals. That seemed to reassure Bente and Dirk. It certainly *looked* like a real hospital. They entered through the emergency room door, and Bobby saw them immediately, looking relieved to have them there.

"They haven't told me anything yet. A nurse came out and got some information about Ilse, but wouldn't say anything about her condition." Bobby was suffering from the anxiety, born of helplessness, that thrives in hospital waiting rooms.

"I'll see what I can find out." It sounded good, but Vincent really only wanted an excuse to leave. He needed some space, and knew there would be a designated smoking area. Soon a cop came out. Vincent hoped he wasn't the smoke police.

"You Vincent Malone?"

"Yeah."

"Chief wants to talk to you." He handed Vincent his phone.

"Malone."

"Got word Ilse tried to kill herself. What can you tell me?" The chief was direct, and more than a little demanding, which annoyed Vincent.

"Nothing you don't already know, I'm sure. She locked herself in the bathroom in her room at the Inn and took some pills—I'm not sure what they were—and passed out, fast. I picked the lock and found her on the floor, called 911. The hospital hasn't told us squat, so I don't know how she's doing. But she didn't look good when they put her in the ambulance."

"I know this is going to sound heartless, but we have enough evidence at this point to charge Ilse for the murder of Anna Marks. We won't actually do anything about that just yet, not under these circumstances. But I'm placing a guard on her room at the hospital."

"What's the evidence?"

"Not going to discuss every detail right now, but she told us she was in her room at the Blue Door Inn the whole night—didn't leave. We have video evidence that's not true—she was at the gallery during the night. That and a few other items give us probable cause to charge her. I'm sorry she tried to kill herself, but it's my job to enforce the law. And that's what I'm going to do, even at the hospital."

"Understood. She retained Jack Hill to help with some financial and legal issues to do with her art. I'll let him know where things stand."

"Hiring Jack Hill sounds more like someone expecting to be charged with murder than safeguarding money." It was true, but it still sounded snarky.

"I'm sure he'll be able to handle both. They also hired me to help with any investigating they need."

"Sounds like you're turning into a permanent local."

"Maybe." Vincent liked the chief, but the conversation had turned awkward. "Guess that makes me a potential voter. You're going to have to be more considerate."

"That's the mayor's problem, not mine. I'm hired, not elected, thank god. Take care, Vincent."

Vincent returned the phone to the officer. Ilse had lied to the police about her whereabouts on the night of the crime. That would put her at the top of the suspects list, for sure. And once you're on that list, it can be damned hard to get off. And if they had enough evidence to arrest her, then more likely than not they weren't going to put maximum effort into looking for other suspects. Vincent called Tucker.

"Shit. You think she'll make it?"

"Don't know. Probably depends on what the pills were, and how long they were in her system. We'll likely know something in the next thirty minutes or so."

"Any thoughts on why the body was moved to the park?"

"Not really. It was obviously intended to be found quickly, sitting in the middle of a high-traffic tourist spot like that. It's not far from the gallery, so that's probably a factor. If someone killed her at the gallery, but didn't want the body to be found there for some reason, they could just move it to a spot not far away, and walk back. I'm sure Hill will have good background information on the police chief, but I think there is no question, based on my limited experience with him, that he's a good cop who knows what he's doing. If he's moved this quickly, then they have something. Which means your client is not only fighting for her life in the hospital but, if she recovers, she has one hell of a problem with a serious murder charge."

"I'll get with Jack and give him this information. You know how this works—we're going to need other suspects—realistic, plausible suspects—if we're going to help Ilse. You need to get as much information as you can on who that could be. If she actually did it, we'll start looking at possible defenses. But if she didn't, then we need a murderer."

"Yeah. If the cops are convinced Ilse's their killer, they'll stop looking. So, I guess it's up to us to keep things going. For good or ill, Anna Marks was living in the middle of what looks like a firestorm, with all sorts of financial entanglements and a few sexual ones. So, there'll be other suspects. I'll get to work on gathering what I can. Any cost limits?"

"None. Hill isn't the cheap-ass I am, so he'll want a full-throated effort, on all fronts."

"On another matter, I talked to Rick Flores. He's moved

back here from Denver. He didn't give me the details, but I believe one reason he left Denver was that he was threatened by Ken Simpson. Simpson's a small-time hood. He bullies anyone and everyone, whenever he thinks he can get away with it. I really don't like bullies, Tucker. I'm thinkin' about a quick trip to Denver, on my own nickel, to make it clear to Simpson that any threats to Flores are a threat to me. I know this is do-gooder shit, which I normally avoid, but I can't help it."

"You're a complicated man, Vincent." Tucker went silent for a minute. "Let me tell Hill you need to look into Ilse's boyfriend, and that you need a trip to Denver to do that. You can check in with the firm's office in Denver, and Hill will pay your time and expenses. Okay?"

"I like the way you think, Tucker. Plus, I think I *will* check on Bobby. I don't know if he's a possible suspect—no motive that I can see—but there's something about him that's off-center. Could be good to know a bit more about him."

"Keep me informed about Ilse's medical status. I'll talk to Jack about you going to Denver, but don't worry about it—he'll say yes, so, you can keep your nickel."

They disconnected. Vincent thought about asking Nancy if she wanted to go with him to Denver, but decided that would be selfish. *Hey, how about a trip to Denver, where you'll wait in a hotel room while I go out and hassle some folks?* It would be better to go by himself and keep it quick.

Vincent wandered back into the waiting area, and took a seat near the others. He concentrated on his phone as a way of avoiding conversation. Soon a doctor entered.

"My name's Doctor Jackson. Ilse's doing much better, and she's out of immediate danger. She was on the verge of cardiac arrest when she was brought in, and she's experiencing some neurological problems from the overdose of her anxiety medication. At this point, we're hopeful, though, that there won't be any long-term damage."

She wasn't doing well, but at least she wasn't going to die. Everyone in the group relaxed visibly.

"When will she be able to leave?" Bobby asked.

"I'm not sure. She's out of immediate danger, but we'll still need to monitor her for a few days, at least. There could be complications related to her kidneys. I think that if everything checks out, she should be able to leave the hospital in four or five days. Now, at least on the surface, this appears to have been an attempted suicide, so our procedures require that she be analyzed by one of our staff psychologists, who'll make recommendations about further treatment, and that could add a few days to her stay. We'll see how everything goes."

"When will we be able to see her?" Bente asked.

"She'll have to stay in intensive care for six to twelve hours. After that, if there are no complications, she'll be moved to a regular room, and you can see her then. We don't want her disturbed at this point, and she'll remain under sedation for now."

The doctor left, and with no more concern that Ilse might die, they managed to cooperate and be civil to one another. They developed a plan. Bobby would stay at the hospital, just in case. Bente and Dirk would go back to the Inn and rest, and return later to relieve Bobby.

After returning to the Inn, Vincent discussed his own plans with Jerry, though he left out the part about confronting Simpson—there was no reason to involve him in something like that. Jerry said he would ask Rick to shuttle the guests between the Inn and the hospital, and wished him a safe trip. Next, Vincent called Nancy, but got her voice mail. He left a message letting her know that he was headed to Denver briefly on business for the Hill law firm, which he figured sounded less threatening than saying he was going to beat up an old enemy.

Tucker arranged for Vincent to stay at the downtown Grand Hyatt, an extremely nice hotel in a convenient location. He checked in late and went straight to bed. He really was getting old—no late-night drinking for him, these days. The next morning, after a luxurious breakfast at his hotel, he walked the few blocks to the offices of Johnson, Johnson and Hill. He was met by Allan Travis, the managing partner of the Denver office. The meeting was cordial, and mostly a formality, but it did establish that he was in Denver doing work for the Hill firm—so, mission accomplished.

Ken Simpson had inherited his father's trucking business, R&R Trucking, after his dad died suddenly of a heart attack. He'd never been involved in the business before that, and was generally despised by the rest of his family, all of whom he hated in return. But because of poor legal planning, and his mother's death the year before, Ken was the sole heir. His father had been a tough, no-nonsense, former truck driver who ran an honest business. His good-for-nothing son soon changed everything. The business quickly developed a reputation for cutting corners, cheating customers, and screwing employees. And Ken brought in new personnel, turning R&R from a business into something more like a gang.

One of the law firms Vincent had done investigations for had hired him to get dirt on Simpson. Their client was suing Simpson and R&R Trucking for refusing to pay them for services related to truck maintenance. Vincent's snooping uncovered not only a deadbeat business, but what amounted to a small criminal empire involving the illegal shipping of a variety of contraband. During one of Vincent's intelligence-gathering ventures, he was confronted by Simpson and one of his stooges. Simpson had been under the impression he was a tough guy, but was quickly schooled in what tough guys were really like. He spent a week in the hospital along with his companion. After that altercation, Vincent alerted police to Simpson's illegal activities. From that first encounter came a mutual dislike, and years of hatred and threats. Vincent had always said that if one day he was found dead, the first suspect should be Ken Simpson. Now he was going to pay the man a personal visit—which he thought should be interesting.

15

Keep On Truckin'

Vincent drove along I-70 to the industrial area north of downtown Denver. R&R Trucking had a large lot, presumably for parking trucks, but it was conspicuously empty. He parked in front of the plain metal building. There were a couple of cars in front, but no obvious activity. Times didn't look good for R&R Trucking.

"What the fuck are you doing here?" Not your typical company greeting, but the meaning was clear; you're not welcome.

"Good to see you, too, Simpson. How about a little talk?"

Vincent eyed his enemy, who sat at the front desk, the first thing you saw as you entered. There were three other men in the office, all of whom immediately turned their attention toward him. He fingered the gun in his pocket for a little reassurance.

"Why the hell would I talk to you, asshole?" Simpson grinned. He was putting on a show for his employees, but his antagonism was real. And Vincent was sure he'd be uncooperative, with or without his cronies around.

"Rick Flores is a friend of mine. You go after him, you'll

have to deal with me." Vincent slid around to the side of the desk for a better view of the other men.

"Listen, you old fart. I have no idea who the fuck Rick Flores is, and you're nothing but a pain in my ass. I don't usually beat up golden old-timers, but unless you want to end up bruised and broken, you should get the hell out of here."

Simpson made a move to open the desk drawer. Vincent pulled his gun and busted it across Simpson's nose. The thug screamed in pain. Vincent aimed the gun at the others, who had yet to make a move. He ordered them into a side office. "You come out of there before I've gone, I will shoot your ass, got it?"

He got nods in return. He shut the door on them. Simpson, meanwhile, had fallen to the floor. He looked like he might pass out.

"You know who Rick Flores is, and you know I don't take shit from people like you. I know lots of shit about your operation in Durango, and I can cause you a ton of grief with the feds. But Ken, old buddy, I don't give a fuck about that. You leave Flores alone, and I'll just forget what I know about your two-bit criminal activities."

Vincent started to leave.

"This ain't over, you bastard." Simpson's voice sounded pinched. He held his nose to try to stop the bleeding, with little success.

Vincent turned back to Simpson and pointed the gun. Simpson's eyes widened. "Yes, this is over, unless you do somethin' real stupid. You do somethin' stupid, and the feds will have all of the info they need to lock your ass up for a long time. Or you'll be dead. Depends on what kind of mood I'm in."

Vincent went outside and began driving away, then noticed that he was almost out of gas. He pulled in at a truck stop down the street a few blocks, thinking how he was going to have to plan ahead a little better if he was going to go around threatening people, and needed a quick getaway. He headed back to the hotel and sat down to lunch. Once he'd ordered, Vincent took out his phone and placed a call. "Mister Younger, how the hell are you today?"

"Could this be my good buddy Vincent Malone?"

"Thought I should let you know I just threatened Ken Simpson with information I had about his operation in Durango. Told him to leave Rick Flores alone or I would spill the beans to the feds and have him locked up forever. Don't know if any of this will get back to your neck of the woods or not. But, I don't have any beans to spill. I just made that up."

The Durango attorney laughed out loud. "Any fallout so far from that exchange?"

"His nose might be broken. The man's clumsy."

"When I grow up, I want to be just like you, Vincent."

"Keep drinking beer and eating fried foods, and you'll make it."

"Don't worry about anything here. What I'm being told is that there was a falling out between the Franks Law Firm and Simpson. Apparently, Franks Junior had some kind of ownership interest in his trucking company, and after they went their separate ways, he had all their trucks repossessed. Don't know if this thing is going to be settled in court or in the street, but it could be Ken Simpson has bigger problems than a rampaging Vincent Malone. Word on the street is that he owes some very bad people some very big sums of money, and they want it yesterday."

"Couldn't happen to a nicer guy. Thanks for the information, George. Gotta go. Don't do anything I wouldn't do."

"That leaves me with plenty of options. See ya."

Vincent liked Younger—he reminded him of himself, but uglier. He got directions to Bobby's business, as well as the address of his apartment, both of which were on the west side of the city in an upscale neighborhood. Spotting what looked like a trendy bar a few doors down from Bobby's apartment, Vincent availed himself of the valet parking and entered a drinking man's heaven. It was the nicest bar he'd ever been in, and he'd been in quite a few. Everything was leather and brass or in some cases, gold. When you don't know something, you ask a bartender—it was a rule that had worked for him for years. Still, maybe posh joints like this one hired more discreet people to pour drinks than his usual watering holes did. He slid onto a stool and leaned his elbows on the mahogany bar. The bartender was a very attractive young woman who walked like she was modeling high fashion—this wasn't really Vincent's world. Not ready to give up his view of the world just yet, he pulled out a twenty and eyed the beautiful woman.

"I'm looking for information on a Bobby Hawkins. Lives in the building next door."

The cold-eyed woman gave Vincent a look that suggested

she was contemplating pulling a secret lever that would cause him to drop straight through the floor and into hell. Never one to give up quickly, he pulled out another twenty and laid it on the bar. Her manner changed, and the forty bucks disappeared discreetly.

"Sure, I know him. Good tipper. Owns a business around here somewhere. Comes in with his employees. Very generous, and it seems like they all think he's a good boss. Only bad rumor I've ever heard was that he had some drug problems in the past—but fuck, who hasn't?"

Vincent was reassured by her willingness to talk to him. The old ways die hard. He left, and tried to enter Bobby's apartment building, but was told by a stern security guard that Bobby wasn't home, and that he wouldn't be allowed in. The entire conversation took place through a video hookup at the entrance. Everything looked very expensive and well protected.

Next stop was Bobby's business. SMY Graphics' offices were in a large building with an open design that also housed a number of companies sharing a common area and support services. The central receptionist asked Vincent who he wanted to see, and he asked for the office manager. Soon a bespectacled young man approached.

"Mister Malone. My name is Carl Long, I'm office manager for SMY Graphics. How can I help you?"

"Carl, I'm looking for a company to help me develop a new product. I know you must have salespeople, or a president, or something, but I prefer to talk to one of the real people before I get fed a bunch of bullshit. Is this a good company to work for?"

Carl Long stared hard at Vincent, then grinned. "I don't believe a word of that, but I'm perfectly comfortable talking about SMY Graphics. It's a great company to work for. We do wonderful design and production work. You couldn't find a better graphics company anywhere, much less in Denver."

"How about the owner? Typical rich asshole?"

Long actually laughed. "This is a joke, right? The owner's name is Bobby Hawkins—I imagine you already knew that—and he's a great boss and an outstanding graphic designer. I think he is rich, as you say, but you'd never know it by anything he says or does. And he's not an asshole—as for you, though, I'm not so sure. What are you really doing here?"

"Good to have met you, Carl. I know Bobby, and this was just a little joke. I'll suggest that he give you a raise."

Vincent left. Time to drop in on one of his old cop cronies, Lieutenant Romano of the Denver Police Department. He found him at his desk.

"Sonofabitch, if it isn't Vincent Malone. I thought you'd died. Or retired to the desert, or something."

"Good to see you too, Lieutenant. Didn't die, but I did leave town for a while. Just back visiting, and thought I should drop in and say hi."

Romano chuckled. They were more like enemies than friends, but you could miss an enemy, too, like a toothache—once it's gone, and you start to forget how much it hurt.

"Doin' a little snooping. Know a guy named Bobby Hawkins?"

"Nope, but if I did, I wouldn't tell you. Snooping does not mean dropping by the police department to dig up dirt." Romano chuckled again—he seemed to enjoy seeing his sort-of pal again. "Hope you're not in town causing any trouble. There's people here who would like nothing better than get something on you and lock you up."

"Yeah, I know. I make friends wherever I go. Thanks for nothing, Romano. Don't get killed before you reach retirement, okay?"

"Why do you want to know about Hawkins?"

Vincent's radar lit up. *He* does *know Hawkins.* "Just domestic snooping for the rich and famous. He's involved with someone, and her family's checking on him. It's lousy work, but I have to make a living."

"They *should* be checking—he's not what he seems. Look Vincent, I've already said too much, but just tell that family to grab their daughter, or whatever she is, and run. Run away as fast as they can."

"My god, Romano, you can't just say that and not give me somethin' more definite."

The cop looked unhappy. "I shouldn't have said anything. You've got to promise me—this is just between us. He's never been arrested, and I haven't been involved in anything related to him. I've heard his name mentioned. Mostly it's bar talk about him being under suspicion for drug dealing. This is high-end shit, mostly for famous people. But if it gets out that I mentioned anything to you, I'll lose my goddamn job."

"Don't worry, I'll keep it quiet. Who's running the investigation?"

"The feds. As far as we know, he's clean in Denver. This is a New York-and-LA investigation. And I'm not sure the feds really know how he's involved, but they came to us to help with surveillance on him. It was described to me as some kind of club, or group. You pay a big, fat fee to become a member, and then you get what you want in terms of drugs. Plus, there seems to be sex stuff, too."

The whole story reeked of bullshit. "You're making this shit up to just yank my chain, aren't you?"

"Hey, I don't know whether it's true or not. I shouldn't have said anything, okay?" Romano was nervous, which also made him irritable. "Just forget it, will you?"

"Sure, fine. I won't report it to my client. But, look, if something does happen, you need to call me and let me know." Vincent pulled out a card and told Romano he was still using the same cell phone number he'd had for ages. "Remember, if you find out something for sure about this guy, call me. Maybe I can help the girl if he's really bad."

Romano groaned like he was in pain. "Me and my big mouth. Yeah, if I find out anything for sure, I'll call you. Where the hell are you now, anyway?"

"Santa Fe. Call me."

Vincent went back to the hotel and checked out. He knew he should stay one more night and head back in the morning, but something told him he would sleep better if he wasn't in Denver.

Bobby involved in drugs? That doesn't make sense—but the part about hobnobbing with the rich and famous does. Jeez, is everybody pushing some kind of scheme? Probably. You'd think I'd know that by now.

So, is he giving Ilse drugs? Should I call Tucker and let him know about this little bit of gossip? I need facts first—real facts, not just rumors. How'm I going to separate the truth from the bullshit? Well, if you want to know somethin' about a horse, go to the horse's mouth.

16

Caution Be Damned

Vincent spent the night at a Holiday Inn Express in Pueblo, where he got a great night's sleep, and woke up before dawn feeling energized. He grabbed a McDonald's breakfast sandwich at the drive-thru, and headed for New Mexico. He thought about his preference for McDonald's, and decided it was just plain smart—the best bargain available, and Vincent was no food snob. He sipped his coffee, and wondered why the hell they always made it so hot.

He decided his first stop in Santa Fe would be the hospital. No one had called with an update on Ilse, which could mean nothing had changed, or simply no one thought of telling him. He needed to know her condition before going ahead with his other plans. He entered the hospital and stopped at the information desk in the main lobby.

"Ilse De Vries' room, please."

The elderly lady smiled at Vincent and began typing into the computer. "Sorry, sir, we don't have a patient by that name. Maybe I spelled it wrong. Is it DeVries?"

"I think it's two words, 'D-E and V-R-I-E-S."

She typed again. "No, no one by that name. Maybe the

patient was discharged?" She seemed to want to help.

"Thanks, maybe so." Vincent walked away, pulled out his phone and called Jerry. "Hey, Jerry, this is Vincent. Just got back into Santa Fe and stopped by the hospital to check on Ilse, but they don't show her as being here now. Did she check out?"

"No. Well, I guess I don't know. She's not here, and her mother didn't say anything about it this morning. Something sounds wrong."

"Yeah. Is Bobby there?"

"I haven't seen him this morning. Hold on, let me look outside and see if his car is here." There was a pause, and Vincent could hear Jerry open the front door. "No car. Want me to check his room?"

"Nah, not right now. If his car's not there, then I'm sure he's gone. Let me get more information, and I'll call you back."

He returned to the smiling information lady. "I wonder if I could talk to someone who would know about the patient I mentioned?"

"Well, let's see who the doctor is." She began to type. "Hm. Not sure about this information. Maybe if you could just wait over there I will get someone to talk to you. Your name, sir?"

"Vincent Malone. I'm a friend of Ilse and her mother."

He walked over to a waiting area and took a seat. He was getting a bad feeling. When the wait stretched into ten minutes, he figured something was up. He was about to get up to ask the nice lady what her game was when he saw the police chief headed his way. Something was definitely wrong. "What's happened?"

"She left. Not sure exactly when, but hours ago. My guard was apparently having some bathroom issues, and was in the john several times during the night. During one of his breaks, she took off. I was just going over the security video when they told me someone was here asking about her. I was up to the point where Bobby Hawkins came into the hospital at about three-thirty in the morning. I think we'll soon see what time they left. Want to join me?"

"Sure." Vincent followed the chief to the basement and a cramped, dark security room with numerous monitors. The chief introduced the security officer for the hospital and asked him to restart the video. Soon they saw Ilse and Bobby leaving the hospital, with the video showing a little before four a.m. timestamp. Ilse didn't look good.

"The nurses didn't realize she was gone until almost six in the morning. And my guard never thought to check the room until then, so that's when he found out he'd screwed up. We put out an alert on the car and both parties and contacted the state police, all around seven o'clock. But a head start of three hours could put them close to another state by then. So far, we haven't informed any other states."

Vincent caught a whiff of something and looked at the chief. "Now it's almost ten. What's the issue with contacting the other states?"

The chief looked unhappy. "I've asked someone in the AG's office to clarify something for me. You see, technically, we never charged her. Because she was in the hospital and unconscious at the time we determined we would charge her for the murder, we never had a chance to actually follow through. I was reluctant to put out an APB regarding a murder suspect when we had hardly even questioned her, or read her rights to her. Sure would hate to have some overly eager Colorado Highway Patrolman shoot her as a murder suspect, and then find out she had a solid alibi. But I'm going to have to do something real soon."

Vincent nodded. "Do the doctors think she's at any risk medically?"

"They're hedging their bets, giving me wishy-washy answers, so I'm guessing she is. But they're just not sure how serious. They were running an IV, but apparently it was mostly to rehydrate her after the procedures they used to clean the drugs out of her system. They said she'd definitely be very weak and sleepy."

"If she hasn't been charged, I guess that means that Bobby didn't aid a fugitive. Are you going to charge him?"

The chief shook his head. "This is one big fuck-up. I'm not sure what I'll do. Probably won't charge him if we can get her back. Where do you think they might go?"

"I really have no idea. Bobby lives in Denver, but I think that'd be the last place they'd go. Ilse is from the Netherlands, and as far as I know, her only connections to this part of the world are Bobby and Santa Fe. So, if they're running, I guess they could head anywhere—there's no place that's more or less likely than any other. The big question in my mind is, why run? Does that mean she killed Anna?" The chief stayed silent, which let Vincent think a moment before he went on, "There are other possibilities. Bobby may be rescuing her from her mother as much as the police. She just tried to kill herself. It may be her mental state that they're trying to run from."

"Whatever the reason, they've made a huge mistake."

"What are you going to do about your guard?" Vincent smiled, even though it wasn't really funny.

"The doctor gave him something for his stomach problems, and I sent him home. It's hard to find anyone to take these jobs, and this guy is actually one of my better men. Guess I just ignore it and hope he's learned a lesson." The chief chuckled, also with little humor.

Vincent left the hospital and sat in his car a while, thinking. He pulled out his phone, but his call went straight to voice mail. "Bobby, this is Vincent Malone. You should know that you could be making a big mistake. The police aren't certain yet what to do, but this isn't going to just blow over. Once they decide on a plan, they can track your phone and your credit cards. Your smartest move would be to come back to Santa Fe. I'm pretty confident that if you come back now, there won't be any consequences." He wasn't so sure about sticking his nose in, but getting them to come back still seemed like the best course, so he went with it, but added an option. "On the other hand, if I needed a place to rest and recuperate, I'd look at Durango. If you ever happen to be in that neck of the woods, you might want to look up my good friend George Younger. He's in the book, under 'attorneys.'"

Vincent couldn't think of anything else to say, so he disconnected. He called Younger and left a voice mail saying a friend might be calling, and if he did, to let him know. Finally, he called Tucker.

"Sonofabitch, that is so fucking stupid. The police will zero in on her for sure, now. What do you think the chief will do?"

"I think all he wants is Ilse back, either in jail or in the hospital under guard. I don't think he cares about charging Bobby, mostly because he's not real sure there's a charge that would stick. He'll probably sit on this for a bit, but eventually he'll go after Ilse because he thinks she did it. And at that point he'll go after Bobby, too, if he gets in the way again. What do you want me to do?"

"Not sure yet. How did things go in Denver?"

"Okay, I think. I'll give you a more complete report later."

"Sure, that's fine. Ilse's hired us to help with the money side of things, so I think that's what we should concentrate on until we know more about the murder charge. I'll talk with Jack, but for now why don't you nose around the gallery, and talk to that butterfly Clive to see what you can find out?"

"You know, I think calling Clive a 'butterfly' is some kind of slur."

"Who gives a fuck?" Tucker clicked off. He was getting back into his old ways.

Vincent parked across the street from the gallery. He could see a lot of activity. Occasionally he would glimpse Clive directing some workmen who seemed to be crating the large paintings, but he wasn't sure if that was what should be happening. They might have been some of the paintings that were sold, in which case they'd be packaged up for shipping to the new owners, which would be perfectly normal. Clive, butterfly or not, seemed to be in complete command. Vincent had gotten some background about Clive online, and knew he was well respected in the fine art field. One article said hiring Clive had probably saved the Howard Marks Gallery from bankruptcy.

He'd done some research on Francis Mitchell, too, but hadn't found anything other than court documents from his divorce, besides bits and pieces related to his CPA practice and his Santa Fe address. He didn't notice Francis at the gallery, and decided to drop by his house to see if he was home.

The address wasn't far from downtown, in a quiet neighborhood of small, mostly adobe houses. They were different from what Vincent was used to. Most of them had an enclosed courtyard in front. *Not a bad idea.* As he approached, he noticed a doorbell button and intercom speaker next to the gate in the tall, adobe wall around the yard. He pressed the button. There was some delay, and he was about ready to conclude no one was home when he got a response.

"Yes, what do you want?" The voice wasn't very friendly.

"My name's Vincent Malone. I'd like to speak to Francis Mitchell." No answer. He was about to say something else when the voice came again.

"I don't want to talk to you, go away." If a door had been opened, metaphorically, it had just been slammed in his face.

"I work for Ilse De Vries. I'm with the Johnson, Johnson and Hill law firm. We've been hired to look into some financial matters. If you don't want to talk now, we'll have a summons issued by the court. It's your choice."

A wise person would have just left Vincent standing there and gone about their business. But many people had an irrational fear of courts and the law. A summons, they imagined, meant they'd done something wrong. A page straight out of the lawyer's—and politician's—playbook; feed people bullshit to get them to do what you want.

"Okay, just a minute."

Vincent wondered if Mitchell was calling someone to see what he should do. Or maybe, as was often the case, the mousy guy would turn out to be more dangerous than he seemed. Maybe old Francis was getting his twelve-gauge and would come out blazing. The thought wasn't entirely serious, but he tensed, anyway.

He heard an electronic *buzz-clack* that meant a remote lock had been released. The gate was apparently more than just ornamental. Why such a secure barrier in such a peaceful neighborhood? The voice came from the speaker. "Come in."

The thought crossed his mind, again, that one of these days he was going to walk into something he regretted. How many times in your life could you open a door, not knowing what was on the other side, without eventually getting yourself killed? He shuddered, but he went in.

The courtyard he crossed before reaching the front door was beautiful. Vincent wasn't really much for noticing beauty for its own sake, but the flowers were gorgeous. He wondered at the effort it took to grow plants so lush, with bright blue flowers, in high-altitude Santa Fe. The door to the small house was bright red, set in white adobe. While not uncommon in many places of the world, it still surprised Vincent to see how many people hereabouts used very bold colors for their front doors. It was both refreshing and unsettling.

As he approached the colorful door, it opened. Standing in the entrance was Francis Mitchell, dressed in a flowery housecoat that was quite beautiful and very feminine. He wore enough heavy makeup to make a Vegas showgirl blush. He also was packing what appeared to be a Smith & Wesson .44 Magnum handgun in a side holster slung on over the housecoat. The combination was unsettling. Even by itself the Dirty Harry pistol was serious business. More a cannon than a gun, it could blast an impressive hole right through that heavy front door, and what it would do to a human body was an ugly thought, indeed. Unsure how to start, Vincent fell back on banality, ignoring the gun as best he could.

"Hello, Mister Mitchell. How are you today?" Might as well be polite if you're about to die.

17

Lazy Crazy Days of Summer

"I don't have to talk to you. You're not the police." Mitchell looked smug and defiant, but his body language contradicted him. He repeatedly jerked his left shoulder upward in a nervous twitch.

"You're absolutely right. I'm not the police. I just want to talk to you a bit about the gallery business. It's my understanding that you've been the company's accountant for quite a few years, right?"

Mitchell nodded. "Yep. I worked for Howard for a lot of years. He was my first real client back in LA." There went the shoulder twitch. "I helped him a bunch, especially in the beginning. Howard knew how to sell—really a great salesman—but he didn't know much about accounting, or how to read financials. I worked with him on basic business stuff, teaching him how to use the numbers to run a better business. He was a big drinker, and sometimes when he'd get drunk, he'd tell me I was the reason he'd become so successful. I didn't know whether to believe him or not. Howard was something of a con man, always playing the angles in one way or another—he even conned himself." Mitchell turned a little sad.

"You helped him open up his other galleries?" He wanted to keep Mitchell talking because it seemed to mellow him out a little.

"Yep. I put together all the presentations for the banks while he was borrowing money to expand. I usually went with him to help with the meeting, in case there were financial questions. He'd often refer to me as his partner, although at that time I didn't actually own anything. He just used me to make the banks feel more comfortable." Mitchell looked up at Vincent as if he'd only just remembered who he was talking to. "What is it you want, anyway?"

"Just a little background information, is all." Vincent paused and gave Mitchell his best I'm-a-good-guy-and-you're-not-crazy smile. "So, when Howard Marks died, and his daughter inherited the business, you stayed on to help her?"

"Fuck, help *her*? *Nobody* could help her. She knew everything—at least, she thought she did. And I didn't *stay on*. Howard left me an ownership stake in the business, and I was looking out after my own interests." Mitchell's rouged cheeks got redder.

Now, this was news. Mitchell owned a portion of the business? Vincent went ahead cautiously. "Did it surprise you that Howard Marks left you a piece of the gallery?"

"A little. He'd always said he was going to take care of me in his will. But I thought that was just Howard bullshitting me, the way he had for years. Anytime I tried to raise my rates, he'd say something along the lines of, I was helping him build the business, and he would take care of me when the time came—whatever the hell that meant. That was just Howard, though. Even when he had money, he was cheap. I'd sold my practice before he died, but I kept him as a client. I moved to Fresno, where my new wife lived, and after that I more or less worked full-time for Howard. So, I guess I thought he might leave me a little something. But I was shocked that it was a share in the business. And I'll tell you, Anna went ballistic. She inherited all of her father's stinginess, without any of his charm or smarts."

Mitchell had gradually led him into the house's small living room, and they now sat in high-back chairs. Jackpot. *Keep him talking.* Vincent nodded like all this was old news to him. "I've heard Anna was hard to work for. That true?"

"Everybody had problems with Anna. She was a difficult woman. But I tried to help her, every way I could. I worked out refinance deals with the banks so she had the cash flow she needed to run the business. And if she hadn't screwed up with those forged paintings, everything would have worked out just fine."

"I've read about that. News reports said she was sold fake paintings, and then resold them to her customers as authentic."

"In a nutshell. Little Miss Smarty-Pants got conned, bigtime. Clive says any gallery owner worth their salt would have known the paintings weren't real. Said it was a pure rube move to have bought those awful fakes. And to turn around and guarantee their authenticity to your top customers was beyond anything he'd ever seen. He told me she shouldn't be in the art business at all, and he knows a lot about the business."

"I hear some say that Clive saved the business from bankruptcy."

"You got that right. Without Clive, that business, including my share, would be worthless." The shoulder twitch intensified. Mitchell eyed him and suddenly stood. Vincent's guard went up. "I think I've said enough to you. I shouldn't be talking to you at all. Please leave. Now."

Time to retreat. "Of course, Mister Mitchell. Maybe we can talk again at some other time." Vincent stood, but didn't turn his back on Mitchell. "I wanted to compliment you on the wonderful flowers in your front courtyard. They're really stunning."

Mitchell's look softened and—far more importantly— his hand moved away from the huge revolver. "Thank you. Clive and I spend a lot of time taking care of those flowers. I'm glad you enjoyed them."

The shoulder twitch turned calmer once they were in the garden. Vincent opened the courtyard gate and said goodbye. Closing the gate behind him, he breathed a sigh of relief and hurried to his car. He didn't know exactly where Francis fit on the crazy scale, but the image of the blue flowered robe and heavy artillery was going to stick in his head for a while.

Santa Fe sits at a very high altitude, which often means cool nights, even in summer. But that doesn't prevent serious heat during the day, and it was going to be one of those days. Vincent cranked up the AC in his old Mustang, watched the gas gauge slowly sink toward empty, and called Tucker to give him an update on Francis Mitchell. Tucker laughed several times during his account, evidently enjoying Vincent's discomfort.

"I'll get someone to research public records regarding Marks's will, plus any filings that might indicate ownership. Does that make a suspect of Mitchell? Or Clive?" Tucker had a single focus; getting his client off.

"Absolutely. That much motive alone, plus opportunity, would put them on the list. And there's no doubt that Mitchell's a few bubbles short of plumb. I don't have proof yet, but judging by appearances, it looks like he and Clive are in some kind of relationship, most likely a romantic one. And they both, according to Mitchell, hold Anna responsible for all the problems at the gallery. They hate her. Hate by itself doesn't say much about a willingness to kill, but you toss in a bunch of money and a secret romance, and that's a lot more convincing."

"Where are you headed now?"

"To the gallery. I haven't been able to talk to the business manager, a guy named Trent Taylor. He's around, but hard to pin down. I thought I'd run by and see if he's there. If not, I'll try to find out where he lives. Got anything else for me?"

"We're getting word that Santa Fe PD will be putting out a 'be on the lookout' alert for Ilse and Bobby sometime today, going out to surrounding jurisdictions. They'll describe them as 'persons of interest,' wanted for questioning only. The talk out of Santa Fe is that the chief is reluctant to charge Ilse at this point, even if he was ready to do so while she was in the hospital. That might mean they have new evidence implicating someone else, or what they thought they had on Ilse didn't pan out. At this point, we just don't know. It might be useful to drop by and see if your buddy the chief will talk to you."

"Will do." Vincent disconnected, then called Jerry at the Inn. "Just wanted to give you a heads-up on my schedule. Looks like I have a pretty full day doing some digging for Tucker, but if you need anything you can give me a call. Anything going on?"

"Nope. Pretty calm here. Maybe I'll see you tomorrow morning at breakfast?"

"Sounds good." Vincent thought about how comfortable he'd gotten with Jerry and Cindy, and it made him smile. His next call was to Nancy, which went to voice mail.

"I'm back in Santa Fe. Got a couple of stops, and then I was going to run by the bar. Thought I'd just give you a warning. See ya later." All his voice mail messages sounded stupid to him. He frowned.

There was less activity around the gallery now, but workmen were still moving things around. He entered and immediately saw Clive. "Hey, I was looking for Taylor. Is he around?"

"You! You stay the fuck away from Francis or some bad shit could happen to you!" Clive did what he could to seem threatening.

Vincent wasn't exactly alarmed. He gave him his best blasé thug look, and Clive seemed to realize his bluster had no effect. "You need to watch your mouth, Clive. All I did was talk to Francis. And if I want to do it again, I will. Where's Taylor?"

Clive seemed confused about what to do next, and decided to exit, stage left. "I don't know," he said, quickly heading for the storeroom.

Vincent looked around, but didn't see Taylor, and now Clive had left, too. He headed to police headquarters.

"Yes, we're putting out a BOLO. You wouldn't happen to know where they are, would you, Vincent?" The chief didn't treat him like a germ, the way most cops did, and he wondered why.

"If I knew, I'd tell you. Had a strange conversation with Francis Mitchell today." Vincent related the gist of his encounter.

"Owns part of the business? That *is* interesting. Wonder what that means now that Anna's dead?"

Vincent had wondered the same thing. "Not sure. But it does open up some areas of inquiry that seem relevant." He let that soak in a moment. "At one point, you seemed ready to charge Ilse with the murder, but now she's just a person of interest. Something change?"

"Fair question." The chief's initial friendliness was ebbing, but it also could have been that he just didn't like being questioned, like anyone else. "I was prepared to charge her because we couldn't hold her unless we did. I was concerned, as was the DA, that she could skip out on us. If she made it back to Amsterdam, we had no idea if we'd ever get her back. Well, that ship has sailed. So, once she's found, we'll see where we are, and decide what to do."

"Does that mean she's still your most likely suspect?" Vincent knew he was pushing his luck.

The chief actually laughed. "You know I'm not going to

discuss our investigation with you, Vincent. But, nice try." He wandered off, still chuckling.

⸻⦾⸻

Vincent took one of the few empty barstools. Nancy's business always did very well on hot days. Cold beer was in high demand.

"Hello, Mister Malone." Nancy placed a cold Coors draft in front of him.

"Hello to you, Miss McAllen." Nancy was looking very attractive today, or maybe Vincent was just paying more attention. "Is it free Coors day?"

"Special for you. I know it's not exactly highbrow, but I think Coors on tap is some of the best beer around. Bartender approved."

"How about you join me?"

Vincent smiled, Nancy smiled. They went to one of the back booths, where they sipped at their beers. Vincent gave her a brief rundown of what he'd been up to, but he left out Francis and the huge gun—he didn't want to worry her too much. Eventually they came around to when Vincent would move in.

"Is tomorrow too soon?"

"Today is okay with me." She smiled one of those beautiful smiles. "But tomorrow's probably better. I'm on the late shift tonight, so you might as well go to the Inn and get a good night's sleep."

"You look beautiful tonight." Vincent surprised himself

by saying it out loud. He really must be in love.

"Now, you be good. I have to be here tonight. Move in tomorrow, and we'll celebrate, okay?"

"Okay, celebration tomorrow."

Vincent leaned over and gave her a kiss. She didn't flinch, despite the public setting. *She is a brave woman*, he thought.

Busy day, and I'm exhausted. Hard to believe the hours I used to work, and then go drinking. Going to be an adjustment, moving in with Nancy. I hope this is the right thing to do. Not sure I could handle the pain if she asked me to leave. I might screw things up on just about any given day, and not even realize I've done it. Dangerous new ground.

18

You're On Your Own

"Hey, Vincent. How you doin'?"

Jerry was moving busily about the kitchen, his large chef's apron dusted with flour, preparing a tray of fragrant muffins for the guests, or himself, or maybe for Vincent.

"You know I've gained ten pounds since I got to the Inn, right? You're one great cook. Or baker. Or whatever you are."

"Is that maybe a compliment? Thank you. I'm having the same weight problem. May have to convert one of the bedrooms into a gym." Jerry was grinning. "Of course, we both know it's Mary's fault, not mine. She's the one who's taught me how to cook."

"Sure, typical businessman—blame the help." Vincent smiled. "Have you seen Bente this morning?"

"No. Talked to Dirk. He came into the kitchen to get coffee and some muffins for the two of them and then took it all back to the room. Said Bente was still not feeling very good." Jerry hesitated. "This is going to sound like innkeeper gossip, but maybe it's something you should know. Bente and Dirk have only been using one room the last few days. My guess is they've only been using one bed since they arrived, but lately they're not bothering to try to hide it."

Vincent chuckled, raising his eyebrows. "It's probably the romantic atmosphere."

"Yeah, maybe so. Dirk asked me, if I saw you, to let you know that Bente wants to talk to you."

"Probably looking for a better man."

"You really are a bad person, no matter what Cindy thinks."

Vincent extended his hands palms up smiling. "I'm innocent, officer." He selected a muffin and got a cup of coffee, then headed out back to the gazebo to enjoy the beautiful morning.

"Good morning, Mister Malone." Dirk had approached without Vincent noticing. "Mind if I join you?"

Vincent thought of a couple of wiseass answers, but held his tongue. "Sure, have a seat."

"Nobody is telling Bente anything about her daughter. Do you know what is going on?"

"I don't know where she is, if that's what you mean."

"We didn't even know she'd left the hospital. The police came and questioned us about where she might have gone. They were very rude to Bente, treating her like a suspect or something." Dirk hesitated. He seemed unsure whether to say more. "Ilse is a very troubled person. She's had problems with drugs and alcohol, and is totally irresponsible. I'm supposed to be her manager, handling scheduling and money matters, and so on, but she just ignores me. There are days I'm not sure she's sane."

"She does seem troubled. Do you think she killed Anna?"

"No! What a question. Of course, she didn't kill anyone. She and Anna had some sort of affair, and Ilse ended it. Bente talked to Anna, and it was Anna who was angry and hurt. I don't think Ilse gave a shit. She surely wouldn't have killed her, not before the show. She had everything riding on the success of this show."

"Why did she try to kill herself?" Vincent was developing a strong dislike for Dirk. He was a tall, handsome man who projected an air of strength. But after only a short time talking to him, it was apparent he was not strong, and probably not very bright.

"Well, I don't know. Bente says she didn't. She thinks it was just an accident. She took the pills by mistake or something. Bente has told me Ilse has everything to live for, money and fame. Why would she kill herself?"

"Did you have any dealings with Anna?"

Dirk gave Vincent a dirty look. "I called her numerous times about the money she owed Ilse. It wasn't just this show—she still owed money from previous sales. I had advised Ilse to drop the Howard Marks Gallery as her U.S. representative, and to sue Anna. I believe that is what she was going to do if she did not receive all of her money immediately after this show. The problem, I believe, was that Anna had spent the money she owed to Ilse to prop up her business, which was failing. She didn't have the money to pay what she owed."

"You and Ilse's mother have a relationship that's more than just business. Did Ilse know that?"

Dirk's face reddened, and he glared at Vincent. "All

Americans seem to be rude—but you, sir, are an asshole."

And with that, he left. Vincent had been called an asshole more times than he could count, but never with such perfect diction. In any case, Dirk's opinion had no effect on him. Aside from his phony regal manner, something seemed odd about Dirk. Vincent wondered why he'd been hired in the first place—why they'd chosen him specifically. He didn't seem to have any connection to Ilse or to the contemporary art business.

Vincent went to his room and began packing. There was a small knock on his door, and he opened it to find Bente.

"Sorry to bother you, Mister Malone. Do you have a minute?"

"Um, sure. Do you want to come in?" She entered, her eyes taking in the very small room with its one chair. She took a seat on the untidy bed. Vincent pulled out the chair for himself.

"I don't give a damn that Anna is dead," she began. "She was an evil person who tried to cheat my daughter. She was good at manipulating people, and Ilse fell for it. That bitch even threatened me once. She knew about Dirk and me, and she was going to tell Ilse unless I backed off my criticism of how Anna and the gallery were handling Ilse's art. This will come out before long, so I'll tell you now. I had Dirk hire a law firm in New York to sue Anna for fraud. She probably got the paperwork the day before she died. Ilse didn't know about it. I was going to tell her, but then she disappeared." Bente put her head in her hands as if she might cry, but looked up at Vincent with a challenge in her eyes instead of tears. "I didn't kill her. Dirk didn't kill her. We had nothing to do with her death. But I hated her."

"Did you talk to her the day of the reception?"

"No. We made eye contact, but she turned and went the other way. Do you know where my daughter is?"

"No. She's with Bobby, but I don't know where."

"Do you think she's safe?"

"I have no way of knowing. It's my impression that Bobby wouldn't hurt her, and more likely he'd protect her, so I think you can assume she's fairly safe. But the Santa Fe police will put out bulletins to other jurisdictions soon, requesting that they detain her. And that will put her at risk. If you talk to her, you should encourage her to turn herself in. At this point, the police just want to talk about Anna's death, and she's only making things worse by running away."

"I've called her number and Bobby's. They're not even taking voicemail now, so I doubt I'll get to talk to her. Who do you think killed Anna?"

"I'm not going to run down a list, but there are other suspects. Ilse's still a suspect, too, though. I'm an investigator for her legal team, so the police aren't going to tell me anything, but we're working very hard to figure out who did it. She should come back to Santa Fe and face whatever's going to happen. If she's thinking about trying to get out of the country, she could be putting herself at real risk."

"Dirk and I are thinking about going home. Do you think that will be okay?"

"The police can't stop you unless they arrest you for something. They may not like it, but they can't do anything about it. I think the more important issue is that Ilse might need your support here."

She nodded. "I guess that's right. We'll decide in the next few days. I'm really tired of this place. Not the Inn—these people have been wonderful—but just being away from home is so stressful."

"I can imagine."

"There's something else you should know. Several weeks ago, Clive Walton called me. He told me he had plans to take control of the gallery from Anna, and that if Ilse held off on any big decisions now, then in a short while she would be dealing only with him. He said he would make a new deal with her that would be very attractive. At the time I thought he was just trying to bullshit Ilse into some kind of deal. I don't like him very much, and in some ways I actually trusted Anna more, especially with him going behind the back of his employer. So, I never said anything to Ilse. Now, with what's happened, that whole conversation takes on a new light." She looked directly at Vincent, and he saw a strength in her that he hadn't seen before.

"That's very interesting. Did you tell the police about this?"

"No, but only because they haven't questioned me yet. I didn't want to bring it up myself, and have it look like I was accusing Clive of something. Maybe you could pass it along, and not mention me?"

"I understand not trusting cops, believe me. But the Santa

Fe Police Department is run by a good guy. You should call him and tell him what you just told me. It's very relevant, and I'm sure they'll keep it confidential for now. I can't withhold information from the police. I live here, so they can make my life very uncomfortable if they think I'm not playing straight with them."

Bente looked thoughtful. "I guess I should call. What's the police chief's name?"

Vincent took out his phone and gave Bente the chief's name and number. She stood, smoothed her clothes, thanked Vincent for his help, and left. Clive Walton was going to move from a bit player in this investigation to a lead role before long.

Vincent went to his computer and searched for a number for Trent Taylor, but didn't find one. He Googled the man—not much. Some background professional stuff. He had an MBA from New Mexico State University in Las Cruces. Nothing else leaped off the screen. Then he saw a search result for a Taylor Art Gallery in Las Cruces, clicked on it and did an online search of state records. He found the name of the owner, a Gloria Taylor, of Mesquite, New Mexico. Maybe Trent's mother? His wife, ex-wife, sister—Vincent couldn't be sure. For all he knew, it might be no connection at all.

He packed his few belongings into the Mustang and went to find Jerry and Cindy. He gave them the good news—also bad news—about moving in with Nancy, and they all hugged.

It felt like he was leaving home for the first time. Cindy actually cried a little.

"Tell Rick, anytime he needs some help with picking up or dropping off passengers, just call. I'll always help when I can."

Jerry smiled. "You better get going before we all break down."

"Guess so. I know I'm probably going to see you as much as I did before, but you both should know how grateful I am. You really helped me when I needed it. I won't forget that." He shook Jerry's hand and gave Cindy another hug, then left. He hoped mom and dad wouldn't be too sad, and he promised himself he'd call often.

As he drove—violating both common sense and the law—he called the chief and told him what Bente had said about Clive Walton.

"Do you think he was suggesting that he'd take over the existing gallery?" the chief asked.

"The way she described the conversation, it seems clear that's what he was suggesting. If he was going to leave Anna and start something on his own, I think he'd have worded what he said very differently." Vincent waited on the chief's next question, but none came. "Do you happen to have a contact number for Trent Taylor?"

Another moment of dead air. "No. We're looking for him, too. Apparently, he was staying at one of the downtown hotels.

He doesn't have a home in Santa Fe. We should be able to get a number pretty quick. Call back later, and I'll let you know what we found."

The chief disconnected in a way that seemed abrupt. Vincent was on his way downtown to the Crown Bar to see his favorite bartender when his phone vibrated. "Vincent Malone."

"Mister Malone, this is Trent Taylor. I need to talk to someone about Anna's death. Can you meet me?"

"When and where?"

Taylor specified the La Fonda bar in an hour, then disconnected. Vincent thought about calling the chief back, but decided that would be carrying civic duty too far.

19

That's My Story and I'm Sticking To It

To Vincent the La Fonda was emblematic of Santa Fe. The colors, the music, and the general hubbub seemed to represent all the qualities, good and bad, of New Mexico's capital. It would never have been one of Vincent's hangouts during his drinking days—way too bright, colorful, and cheerful for the old Vincent to feel comfortable. The places where he'd spent time drinking in those days tended to be dark and moody, with jazz or blues playing in the background while people drowned their sorrows. La Fonda was for tourists, so everything was happy and upbeat.

He found an empty spot at the bar and ordered a beer. He was a little late, and looked around for Taylor, but didn't see anyone who looked like him. He hadn't met the man, but was fairly sure he'd recognize him when he saw him. He was on his second beer when Taylor showed up.

"How about we go to a booth?" Taylor suggested that in a conspiratorial, nervous way, looking around in a manner that suggested he was concerned about being seen. He was a very plain man, the sort of person people would describe as ordinary—the sort of person who remains invisible until, one day, he explodes.

"Sure." Vincent followed him to a more secluded location, and slid onto the bench-style seat. A waitress appeared and took their order—Diet Coke for Taylor and another beer for Vincent.

"I didn't kill her. Should have a long time ago, but I didn't. Can you help me?" Taylor sounded stressed. His eyes looked wild—or maybe he was on something.

Vincent hesitated. Taylor had called him—why? "I guess you mean you didn't kill Anna? Has someone accused you?" He was tiptoeing, trying not to push the wrong button and have this guy blow up.

Taylor opened his mouth to answer just when the very efficient, and annoying, waitress reappeared. She did her thing and left. Nothing of any consequence had changed, but the interruption seemed to put Taylor even more on edge. "No, nobody's accused me of anything. I'm a nobody—people don't even notice me. That bitch would have been flat broke—maybe even in jail—if not for me. But she treated me like dirt. Never said 'thank you,' or 'good job'—nothing. Just ignored me, like everyone else."

"How long did you work there?" Vincent wanted to keep him talking, but he also needed to know some things, not just to listen to the guy rant.

"Five years—five very long years. I was hired by Howard, not Anna. He was hard, but he knew what he was doing. It was different when he was alive. But Anna, she thought she knew everything. She didn't know squat. All she knew was how to spend Daddy's money and complain. After he died, everything went to hell."

"Why didn't you quit?"

"Yeah, I should have. And actually, I did quit, right when Howard died. About a month after Howard had gone, I told Anna I thought it was time to move on. She begged me to stay, said she needed my help. I believed her, but it was all lies. She needed me to take care of things, all right, but no more money for me—just more work, while she proceeded to run the business into the ground." Taylor took a sip, and looked around nervously, again. "Plus, all I know is the gallery business, really. It's not easy to find jobs in this industry, especially without a good reference. And there was no doubt that if I'd quit, she would have made sure I couldn't get another job."

Everybody had a story, even the invisible people. "Do you know who killed Anna?"

"I don't know, but my guess is that the crazy Dutch artist did it. She and Anna were always fighting, and her stupid manager would call almost every day, yelling about the money we owed them. They may have been all smiles when the customers were around, but it was obvious they hated each other."

"Where were you that night, after the reception at the B&B?"

Taylor gave him a dirty look. "What, you think I killed her? I didn't even see the bitch. I was waiting at the gallery for Clive to have the paintings brought back. It was part of the security procedures—which, I might add, I put in place. The paintings had to be returned and inspected before they were secured. That's what I did, then I left. But I know someone's going to accuse me sooner or later, because I'm a nobody, right? So, go ahead and hang me for what these nutcases do to one another."

People might accuse him simply because he's so bloody annoying. "Why did you call me?"

Taylor looked confused at the question. "I needed to talk to someone. I heard about you from Clive. He doesn't like you much, but it sounded like maybe you were kind of independent. I can't go to the cops. So, I called you."

None of that actually answered the question. "What did you need to talk about?" There was a long pause, and Vincent wondered if Taylor was rethinking this whole meeting.

"I heard you're an investigator, and were looking at everyone. I figured sooner or later you'd look at me. It's nothing to do with Anna's death—but if someone starts to look, there are some things that might seem a little odd. I don't trust the cops here. If they find out about it, they'll find a way to railroad me. Guess I wanted someone else to look at it and see that it wasn't related to Anna's murder." Taylor started his nervous search of the room again. If he wasn't guilty of something, he was sure doing a good impression of someone who was.

"I don't know what you're talking about," Vincent said. "I'm a *private* investigator. I work for the law firm representing Ilse De Vries. If you have information about this crime, you need to talk to the police. If you tell me anything about the crime, I have to tell the police. I can't hide evidence or any relevant information." He paused to let that soak in. "Before you tell me anything, my advice to you is to hire a lawyer, and tell them what you were going to tell me. That way, it's a privileged communication, protected by the client-attorney relationship. Anything you tell me, I can't withhold."

Taylor sipped his Coke. It was obvious he wanted to tell someone what he knew, but now he wasn't sure about going ahead with Vincent. "Okay. Well, thanks. Excuse me, I need to go to the washroom." He got up and left.

Vincent knew he wasn't coming back. He called Tucker and gave him an update, including the meeting clearly just adjourned.

"Have any idea what he's talking about? His big secret?"

"I don't know for sure, obviously, but I'd guess it has something to do with money. He's a disgruntled, underappreciated employee who handled the company's cash. The first guess is that he was stealing, and now he's worried about the police finding that out and jumping to the conclusion that he killed Anna because *she* found out."

"Strange that he would call you." Tucker was always direct.

"Hey, I'm a charming man. Good company, too. Maybe he was looking for stimulating conversation."

"Yeah, right." Tucker hung up.

Bobby watched as Ilse slept. She looked small and vulnerable, but he knew—maybe more than anyone—that she could be dangerous. He didn't believe she'd killed Anna, but he couldn't be sure.

He'd awakened the night Anna was killed, and Ilse hadn't been in the room. He'd been concerned about her after the ugly exchange at the reception, and when he saw she wasn't there, he'd gone looking for her. He didn't find her, but did discover his car was gone. He'd thought about calling her, but wasn't sure whether it was the right thing to do, and resisted an urge to call someone and report her missing. If she turned out to be fine, she'd probably be furious. He went back to the room and waited. He didn't know when she'd left, but it was almost an hour after he awakened that she returned. He wasn't sure he wanted to know where she'd been, so he'd pretended that she woke him up when she came in.

"Something wrong?" He'd acted drowsy.

"No, everything's fine. I just got a glass of milk. Go back to sleep."

The next day, he'd confronted her about it, and that was when she locked herself in the bathroom and tried to kill herself. They hadn't talked about any of it since. Now, holed up in Durango, wondering if he'd done the right thing when he let her pretend like nothing had happened. He knew he shouldn't bury his head in the sand, but he'd done it, anyway.

He went to the hotel lobby, got coffee, some tired-looking donuts and a Denver newspaper, and returned to the room. He glanced at the front page of the paper, and when he didn't see his picture, breathed a sigh of relief. What a strange life.

Ilse stirred. "Do I smell coffee?"

Bobby brought her a coffee and a couple of donuts. "Donuts are a little shopworn, but they'll help get you started."

Ilse giggled. "I'm so hungry, these look wonderful." She grabbed one and took a big bite. "What's the plan today?" She actually seemed to be enjoying herself.

"Maybe a big breakfast downtown. Saw a place yesterday that I thought looked interesting." He was rewarded with a big smile. "Next, I think we contact the attorney Malone recommended."

"Why?" Ilse clearly preferred to ignore everything and continue to pretend nothing was wrong.

"This isn't going to go away. We need advice, and I think Malone is being straight with us. I think we can trust him, more or less." Even assuming she hadn't done it, he knew she needed help dealing with the situation.

"I don't think I trust anyone but you. Maybe we should just stay in the room and wait."

"Ilse, I know you want this to all just disappear, but it won't. We need to deal with it, now, before it gets worse. If you don't want to talk to this attorney, fine, but then we should go back to Denver and contact someone else. Or get in touch with those lawyers in Albuquerque. It's the smart thing to do."

"Okay, okay. I know you're right. I just wish I'd never gotten you involved in my messed-up life."

"I want to be involved. And I'm not going away—not unless you tell me to. Let me help, okay?"

She smiled. "Maybe we should call in a little while." She grabbed his hand and pulled him onto the bed.

"Sure, I know who you are," Younger told Bobby over the phone. "Malone gave me a heads-up that you might call. Why don't we meet at a restaurant downtown?"

"Great. We haven't had breakfast yet."

"The Lone Spur Café is on Main Street. It's easy to find, and has the best breakfast in Durango. Say in about thirty minutes?"

"We'll see you there. How will we know you, though?"

"Big, ugly guy with intelligent eyes."

Bobby laughed. "Great, see you in a bit."

He went into the bathroom where Ilse was getting ready. "Guy sounds like he should be entertaining at the very least. For some strange reason, even over the phone, he made me more comfortable that we're doing the right thing."

Ilse gave him a kiss on the cheek. "Let's hope so."

Vincent's phone vibrated.

"Malone."

George Younger filled him in on the phone call and his plan for breakfast. "What do you want me to tell these people?"

"Give them your best, most honest assessment of their situation. Don't pull any punches. I believe they're both in-nocent, but they're in a lot of trouble. Ilse's hired the Hill firm

to represent her regarding financial issues related to her paintings, but someone else might be better for anything about the
murder. They need a good criminal attorney, and that's you.
Also, I might not have mentioned this, but they're both rich—
try not to let your glee show too much."

"I'll do my best."

20

Confessions All Around

Hungry or not, once a person walked into the Lone Spur Café, the aromas insisted they order something immediately. The atmosphere was rustic, and promised wonderful food. Bobby and Ilse looked around for the self-described large, ugly man. They soon spotted a big guy, though he wasn't very ugly, talking with several others. He saw them, and headed their way.

"Hi. You must be Bobby and Ilse. I'm George Younger. Come on in—we have a booth in the back."

As they headed that way, several people waved or said hello to George, who clearly was well known at the Lone Spur.

"Thanks for meeting with us." Bobby was polite, Ilse reserved.

"No problem. I usually eat breakfast here, and it's nice to have company. When Vincent called and said you might be in touch, he told me you're both involved in the arts. But he didn't get specific. Can you tell me a little more about that?"

Bobby gave George some background about himself and Ilse, who still hadn't said a word.

"Holy cats, a world-famous artist right here in Durango." George moaned at himself inwardly. Could he possibly sound more small-town?

Ilse smiled. "'World-famous' is probably a bit of an exaggeration," she said, picking up a menu. "I love this place. What do you recommend?"

"Either the southwest omelet or the cowboy benedict. Either way, it's a lot of food, but I guarantee it'll taste great. Might have to take a nap if you eat the whole thing, but I'm all in favor of naps." *In favor of naps?* Unbelievable. He was completely at ease defending bikers, confronting cops in court, and even standing up to judges when they ruled against him, but here he was, acting like a teeny-bopper fan meeting a rock star. The simple fact was that, in his element he could be fearless, but outside it he sometimes wasn't sure of himself, and it could put him off balance.

Ilse and Bobby chuckled. They ordered from a friendly and efficient waitress. Anticipating their meals, they stayed away from the business at hand for the moment, talking about Durango history, the hotel, how long George had lived there, Bobby's graphics business, and local matters in Denver. Soon the food arrived, and no one was disappointed.

"I have a question." That came from Ilse, who was becoming more comfortable with George. "Can I hire more than one attorney?"

"Sure. You can hire any number of attorneys to help you in the same matter, or different attorneys for different legal issues, or a whole truckload. You can also fire attorneys anytime you want. Are you thinking about the Albuquerque firm you hired?"

Ilse nodded. "Yeah. I was just wondering if hiring you canceled that, or if we need to tell them about you?"

"You can hire me without firing them or notifying them, but I'd be a lot more comfortable if you let them know I've joined your team. I think it's always best to let everyone know what's going on, even if each attorney's dealing with what seems to be a distinct matter. Sometimes there's overlap you don't expect. And you don't want your lawyers keeping secrets from each other, and maybe doing you harm in the process."

Ilse looked at Bobby and nodded. Bobby grabbed her hand and squeezed. "I have something we need to discuss, but I'd like to talk to Ilse first. Could you give us a few minutes?"

"Of course. I have a couple of calls to make." George got up and walked away.

"What's that about?" Ilse looked concerned.

"I know you left our room that night. You took my car and went somewhere, but obviously I don't know where. When I asked you about it, you exploded at me and then tried to kill yourself." There was a moment of silence between them before he went on, "Wherever you went, I think the police have a witness or a video, because that would explain some of their actions, like putting a guard on your hospital room. This has to be dealt with in some way." Ilse had her head down. Bobby talked softly. "I like this guy. I have no idea if he's a good lawyer, but he seems like someone who won't lie to you. You need to tell him everything, including what happened that night, and that might mean I shouldn't be here."

Ilse began to cry, softly. "I'm sorry, Bobby. I'm so scared."

He hugged her. "I'm scared, too. Did you kill her?"

"Oh, no. No. I should have just told you what happened as soon as I got back, but I just wasn't sure what to do. I didn't kill her, though. I know I've done some crazy things, so maybe you have a right to wonder what I might do, but I'm not that far gone. I hated Anna, for sure, but I didn't do anything to her."

"Do you want to tell this guy what happened, and see what he says?"

"Yes, I think I do. I'm sorry, Bobby. Maybe you should leave and go back to Denver. I should have never gotten you so involved."

"I'm not going anywhere. If you want to talk to the lawyer in private, I understand, but I'm staying with you until this is resolved."

They hugged again and hung on. After a moment, George returned.

"Need more time?"

"No. We're ready," Ilse said. "I want to hire you, and I need to give you some information about what happened on the night the art gallery owner was killed. I haven't told anyone this, including Bobby, or the police or the Albuquerque attorneys."

"Maybe we should go to my office. It's just around the corner."

Vincent entered Nancy's house with the key she'd given him.

Even so, he felt like he was trespassing. The place was very orderly, amazingly clean—he felt like he made a mess just standing in it. It crossed his mind—again—that this might not be the right decision. But the moment passed, and he unloaded some of his stuff. The house was too quiet, so he headed to the Crown as soon as he was done.

"Hello," Nancy greeted him with a smile.

"Hello."

"You seem a little down."

"Took some stuff by your place. Are you real sure this is what we want to do? Everything's so clean and orderly. I'm just going to mess stuff up."

She laughed. "I spent hours last night cleaning the place just because you were coming. I should have left it the way it was. That way, you'd have felt right at home. This is going to take some getting used to. But I'm willing to try, if you are."

"So, it's not always that neat."

"It may never be again."

"Then I think we can make this work."

"Me, too."

Ilse and Bobby were surprised at the size of Younger's office. He explained that he'd had a couple of partners, but the arrangement hadn't worked out, and he simply held onto the space. He showed them into a conference room lined with an impressive assortment of electronic communications gear, and they settled into luxurious leather chairs.

"Do you mind if I take notes?" George had taken a leather-bound pad from his briefcase.

"No, that's fine."

"Should I be in on this or step out?" Bobby wasn't sure what it might mean if he heard confidential information.

"If you don't mind, I think it's best if I have this conversation one-on-one with Ilse."

"Sure, not a problem." He touched Ilse on the shoulder and left.

"Okay, tell me what happened."

"After the fight with Anna at the Inn reception, I was pretty upset. I grabbed a bottle of wine and went to my room. I just wanted to hide. I knew that a lot of the problem with Anna was because we'd had sex. I know you'll think I'm an awful person, but it just didn't mean that much to me. But, obviously, it was different for her. She said she was in love with me. So now her behavior was all mixed up, with the sex and the money. We both needed the show to be a financial success to fix our money problems. I didn't know what to do, so I drank."

"You must've been angry with her."

"Yeah, I was. But there was something else. I was angry with myself. Everything had been going wrong for me for some time, and I knew I was causing problems with Anna, and my mother, and just about anyone else I had anything to do with. I felt like I was going crazy, and it scared me. I knew Anna was vulnerable. She was way over her head in the business. She really didn't know what she was doing. The last thing

I should have done was have some kind of stupid fling with her—I should have fired her, and moved on. It was like I was playing with people, and it made me feel horrible—I really started to hate myself."

George wasn't sure what to say. He knew all about the law. But this was personal, enough so that it made him uncomfortable. "Sounds like you both had a confusing situation. Did you just stay in your room that night?"

Ilse gave George a look that suggested it was a stupid question, giving him a brief glimpse of the harsher Ilse, the one she'd just been talking about. But she continued, "I drank enough to make me sleepy—that's what wine does to me. I'd shunned Bobby, so he'd left me alone. I went to sleep—the ultimate escape. I had my phone on mute, but sometime in the night it vibrated, and I woke up. Someone had called and left a message. I was going to just go back to sleep, but I thought it might be something important. I don't know who left it. It was from an unknown number, and I didn't recognize the voice. It was a man, though. He said one of my paintings had been damaged, and that it was Clive's fault, that he'd been careless. He hung up, and that was it. Bobby was in bed, sound asleep. It wasn't the brightest decision in the world, but I decided I'd go to the gallery. I thought maybe someone would be there doing something about the damage—I was still drunk, so I wasn't really thinking straight. I took Bobby's car."

"What time was this?"

"Sometime after eleven, maybe eleven-fifteen or so. I got to the gallery, and it was obvious there was no one there.

I parked in front, and tried the door, even knocked on the glass, but nothing. Went around the side where there's a small parking lot and a side entrance, and I saw Anna's car there. I knocked on the side door, but still nothing. By that point, I felt kind of foolish standing out there in the middle of the night—maybe I was sobering up a little, too—so I left, and returned to the Inn."

"Were there any video cameras that you saw?"

"No, I don't remember any. But of course, I wasn't looking for them, either."

"Did Bobby know you'd been gone?"

Ilse hesitated. She couldn't be sure if it was the right decision, but for now she decided to lie to protect Bobby. "I went back to the room and changed into my pajamas again, as I was getting into bed, he woke up. I told him I had been to the kitchen for a glass of milk, and he went back to sleep."

"Did you see anyone else at the Inn when you were leaving or returning?"

"No."

"Does the Inn have video cameras?"

"I don't think so."

"Since that night, have you been able to determine whether any of the paintings were actually damaged or not?"

"No. The police haven't let me near them, so I don't know if that was true or not."

"Is there anything else I need to know about Anna's murder?"

"Nothing that I know about. I didn't kill her, and I don't

know who did."

"Based on what Malone has told me, I'm guessing the police have some kind of evidence, probably a security video, putting you at the gallery that night. But more than likely, they cannot put you *inside* the gallery, and it's clear that's where they think she was killed. So, you're their number one suspect, but they still don't have enough evidence to charge you. If they come up with something inside the gallery, or in the car, or on the body, then they'll probably go ahead with the charges. Based on what you've told me, I think the best approach for us is to provide your side of what happened that night. Without something further, other than the possible security video of you at the gallery, I don't believe they have enough evidence to charge you with a crime. We need to talk some more, but right now I think you need to consider turning yourself in to the Durango police. I can arrange for you to have an interview here, in which case you might not have to go back to Santa Fe."

Ilse wasn't sure what she wanted to do. She didn't want to be charged for murder, but she also had a huge amount of money hanging in the balance, and the solution to the money problem was in Santa Fe.

"I need to talk to Bobby."

21

The Truth Will Set Us Free

Vincent opened his eyes, still half asleep, and didn't realize for a moment where he was. Then he heard Nancy in the kitchen, and it came back to him. He wasn't sure he wanted to get up, just yet, but lying in bed seemed wrong. He went to the bathroom, freshened his tired face, and ran his fingers through his hair. He still had an impressive mane, though it was now mostly silver. It made him think of his brother, who had taken after their mother, while Vincent looked exactly like their bear of a dad. His poor brother had always felt undersized, and it had affected everything he did in life. Then, to top it off, he lost all his hair while he was still in his thirties. Life can be cruel.

"Good morning." Vincent stood at the door, watching Nancy prepare coffee. "Can I help?"

"Help is always welcome. How did it feel to wake up in a strange house?" Nancy seemed to be a morning person—a definite potential conflict.

Vincent hesitated a moment. "Well, strange, I guess."

Nancy laughed. "Not a morning person, are you?"

"More like mid-morning, post-coffee." Vincent found a cup and poured himself some, placed his cup on the table, and walked to Nancy. They embraced. "Last night was wonderful. Thank you for letting me be in your life."

They held on a while. Nancy sniffled a little. "So, where are you on your investigation of the art gallery murder?"

She turned away. She did not want Vincent to see her tears.

He played along with the change of subject. "Well, I've got a substantial list of suspects. Seems Anna Marks wasn't an easy woman to be around, and a horrible boss. Combine that with all sorts of money entanglements and, of course, that old standby—sex—and suspects start to come into focus. Ilse's disappearance has put the spotlight on her, but I think there are plenty of other people who had some reason to wish Anna the worst."

Nancy frowned. "I almost feel sorry for her. Why was she so difficult?"

"Not real sure. Her father was a hard man, at least toward her, so there were bound to be some psychological problems associated with that. And she didn't seem to have anyone in her life. Being alone isn't good for the human soul, so she probably resented anyone who had a more normal life than she did. Yeah, the more I think about it, the more I feel a little sorry for her, too."

"I'm glad you're here, Vincent."

"I've made up my mind." Ilse stood at the foot of the bed, a cup of coffee from the hotel breakfast bar in each hand.

Bobby sat up and took one. "About?"

"I like this George guy, and it definitely feels safer to stay here and try to defend myself without going back to Santa Fe. But I've decided I'm not going to hide. I didn't do anything wrong, other than kick her in the knee. I want to go back to Santa Fe, and turn myself in to the police. There's too much money involved for me to stay hidden. I want that money, and I want to be free to go and do what I want." She looked defiant.

Bobby smiled. "You are one strong, beautiful woman. Let's go fight!"

Ilse called George Younger and told him what she'd decided. He said if she needed anything from him, to call anytime. She could tell he wasn't pleased, but she couldn't tell if it was because he was losing a client or because he thought her decision was wrong. But in the end, it didn't matter—her mind was made up.

They packed, checked out of the hotel, loaded the car, and headed for Santa Fe, a little more nervous about what might happen than they'd been just a few hours before.

Vincent's phone vibrated.

"Malone."

"Mister Malone? This is Ilse De Vries. I'm in the car with Bobby. We're headed back to Santa Fe. Do you have a minute?"

"Sure."

"I told George Younger everything that happened that night. Now I want to tell you. Can we do that over the phone?"

"You know your communication with Younger is protected client-attorney information, but it's not the same with me."

"I understand. I want you to know this." Ilse gave Vincent the same details she'd related to George about what happened on the night Anna was killed.

"What are you going to do now?"

"We're headed to the Santa Fe Police Department. I'm going to give them a statement about what happened. If they arrest me, then I'll need someone to get me out of jail. And no matter what happens, I still need help with my money. I don't know what Clive is trying to do, but he's up to something, and the business manager at the gallery hasn't been cooperative at all. I think his name's Taylor. I know I signed a representation letter with the Albuquerque law firm, and they were going to hire you to do some investigation into the money and the paintings. Is that still true?"

"It is. I've done some work on it, but when you disappeared, things slowed down."

"Okay. I want an all-out effort to protect my financial interests, and that includes any money anyone's holding, and possession of my paintings. I'll pay whatever it takes to get this sorted out. Should I call Mister Hill or Mister Tucker to tell them this?"

"I can pass your message along."

Ilse seemed to have transformed into a different person—someone who was going to take charge one way or another, and set things right. "Good. Also, could you call the police chief and let him know that we should be there in about three hours? If he wants us to do something else for some reason, then just call me back."

"I'll let him know." Vincent was in his car, but had pulled into a parking lot when the call began. "Ilse, I'm not a lawyer, but I'll be at the police station when you get there in case I can help in some way. Tucker and Hill are going to want you not to say anything to the police without them present, apart from just identifying yourself. My guess is they'll call you to set that up, and my advice is to take *their* advice. Wait for them to get there before you answer any questions or volunteer any information."

Extended silence followed. "Look, Mister Malone, I know I should take that legal advice, but I just want to tell my story. If they advise me to just shut up and not say anything, I'm sorry, but I'm not going to. I didn't kill Anna, and I don't know who did. Now that I'm thinking more clearly, I'm not worried. I don't want to run. I want to deal with it head-on."

"I really do understand. Let me make sure they understand your position. They can't stop you from doing what you think is right, and I don't believe they'll try, but you should have an attorney there with you, okay?"

"Okay, they can be there, but I want you there, too. Bobby and I trust you more than the attorneys. Thank you, Mister Malone."

Vincent called Tucker, but got his voice mail. He left a message to call, saying it was urgent. Next, he called the chief.

"I just got a call from Ilse De Vries. She and Bobby Hawkins are on their way to Santa Fe—be here in about three hours. She wants to make a statement about what happened that night. She told me she did go to the gallery, but didn't see anyone, and then she went back to the Inn and went to sleep. She can give you all the details, but she says she didn't kill Anna, and doesn't know who did."

"Okay. Well, it's good that she's turning herself in. Depending on what she says, we may just let her go. I can tell you, Vincent, we can place her at the gallery, but we don't have any other evidence against her. Will you be here when she arrives?"

"I will, and I imagine either Tucker or Jack Hill will be there, too, but she made it clear to me that she wants to tell her story, no matter what the attorneys say."

"After her statement, maybe you and I should compare notes."

"I'm open to that, unless what you actually mean is that I should tell you everything I know while you tell me squat."

"That was my original plan. But actually, I'm sure I can tell you a few things you don't already know."

On that intriguing note, they disconnected. Vincent was near the gallery, and decided to swing by. He pulled into a parking spot across the street, in front of a medical supply company, got out, and used his phone to take pictures of the two security cameras he could see that pointed toward the front of the medical business. It was possible they could also capture the front of the gallery, or at least a portion of the street in front. He walked across to the gallery. The front door was locked, and bore a sign saying it was temporarily closed.

Looking around, he couldn't see any cameras near the storefront. He walked toward the side of the building, where there was a small, empty parking lot and a side door. One of the spots in the lot had a sign saying it was reserved for Howard Marks. Interesting that Anna never had the sign changed after her father died. Moving to the back of the building, he could see a loading dock farther down, and it had a camera pointing onto it. There was a narrow alley leading to the loading dock, while another building butted up against the gallery on the far side. He went back to the side door. He pushed a button next to a sign reading, "Employees Only," and could faintly hear a buzzer going off inside when he did, but no one came to the door. He walked around to the front. The gallery's display window was empty and, peering through the glass, he couldn't see any activity inside. He went back to his car.

He could tell from the exterior of the building, and the parts of the interior he could see through the window, that there had to be a large storage area connected with the loading dock—a secure area, for storing valuable paintings. He needed to get inside so he could determine what kind of security they had for that section. He pulled out his phone and called Clive.

"Hello." Clive didn't sound happy, even before he knew who was calling.

"Clive? Vincent Malone. I need to get into the gallery. Can you or someone come down and let me in?"

"Are you crazy? I'm not letting you in. You stay away from me, and stay away from Francis, or something bad is going to happen to you, you asshole." With that, he hung up.

Clive sounded a lot more confident on the phone than in person. Maybe Francis had been in the room, making it show time for Mister Braveheart to act like a hero. Vincent didn't bat an eye at being called an asshole—he'd called himself an asshole many times—but it did annoy him that he couldn't get into the gallery. He called Tucker again.

"Hey, Vincent, I was just getting ready to call you back. What's so urgent?"

Vincent filled him in about Ilse returning and going to the police. Tucker said he would chat with Jack Hill about it, but he would definitely be in Santa Fe in time to meet her at police headquarters. "I don't have a problem with her making a statement, but only if I'm there to make sure the questions don't get out of line. You planning to be there?"

"Yeah, I'll be there, but at the moment I'm trying to get into the gallery to see what kind of security system they have. But Clive Walton—I guess he's the guy in charge for now—said hell, no. Can we force him to open it up?"

"Hell yes, we can. Let me file something electronically with the court right now. We need to have access to the building so we can ensure that the paintings are properly safeguarded. I'll file a request to have all the gallery's assets frozen this afternoon, but you're damn right. We need access to the building, immediately. Give me about thirty minutes, and you should be able to let Mister Walton know what we've filed with the court. Maybe he'll be more cooperative."

"You know there are millions of dollars of paintings in

that building under the control of Clive or Francis or Taylor. Should we be concerned?"

"Fuck, yes. Just a minute, let me talk to someone." Tucker was silent. A couple of minutes passed, with Vincent waiting, before he came back on the line. "I've contacted a security firm Hill uses here in Albuquerque—they have a satellite office in Santa Fe. They're sending two cars with guards, and I've given them your name. Make sure nothing is removed from that gallery. As soon as I get the court documents filed, I'll head your way."

"Thanks, Tucker."

Vincent called Clive. It went straight to voice mail. "Clive, we're placing guards around the gallery. Don't try to remove anything, because they'll stop you. The proper documents have been filed with the court to allow us access to the building to view our client's assets, and to make sure the building is secure. If you stand in the way or try to interfere, you'll be held in contempt of court, or could even face criminal charges. If you have any questions, you can call Jack Hill or Peter Tucker at the Johnson, Johnson and Hill law firm in Albuquerque." He wanted to sign off with, "a message from your friend, the asshole," but he knew that would be piling on.

22

Love and Money

Vincent met the private security guards and went over the situation with them, as well as providing descriptions of Clive and Francis. He instructed them not to stop either from entering the building, but that if either took anything out, they should immediately notify him, and follow if the men left. He told them he would be back in touch in a few hours with more on what to do.

Having the guards made everything look secure, but Vincent wasn't so sure. For one thing, the biggest issue had to do with funds, not works of art, and those could disappear in a matter of a few clicks. Still, one thing at a time. He headed for Santa Fe police headquarters.

As he walked in, he spotted the chief and waved.

Stanton came over. "They're not here yet. Come on back."

Vincent followed him into his tidy but cramped office.

"I should let you know, we secured a court order to allow us to monitor the gallery to prevent any of the art from disappearing. Clive Walton seems to be in charge, and I'm sure he'll be calling you soon to have me arrested."

The chief chuckled. "Clive, huh? I thought it was Francis

who owned a piece of the company."

"It is, but Clive's turned into his spokesperson."

"It's been a long time since I took estate law in school, but even I can see this situation's going to get complicated. What do you think happens to the business?"

"Well," Vincent replied, "it can operate, since it's an independent legal entity, and it can survive the owners, if there's a succession plan. The question is ownership. It seems, as best anyone knows, that there aren't any obvious heirs to Anna's ownership interest, and that she didn't leave a will. So, it goes to probate court. A judge will put some effort into a search for any relative of Anna Marks. It might be a cousin, or aunt, or uncle—any relative could potentially have rights. The court would try to determine what Anna would've done if she'd bothered to sit down and draft a will, but the judge can't just say, 'Well, let's give it to Francis, he's a good guy.' There has to be a proper legal basis for whatever the court decides, like the existence of a next of kin. It's rare that someone doesn't have *any* relatives, but it happens. If there's absolutely no one, then the court may decide to settle her estate. It'll sell her interest in the business, pay off any debts she has, and give whatever's left to the state. That'd be a little unusual, and subject to legal objections from wanna-be heirs, but it does happen. In this case, the most likely buyer might be Francis, but that would mean he'd have to come up with a bunch of money. From what I hear, he doesn't have much left after his divorce. So, the bottom line is that this could go on for months, or even years, before the estate is settled."

The chief nodded. "If Ilse knew all this, that would be a reason to make sure Anna stayed alive, rather than kill her. Getting her money out of Anna might take time and effort, and be annoying, but it sounds like probate court would be even worse."

"Absolutely. Anna's death really complicates her world. There are paintings worth millions locked up in a gallery whose ownership is in question, and may have to be decided by a court. And all the cash paid toward purchase of those paintings—deposits, and so on—is also locked up in the gallery's bank account. Ilse doesn't have her art or her money. As far as I could tell, the biggest point of contention between Anna and Ilse was that they both needed cash, and the sooner the better. I suppose some hard-ass cop could say she killed Anna in a fit of temper, fueled by passion or blinded by ignorance and wishful thinking, and never thought through what would happen to her assets if Anna was dead. But I don't buy that."

"So, if Ilse didn't kill her, who did?"

"This is why you get the big bucks, chief—you get right to the point. Unfortunately, I don't have an answer."

An assistant stuck her head into the chief's office to say that Ilse De Vries and Bobby Hawkins were out front to see him.

"Is Hill or Tucker going to be here for this interview?"

"I spoke to Tucker not long ago, and he said he was headed this way."

"Good. I'll put them in a conference room, and we'll wait for Tucker to get here."

"You want to what!" Mary almost never raised her voice, but she did now. "You can't do that. I will not allow you to do that. She's not old enough! What are you thinking?"

"Mother," Rick said, "she's twenty. When you got married, you were what? Sixteen?"

Mary frowned and started to say something else, but hesitated. "Neither one of you has a real job. Her family will object. They sent her here to get away from boys, not to get married."

Hector was about to walk in, but stopped just inside the door. He saw Mary's face and knew there was trouble.

"We're both old enough to get married without anyone's permission," Rick argued. "We're in love, and the jobs we have now aren't going to be the jobs we'll have forever. Mom, I have a college degree. Mariana has an associate's degree in business. She was a bookkeeper. She can find a better job. We'll be okay. Dad, am I wrong?"

Hector usually deferred to his wife, as much out of habit as anything else. He seldom saw things as black and white, which meant a lot of decisions in life could go either way, so why fight about it, unless it was obviously stupid? But on this question, he wasn't going to be silent.

"You need to make sure that you both are emotionally ready to be life partners. Marriage isn't a convenience for a few years. It is a commitment for life. Forget about jobs and money—that isn't important in this decision. What counts is your commitment to each other. Make sure it's more than just physical attraction, and that you both understand what this means—a lifetime commitment."

Rick looked at his dad. In a few words—although more than Hector usually used—he'd summed up the situation, and made clear what was expected. "We'll discuss it and make sure we're ready. I won't do this unless I'm sure Mariana and I are doing it for the right reasons."

"That's all we can ask."

Rick hugged his dad. "Thanks."

Tucker arrived, looking frazzled. "That traffic is idiotic. I thought this state was supposed to be sparsely populated—every one of them must have been on the same highway I was. Anyway—sorry, chief, for being a little late."

"No problem. They're waiting for us in the conference room. They want Vincent to sit in, if that's agreeable to you."

"Sure. I think that would be best."

They entered the conference room, and everyone was introduced. Ilse seemed very nervous—the look in her eyes hinted she might bolt at any moment. They needed to start quickly, and the sheriff could see it. He immediately began his formal introduction for the record. "This is an interview to establish certain facts regarding Ilse De Vries and her interactions with Anna Marks. It is being recorded. Ilse De Vries has an attorney present, Peter Tucker, as well as an investigator,

Vincent Malone, who works for Mister Tucker's firm. Ilse, you haven't been charged with any crime, and you can leave at any time. You've indicated you want to make a statement as to what occurred on the date of your art show involving Anna Marks, and events later that night. Does that state the reason for this interview correctly?"

She nodded.

"Be best if you gave a verbal response for the recording."

"Yes, yes—that is correct." she kept her eyes down, hunched, making herself seem small.

"Please tell us what happened that day and night."

Ilse told her story. It was identical to what she'd told George Younger and Vincent, but with a few more details. By now it sounded a little rehearsed, but that's what happens when someone tells the same story repeatedly—it's not necessarily a sign that what they're saying isn't true. The chief asked several questions, and Ilse answered in a soft voice, never looking up.

"You took an overdose of prescription anxiety medication—was that an attempted suicide?"

Tucker interjected. "I understand why you're asking, chief, but my client volunteered to give an interview today covering a very specific time period—that question is out of bounds."

There was quiet in the room before Ilse spoke. "It's okay, Mister Tucker. I took those pills because I was upset about everything. It wasn't just Anna—it was my whole world. I don't know if I meant to kill myself or not. I just wanted some rest, some peace—I overreacted. But I did not kill Anna." Her voice was stronger now, and she looked directly at the chief as she spoke.

"Thank you for coming in. You should know that you are a suspect in the murder of Anna Marks, but for now you're not under arrest. We ask that you remain in Santa Fe while we pursue our investigation. Thank you again for coming in and talking to us." The chief got up and left the room.

Bobby glanced over at Tucker and Vincent. "What does that mean? Can we leave Santa Fe?"

It was Tucker who answered. "You can leave. The only way the police can stop Ilse is to charge her. I think the only evidence they have so far is the security video of her outside the gallery that night. If they had any forensics that could tie her to the car or the body, they'd have already charged her. So, you're both free to go." Tucker waited a bit for that to sink in. "That said, I recommend you stay in Santa Fe for at least a couple of days—not to deal with the criminal side of things, but to help us resolve the issues regarding the paintings and funds that are being held by the gallery. We expect to have several hearings very soon, and your presence may be required."

"I don't understand," Bobby said, stress in his voice. "Why can't you get a court to order that they pay Ilse what they owe her?"

Tucker answered, "Even without Anna's death, that wouldn't be simple. A business transaction that's gone bad, even if there's a good contract in place, can take time to resolve. The courts don't like to make snap decisions, and they won't make any without evidence, which means that until we've had a hearing, with testimony and documents and all the trimmings, no judge is going to make a ruling. The first step is to get all the assets frozen or in secure custody. That's what we're doing right now. But with Anna's death and no obvious heir, there are added complications. It's not even clear who owns the gallery, which means we don't know who should be taking part in the hearing." Tucker was trying to come off as reassuring, but it sounded ominous, anyway. "We've put security around the gallery, and we're in the process of getting a court order to allow us to enter the building and inspect the paintings. But not long after that, someone—we don't even know who yet—will hire an attorney and try to force us to release those assets so the business can function again. All that can take a fair bit of time."

Vincent looked at Tucker. "Mind if I jump in?" Tucker nodded, so he spoke to Ilse. "It could be that it's in your best interests to try to negotiate a deal with Francis and Clive. Francis apparently has a minority interest in the business, and Clive is advising him. I think we can safely assume they want to keep operating the gallery, which means they want to get all the legal issues behind them as quickly as possible. A long court battle is as bad for them as it is for you. If we can work out an agreement that is acceptable to everyone, it's very possible the court would allow the business to operate until the issue of Anna's estate is settled."

"You mean work something out to continue in the business with Clive and Francis?" Ilse made a sour expression.

"That might be the best solution to the immediate cash flow problems of both sides." Vincent was being pragmatic.

Making a deal with your enemy might not feel right, but sometimes it was the best solution.

"What if they were the ones who killed Anna?" Bobby asked, mainly because he didn't like Clive or Francis.

"Then they'll be charged with murder," Tucker said, going along with Vincent's strategy. "But if we can make a deal, Ilse will have cash and should be able to get back any unsold paintings. Keep in mind that a murder case can take years to resolve, too."

Ilse was thinking. She looked at Bobby, then Tucker. "Let's negotiate. See if we can get some of the cash released."

23

Love Conquers All

Vincent started to head for the Inn before he remembered he didn't live there anymore. He knew Nancy wouldn't be home until much later, and he was uncomfortable with the idea of going to her house—even if it was his, too, in theory—just to wait. He decided to stop by the gallery to see if anything had happened.

He approached one of the security guards, who was leaning on their car. It was a nice night in Santa Fe.

"Seen anyone go in?"

"Yup, the two guys you described were here. One of them came over and asked us what we were doing. I'm pretty sure he wanted to yell at us, but he didn't. I told him we were following a court order, just like you told us to say, and he wandered off mumbling something. They were in the building for about an hour, and then left. Nothing since then."

Vincent walked around the building, not particularly looking for anything, mostly just killing time. Everything seemed normal. He got back into his car and left. He decided to run by the free clinic.

The place was run by Nancy's uncle, Butch Collins, who

most people knew as Santa Claus, due to his impressive white beard. The clinic served the street population, which was substantial in Santa Fe, and there were several agencies who provided services to the homeless in the same area. Homeless people seemed attracted to the city despite its harsh winters, possibly because its multi-cultural makeup and liberal local politics made it seem more inviting than many places. Vincent often found street people to be a reliable resource of information, if you had the cash to contribute.

"Hey, Butch, how's things?"

"'Bout the same, Vincent. Dangerous and mean. How 'bout you?"

"Well, you know, I sure wouldn't want this to get out, but things are going pretty good for me. And a lot of that good stuff has to do with your niece. She is one special person."

"You got that right. You're a lucky man, Vincent. I thought Nancy was done taking heartache from men, but I guess she sees something special in you."

The lighthearted banter suddenly hit home, and Vincent realized all over again that he was exactly that—one lucky SOB. Rather than tear up and give Santa a hug, he changed the subject. "Sure you heard about the murder of the gallery owner."

"Oh, sure. Always lots of gossip in this town. And the cops have been around a few times to find out if anyone saw anything around the park where the body was found."

"Yeah, I figured that. Did they find anyone who saw anything?"

"Nah. The chief's a great guy, and he was friends with one of the most famous street people in this town, but your average cop around here is the same as every other cop in every other town. They come at homeless people with implied threats and aggressive attitudes, even when all they want is a favor. Not the best way to get information. And if anyone did see anything, they probably moved along, just to avoid having to deal with the cops. I once had a cop tell me he couldn't understand why 'these people,' as he called them, weren't more cooperative with the police. 'After all,' he says to me, 'they're citizens, too.' This was the same cop who just a few minutes earlier was hassling these 'citizens,' telling them to pick up their 'shit'—his word—and move on, or he'd toss them in jail. 'Citizens,' my ass. These folks know they're nothing at all to the cops—until the cops want something, of course."

"Do you think there would have been people in the park at that time of night?"

"Oh, for sure. Cathedral Park is a prime location. I have no idea how many, or if they would have been sober enough to remember anything, but if someone parked a car there late at night and walked away, my guess is, someone saw it."

"Do you think they might come forward?"

Butch gave Vincent a look that made him feel foolish. "Seriously? There's nothing good in it for them, and plenty of bad. Ten minutes after they give the cops an eyewitness account of what happened, they turn into a suspect instead of a witness. Cops can't help themselves. You find a homeless guy and accuse him of a crime, and it's perfect. You've solved the crime, and no one gives a shit either way about the homeless guy."

"How 'bout a five-hundred-dollar incentive?"

"Way too much. At those prices, you'll get a couple hundred supposed eyewitnesses—and a few confessions, even. Let me put word out that a private eye is willing to pay a smaller reward for any information about what happened in the park that night. I'll make it clear the information has to be useful and credible before anyone gets paid. You might get something."

"You're a good man, Butch—even with the funny beard."

Vincent decided he'd drop into the Crown Bar next to see if Nancy had time for a drink with him. He knew she was working, and it was rude to just drop in and expect her to entertain him, but he couldn't help himself.

"Vincent, good to see ya. You hear the news about Rick and Mariana?"

"Did they get married?"

"How did you—? Well, they didn't actually get married, but they got engaged. Still, how did you know?" Nancy was grinning—unless he missed his guess, she was glad to see him.

"Hey, I have eyes. It was obvious, just watching them. How did Mary and Hector take it?"

"Mary may still be crying, but I think they're mostly pleased."

"I bet Cindy's already planning the wedding."

"Yeah, everyone seems happy about it. Mariana's mom was really doubtful at first, but I talked to her and told her what a wonderful man Rick is, and she discussed it with Mary, too. I think she really bonded with Mary. Anyway, she seems to be okay with everything, now. What have you been up to?"

Vincent was about to answer when his phone vibrated. "Malone."

"Mister Malone? This is Hank, one of the security guards at the gallery. We've got a guy down here who says he has a right to enter the gallery—not one of the two you told us about. And he's shit-faced drunk. We stopped him before he could go inside, and asked him for identification. He got pushy, even attacked one of my men, and my guy shoved him to the ground. Anyway, the dude isn't hurt, but he did start puking, I think because of how much he's had to drink. What do you want us to do?"

"I'll be there in about five minutes," he told the guard, then turned back to Nancy. "Looks like my day isn't over. Okay if we continue our conversation at home later?" He didn't want to leave, but he needed to find out what was going on.

"That'll be great." Nancy gave him one of the smiles he longed for. He hesitated, but after a moment, he managed to leave.

"Mister Taylor, are you okay?"

Trent Taylor was a mess, lying on the ground, with vomit all over him. He'd been crying when Vincent arrived, and the guards were standing back, watching cautiously while the man collapsed in some kind of emotional breakdown.

He opened his eyes and looked at Malone. "My mother is the greatest goddamned artist in the world, in the whole fuckin' world—and, and nobody cares. How can that be fair? Fuck *no*, it's not fair. I love my mother." Taylor's eyes rolled back into his head, and he blacked out.

Vincent, who'd had years of personal experience with drunks, went to find some paper towels to clean him up. After he finished that—a process the guards watched, but didn't take part in—he asked for help putting the man into his car. As soon as he got in, he regretted it. Taylor was ripe, and his car would almost certainly smell like vomit for days. But it was too late to change his mind, so he drove to the free clinic. Butch helped get Taylor into the building, and put him in a bed with plastic coverings, set aside for just such situations.

"Doesn't look like my normal street drunk," Butch observed.

"No. His name's Trent Taylor. He's the business manager at the Howard Marks Gallery. I know he's plastered, but I also think he's having some kind of emotional crisis that may have prompted it. I want to talk to him once he's sober enough to make sense. How 'bout I rent the bed, and when he wakes you give me a call?"

"Is he homeless?"

"No, not in the sense you mean. He's not on the street."

"Okay, fifty bucks."

"Done."

Vincent went home, although in his mind it still felt like

going to Nancy's. It was a very comfortable house, and after a few minutes of adjustment, he started to relax, digging out a beer and sitting outside to stare up at the sky. There were few lights in the neighborhood, which allowed for a decent view of the stars. It wasn't long before Nancy came out with a glass of milk and joined him. Vincent had never been good at expressing his feelings, but he thought he should try.

"I've been thinking about how lucky I am to have found you."

"I've been thinking the same thing—how lucky you are to have found me." She giggled.

"I guess you know that wasn't funny."

"Yeah, I know."

"The guy at the art gallery was Trent Taylor, the business manager. Drunk as a skunk. Kind of out of his mind, saying stuff about his mother. I took him to Butch's place, and rented a cot for him there. I have no idea what the guy was talking about, but he was in bad shape."

"A lot of troubled people associated with that gallery. Do you think they made each other crazy, or are crazy people attracted to one another?" Nancy was lying on her back now, cushioned by the soft grass, watching the sky.

"Not sure in this case, but most of the people involved are just a wee bit odd. Maybe it's inherent in a creative business. Back in my drinking days, during one of my moments of clarity, I realized most of my drinking buddies were normal. They were accountants, lawyers, salesmen, and they had wives and kids, and maybe a dog—normal, but hating it. They despised being nothing more than normal. They wanted to be special, unusual, gifted, great, super—anything but normal. By definition, most people are normal, but I think most of us don't think of ourselves that way. We pretend we're something special, even if we're not. The drunks were the people who'd figured out the truth—they weren't special. And it haunted them."

"That's pretty deep, Vincent. Have you taken up drinking again?"

"Hey, I was a deep thinker way before the booze." He frowned. "I think a lot of murders are committed by those same people, the ones who wanted to be special but are confronted by the fact that they're nothing but normal. It drives them nuts."

"Did you know that Uncle Butch is a genius?"

"Santa Claus is a genius?"

"Yep. He graduated from MIT at the age of eighteen. Certified genius—very, very special. He met a woman and fell madly in love. She left him for the star quarterback on the football team. The certified genius who knew everything spent the next twenty years drinking himself into a stupor every night, trying to forget the woman he lost. And he's still not over it. I don't know about special, or genius, or normal, but I do know most people live through grief. That's when you start to really know yourself. In the middle of my uncle's amazing grief, he decided he needed to help other people. He still got drunk, sometimes, but he committed his life to helping others rather than being a genius. Does that make him stupid?"

"Not sure about stupid. It does make him someone you

can trust."

"I love you more every day."

Had a four-alarm alert in my head today. I'm too happy, there's too much going right—watch your back! If there's a fork coming up in the road ahead, I sure as hell hope I pick the right path.

24

Crazy Gene

Vincent looked at his vibrating phone. At six am? He answered it, quietly, so as not to awaken Nancy.

"Hey, Vincent," Butch said. "Our guest took off sometime during the night. I got here early this morning, but he was already gone. No tip, no five-star rating, nothing. Sorry."

Santa Claus really did get to work early.

"Wow. The condition he was in, I expected him to sleep 'til noon. Anyway, not your fault, Butch. How about we go ahead with that plan we talked about yesterday? Put word out that I'll pay for info about any unusual activity at the Cathedral Park the night of the murder, okay?"

"Sure, I'll take care of it. See ya."

Vincent disconnected, then glanced over at Nancy, who was still asleep, with a sense of real belonging. He got up to fix coffee and retrieved the Santa Fe and Albuquerque papers from the front porch. He knew that fewer and fewer people were reading actual newspapers these days, but it was one of his great pleasures to enjoy a cup of coffee while flipping through real newsprint, taking in the news of the day—an old-fogey habit.

"Good morning." Nancy said, coming into the kitchen.

"Morning."

"Thanks for making coffee. I love my coffee in the morn-ing, but I hate making it."

"So, that's why you shanghaied me—my coffee-making skills."

"Actually, I didn't know about *that* skill." Nancy leaned over and gave him a playfully passionate kiss, out of sync with the early morning sunlight. "Your coffee-making is just a bo-nus."

If Vincent had been a young girl, he would have giggled—he almost did, anyway. For some time, they sat in silent bliss, drank coffee, and read the papers.

"Think I'll make a quick trip down to Las Cruces. My drunk buddy slipped out of the clinic sometime during the night, and I think he might be headed there. If not, well—I want to meet his mother, anyway. Should be back, late after-noon at the latest." Vincent looked up and saw Nancy smiling. "Are you smiling because I'm going to be gone today?"

"Nope, I'm smiling because you're coming back today."

"How about a date tonight at one of those famous Santa Fe restaurants you can't get into at the last minute without a reservation, unless you call and sweet-talk them?"

"Done."

Vincent took a quick shower and was on the road early. He had a nagging feeling he should visit Taylor's mother, and he'd learned a long time ago to trust those feelings. The drive to Las Cruces took about four hours, and was not very scenic.

Considering the number of miles involved, it amazed him how few towns he passed. After a long stretch of almost nothing after Truth or Consequences, he came to Las Cruces. He knew his exit was University Drive, and the gallery was only a short distance from I-25.

As he exited, he could see the campus and football stadium of New Mexico State University, a big school in a small town. He'd always liked that combination, ever since his OU and Norman days. He felt a pang of nostalgia as he drove by the large campus. Not far down University Drive, he spotted the Taylor Gallery. It was in a small strip center, mostly housing local mom-and-pop businesses. He pulled into a parking spot in front of the gallery.

If it hadn't been for a small sign on a string saying the place was open, he never would have guessed. Of course, it might actually be closed—someone could have forgotten to change the sign. He tried the door, and it opened, so he went in.

The paintings on display were all very similar. The majority were landscapes, with lots and lots of flowers, mostly mountain scenes with large trees. Even without looking closely, he could tell that they'd all been painted by the same artist. Vincent was no expert, but to him the paintings had a period feel, like they'd been painted a hundred years ago. They weren't bad or anything—just not very relevant.

"Oh, hello. I didn't hear you come in. Can I help you with something?"

Vincent could immediately see the woman wasn't all there. Maybe that wasn't the kindest way of putting it, but something about her voice and the look in her eyes suggested he was dealing with someone who had mental health issues. She spoke without stopping what she was doing, dusting the paintings with a bright yellow feather duster. The task seemed to occupy her attention more than Vincent did.

"Would you by any chance be Gloria Taylor?"

"Of course. Who else would I be?"

Vincent liked her logic. "I know your son, Trent, and I was passing through Las Cruces, and thought I'd stop and see if he happened to be here today." Vincent realized he'd begun automatically to speak a little slower than usual.

"A friend of Trent's. Isn't that wonderful! Where is Trent?"

"Uh, I'm not sure where he is just now. I was looking for him. Have you heard from him lately?"

"No, it's been a few weeks since he was here. He's very busy. He runs a large art gallery in Santa Fe—they sell a lot of my paintings. Maybe you've been there? My daughter's usually here, and she's better at answering these kinds of questions than I am."

"Oh, I didn't know Trent had a sister. That's great. Does she live here in Las Cruces?"

"Who the hell are you?" came a loud, angry voice. A large woman was standing in the door, staring at him. Vincent was a big guy, but she had to be about his equal, not only in size, but in disposition, too. "I asked you a goddamned question, mister—who the hell are you?"

"My name is Vincent Malone. I'm a private investigator working for an Albuquerque law firm. I'm looking for Trent

Taylor."

"He's not here. She hasn't seen him in months. My mother gets things mixed up. I haven't seen the bastard in a real long time." The obviously angry, giant woman moved her hand toward her purse, and Vincent had the impression that there was a gun inside—and that she wouldn't hesitate to use it. "I think it'd be best if you left."

"Sure, not trying to upset anyone. Just doing my job. Are you Trent's sister?"

She glared at him. "Half-sister. Now get out, before I hurt you."

Some threats are hollow, but not this one. Vincent left. Now what? He had no contacts in Las Cruces. He didn't think it would be wise to try to contact Gloria Taylor again today, what with her ogre daughter on duty. He had no desire to shoot the monster woman, and sure as hell didn't want her to shoot him.

When in doubt, find a bar.

He headed away from the college neighborhood because bartenders around there would only know about sports and hookups, the two main matters of interest to college students. Passing into a less upscale part of town, he spotted his favorite source of information—a dive.

The Hill Top Bar & Grill was a living stereotype. It was the biker bar you saw in movies, although the real thing could be hard to find. Most bars, he thought as he approached it, couldn't survive solely by serving the kind of person who would frequent a bar that looked like shit both inside and out, but this place seemed to be an exception. There was a busy lunch crowd, judging by the number of parked vehicles. And it wouldn't surprise Vincent to find out they made the best burgers in a hundred miles, and were visited around noon by business people who would never have ventured there at night. He entered, and bingo—suits everywhere.

He settled onto a barstool and ordered a Tecate, then went with his normal routine for these situations, laying a twenty down on the bar and following it with a question. The bartender gave him a blank look and went to another customer. Mr. Blank turned out to be a practiced conveyor of information and a driver of a hard bargain—it took a hundred bucks to pry loose anything useful.

The sister's name was Joyce McGregor. It was rumored that she was the masked wrestler from El Paso known as "Bad Ass Mama," who had a string of victories over women and a few brave men. The bartender provided the totally unnecessary advice that she should be avoided at all costs. Her father was some kind of famous artist from Spain who had moved to Las Cruces to teach at New Mexico State. Her mother, Gloria, was much younger than the old artist. She had been his student, and left her husband and son to move in with the old man. For reasons the bartender didn't know, the artist ultimately killed himself—shot himself in the head. Joyce was born just before that, but the bartender didn't know whether that had anything to do with his suicide. Taylor's mother seemed to lose her mind after that.

Vincent asked how she'd opened a gallery if she was so

out of touch.

"*She* didn't open it. It was her son from her first marriage that did that. Opened the gallery and let her show her paintings. But there's lots of bad blood between the siblings. Joyce almost killed him once with a baseball bat. She went to prison for five years for that. This is one seriously fucked-up family, man. Not sure what your interest is, but I'd avoid the whole lot of them like the plague, if I were you."

Vincent tipped him an extra twenty—you have to respect talent when you find it. He got a burger to go and headed back to Santa Fe with some answers, but more questions. The return drive was, through some mystery of physics, longer than the drive down. He was actually a little shocked when he finally reached the Santa Fe city limits.

Rather than stopping in the Crown, he decided to head home and take a nap. He wasn't really a nap person, but he also wasn't as young as he'd been once upon a time. The nap lasted longer than he expected.

"Hey there, road warrior. All tuckered out?" Nancy was smiling, holding out a cold beer.

"Sorry, it was just going to be a quick nap but—holy crap, it's dark already. Give me just a minute, and we can get going on our date."

"Don't worry. I canceled the reservation, and our pizza just arrived. The favorite food of lovers and old people."

"Do I get to pick which I am?"

"Okay with me if you're both."

Vincent got up, took a quick shower, and joined Nancy

for beer and pizza. He'd rarely felt better in his life. *Must be the nap.*

"So, what did you find out in Las Cruces?"

Vincent gave her the whole rundown.

"Do you think he was actually there?"

"My guess is no. Joyce might have been acting some, but what I saw was real anger, real hatred. I think if Trent was around, he'd be in serious danger from his giant, lethal half-sister, and he has to know that. Lots of things I still don't know, though. Does he really own the gallery in Las Cruces? His mother's paintings were good, I guess, but in a strange sort of way. Not sure you'd sell too many, even if you had foot traffic coming through, and I got the impression not many people wandered in there. Why would he continue to fund it—if he's doing that—just to have a place for his mother's paintings to be displayed? And the big question is, where is Trent now?"

"You know I own a bar, right? You keep saying you can walk into any bar and learn information about the local community just by paying the bartender. If I saw that sort of thing going on in my bar, I'd fire the bartender in a New York second. So, how do you get away with doing that?"

"First, I would never do it in your bar—at least, not anymore. And second, if you could spot a bartender making money on the side, he or she wouldn't be much of a source. You should be proud that your profession acts as a much-needed information clearinghouse for your community."

"You are so full of shit."

"I've been accused of that before, but never by such a

lovely lady."

Comforts of home: a beautiful woman, pizza and beer.
Must be heaven.

25

Looks Like Rain

Vincent's phone buzzed.

"Malone."

"Hey, Vincent, Chief Stanton. Got some time that we could visit?"

"Whatever they said about me, it's a lie."

"You're hilarious—for a PI, anyway."

"So I've been told."

They arranged to meet that afternoon at the chief's office. Vincent went back to reading the morning paper. The national news seemed to be about politicians lying or being accused of lying, although the reporting seemed more focused on assessing the skill with which the bad behavior was conducted than on condemning it. How the world arrived at a place where flat-out lies were okay, as long as your political opponent lied as well, was beyond Vincent. So, one guy was a four-star liar and the other a two-star. How about someone who doesn't lie? He shook his head.

Vincent parked a block or so from the clinic and walked the rest of the way. The weather was perfect. There was a little moisture in the air, which might have been what caused it, but whatever the reason, it seemed to make everyone feel more up-beat than usual. The promise of rain must be something buried deep inside the human genetic code, because everyone he saw was smiling.

"Good morning, Butch."

"I think it *is* a good morning, Vincent. Lots of people out early, and everyone seems to be in a good mood."

"I noticed. Any action on my info request?"

"Nope, a little early. Takes a while for the human grape-vine to spread the word. This isn't cable news, and it sure as hell ain't the internet. I'd say another day or two, and we should start to hear something. Of course, it's possible no one wants to talk about dead bodies. These people mostly survive by not trusting anyone who isn't one of them."

Probably a sound approach. Vincent was debating with himself over a second breakfast when his phone vibrated. "Malone."

"Just got a call from Curtis Howard. He's representing Clive and Francis. We've exchanged some ideas on how to re-solve some of the issues about the frozen assets, and he called to say they want to meet this morning. Curtis Howard was a partner of Stephen Martinez—remember him? Nobody wants to, these days. Even the firm name is now just Howard and Fitch. Anyway, I know this is short notice, but I thought you might want to be there."

"And hello to you, too, Tucker. Sure, I can be there. When and where?"

"At their office, same place as the old Martinez, Howard

and Fitch firm. I told them to give me an hour to get there. That work for you?"

"Yep. Will Bobby and Ilse be there?"

"No. Just got off the phone with them, and they asked me to call you—you seem to have developed a couple of fans. Anyway, they said they didn't see any reason to be there, so we should just do our thing and let them know the outcome."

"Are you in your car? It sounds like you are."

"Yep."

"You know you shouldn't drive and talk, right?"

"So, fuckin' sue me." With that, Tucker disconnected.

The law office was just off the downtown Plaza. Vincent decided to walk, since he had time to kill. A big second breakfast seemed like a bad idea, but he was drawn to the aroma of a small bakery. He chose a sandwich of green chili, pepper-jack cheese, chorizo sausage, and egg on a croissant, and it turned out to be the most delicious thing he'd eaten in a long time. If it hadn't been for his ever-expanding waistline, he would have had another. Instead, he took his coffee and walked around the Plaza. Vendors were arranging their wares on the sidewalk—a daily routine on the Plaza, people hawking a variety of items ranging from cheap trinkets to high-priced jewelry. He found a bench and watched. He never thought he'd become an old man sitting on a bench, watching the world amble by, but he could see the attraction, at least briefly. He felt very content.

After a while, he broke the spell and headed to the law firm. He'd been to the office before to address some problems with the former partner, Martinez. Apart from taking Martinez's name off the sign, not much had changed.

"Good morning. Vincent Malone. Here for a meeting with Mister Howard."

The receptionist was an older woman with a friendly face. "Of course, Mister Malone. As soon as Mister Tucker arrives, I'll show you both to the conference room."

She offered coffee, but Vincent was stuffed, and declined. He took a seat and waited, wasn't there long when Tucker arrived, and they were shown to the conference room. Clive Walton and Francis Mitchell—dressed in a very conservative blue suit, this time—did not get up or even acknowledge them. Curtis Howard stood to shake their hands.

"Will Ilse be joining us today?"

"No. I told her I thought it might be more productive if she wasn't here. She'll be available if we need to consult with her, to get instructions. She did request that Mister Malone, our investigator, attend, if that's acceptable."

Clive gave an odd twitch that suggested he wanted to say something, but stayed silent.

"Sure, that's fine." Howard just wanted to resolve the legal issues, and probably wasn't aware of any lingering personal conflicts. He summarized the discussions and proposals that had taken place prior to the meeting. He was a detail-oriented attorney, often referring to his notes to make sure he was stating the matters correctly. "First, my clients have agreed in principle with your proposals, such as a complete audit of the financial dealings between the two parties for the past twelve months—that's agreeable. We can discuss what approach to use in choosing an independent auditor at a later time. You've requested they release all paintings for which the gallery doesn't have a signed sales agreement with a deposit. We agree that those are your client's assets, but there's been a great deal of prep work and expense put into the showings at the other Howard Marks Gallery locations. The contract between the parties that's in place now calls for those pieces to remain under the control of the gallery until the final show in New York. We think it's still in the best interests of everyone for that to proceed as planned."

"Our concern," Tucker replied, "is related to the complications that will arise due to the death of Anna Marks—ownership issues and management issues of the gallery business. We acknowledge that our contract is with the corporation, but at its heart it was an agreement with the driving force of the business, which was Anna Marks, therefore we—"

Clive slammed his fist down on the table and shot to his feet. "Fuck that. She didn't know shit about the business. I'm the one who made it a success. I'm the one who arranged all these shows and got people to buy this shit artwork. I'm the one who did all the work while Anna and your bitch client were off playing fuckin' footsie, or whatever they were doing. *I'm* the one who will make your client a lot of money. *I'm* the driving force, *not* Anna." He sat down, looking exhausted, angry, and a little embarrassed. Francis reached over to take his hand, but he pushed him away.

Howard cleared his throat. "Maybe we should take a short break."

Tucker and Vincent left the conference room to go outside and get some air after asking the receptionist to let them know when everyone was ready to restart.

"What the fuck was that all about?" Tucker looked annoyed. "I thought we had some general agreement to agree, and that guy acts like he wants to go to war. After that, I'm not sure we can agree to much of anything. He's nuts."

"Well, he's a little volatile, but what he said is probably pretty close to the truth. Clive is the driving force behind the success of the gallery. He's the one who had the contacts, meaning buyers—not Anna. But it was Anna who had the business relationship with Ilse—or more than business, I guess. If we could get rid of all the emotional crap that's getting in the way, I think it'd be clear the business side of this deal will probably be just fine with Clive and Francis in charge. I think the issue isn't so much whether they can accomplish everything Anna would have done. It's more about whether they can be trusted."

"Do you think there's a chance those two had anything to do with her death?" Now Tucker looked more worried than annoyed.

Vincent hesitated. "First, I don't know who killed Anna, or why. My number one suspect from the beginning was Clive Walton. My list has shifted some, but he's still at the top."

"Why would he kill her? Doesn't that potentially leave him out in the cold?"

"Clive's an angry man. He brought this business back from the dead, and he wanted to be rewarded. I don't know what the deal was with Anna and Clive, but I can guess she promised him the world if he'd put together this show and sale of Ilse's work, and make it a success. Plus, Clive's involved with Francis, and I bet he thinks Anna treated Francis like shit. On top of all of that, he has a real temper, as you just saw. If he and Anna came into contact that night, there could have been fireworks."

Tucker looked thoughtful. "This is a mess. I think we should postpone this meeting, use his temper tantrum as an excuse, and consult with Ilse. If this was just about money, then the best course would probably just be to let Clive run the show—but it could all blow up in our faces if he ends up being accused of murder. It's a big decision, and our client needs to give us her instructions on it."

"Okay, but we need an accounting, right now, of how much money was collected on deposit for the paintings that sold. Ilse needs cash, and she should immediately receive some of that deposit money."

"Good point. Let me go talk to Howard and see what we can work out."

Tucker went back in. Vincent thought it was a good opportunity to smoke, even though he had quit just that morning. Again.

"What do you think we should do?" Ilse asked Vincent after Tucker had given her and Bobby a summary of the meeting and what appeared to be the options moving forward.

"Clive will want to do everything possible to have successful showings of your art. From the information I've been able to gather, almost all the buyer contacts are people Clive has brought in. So, if having the paintings sold quickly at the best price is your goal, then it would make sense to go forward with Clive. The risk is if he gets charged with murder, or if he and Francis try to cheat you out of your share."

"Do you think he killed Anna?"

"I think it's possible. I'm not sure what the police have. I'm meeting later with the chief, so I might have an update after that. But as of right now, I think it's a real possibility that he could be charged."

"What would the legal strategy be if I try to break away from this whole mess?"

"First, we try to void the contract because of Anna's death," Tucker replied. "We would argue that the execution of the contract was dependent upon Anna's skills, and that with her death the corporation is no longer capable of fulfilling its obligations. We'd also argue that, due to her death the company does not have the financial resources necessary to complete the contract. All that would have to be argued in court, with the goal of getting the court to order the corporation to return any unsold paintings to you. Any paintings where we have a confirmed contract for their sale would stay with the gallery, but we would request that you receive some portion of any deposits immediately, and we'd ask the court to monitor the actual execution of the contract. No one can ever guarantee what a court will do, but I'm confident we could win on all those points."

"Do you think Francis can gain full ownership of the gallery?"

"That's another question that's not easy to answer. At this point, we're being told that Anna had no heirs. But it's early days for that process to play out. Without a will, and with no obvious heirs, her estate goes to probate court. A judge's first duty will be to do an extensive search for any living relatives. It could turn out there's a relative that Anna didn't even know about who would turn into the new majority owner at the gallery. And how that would play out is anyone's guess. The new owner could try to sell the business, or run it themselves, with or without Clive and Francis. Nobody knows. If no relative can be found, then it really gets complicated. The court might decide it's in the best interests of the estate to sell the business to the minority shareholder, but even if it did, that would be months down the road."

"And if they find a will?"

"Then all bets are off."

26

Too Many Cooks

Vincent excused himself from the meeting with Tucker, Ilse and Bobby so he could meet with the chief. He'd become comfortable with the guy, which wasn't his normal relationship with cops. Even so, the request to meet had come as a surprise. He knew perfectly well that the chief hadn't asked to see him to share information about the investigation. More than likely, he wanted to convey some kind of message. The most typical, based on Vincent's experience with police in the past, was, "Stay out of our investigation."

But he also knew Stanton was an honest cop, just trying to do his job. If he had any kind of underhanded agenda, it was well hidden. So, he wasn't overly concerned about meeting with him.

"Vincent, come in, have a seat." The chief's desk this time was stacked with paper and looked disorganized. "There are two things I really hate about this job, and the first is paperwork." He gestured at his desk. "I never get it all done. I thought computers were supposed to eliminate all this crap—but it never stops." He laughed a little, and cleared this throat. "The second is politics."

"I've pissed off a politician?"

The chief smiled. "Very insightful. Our mayor is very pro-business. He's more like the head of the chamber of commerce than a mayor of the people, but he is what he is. His belief is that if it's good for business, it's good for Santa Fe. One of his country club buddies has complained to him, and then, of course, he complained to me. The guards you put at that gallery are causing someone grief, and they want me to remove them."

"Let me guess. The country club buddy was Curtis Howard. You know this is a legal matter, right? And we have a court order allowing us to safeguard certain assets."

"So I understand. Believe me, I have no desire to get in the way of the courts, but my boss has insisted that I look into whether you can legally have private guards stationed at a business without the business's permission. As it turns out, we have an ordinance for that sort of thing. I have no idea who wrote the rules or when, but they're legal and enforceable. Private guards can only be stationed at a business if they're inside it, or if they're doing a moving patrol around it. Having your guards parked in their cars outside the gallery doesn't cut it."

Vincent stared at the chief in disbelief. "Are you going to enforce that?"

"No, not today. And probably not tomorrow. But after that, we'll issue tickets. The citation can carry a fine of up to a thousand dollars per day, per guard."

"That's fuckin stupid." So much for diplomacy.

"Maybe so. Look, Vincent, I asked to meet with you so we could hopefully avoid any real conflict here. I'm guessing you're close to getting something resolved regarding the gallery, so I'm giving you a couple of days' notice. Now, maybe you can go to the court and they can order me to do nothing. I'd prefer that didn't happen. Despite the mayor's insistence, I don't believe this should turn into a civil war. Just get your matter solved with the gallery, or reach a different solution that doesn't involve those guards sitting in their cars."

Vincent thought about it, and realized the chief was actually trying to help him. He smiled. "You're right, chief. No reason to fight city hall. We'll get the matter resolved or seek some other solution to safeguarding the assets inside the gallery. I appreciate you giving me a heads-up. Sorry if I overreacted there a little." When it's appropriate, you kiss up.

"You should know, we have new information, and we'll be making an arrest in the Anna Marks murder in a few days." The chief said it in a matter-of-fact-way that caught Vincent off guard.

"Wow, can you give me anything on that?"

"No."

Vincent left the police station convinced the chief was a sneaky bastard, but a likeable sneaky bastard. He couldn't figure what the new information might be, or who it implicated. He pulled out his phone and called Tucker.

"Didn't even give you a hint?"

"Nope. Nothing."

There was a lengthy pause while Tucker thought. "Well, you're right about getting some other kind of solution on the guards. We could go to court, but I think the judge might be reluctant to give us permission to violate an ordinance, even if it's a stupid one. Can't believe Howard would go through the mayor rather than just calling me and asking what the hell was going on. But I'll call him and set up another session to get this resolved. I think we're close. Shit, I hate this unknown with the police. You have no idea what they might have?"

"None. Unless it's the same thing I'm trying with the street people. Maybe they found a witness who saw the murderer drop the car off at the park."

"Yeah, I guess that's the most logical. Well, keep digging, and let me know about anything new."

It was the time of day when the old Vincent would have headed to a bar, and he had to admit he missed the comfort of that old routine, and the soothing effects of alcohol. But he sure didn't miss feeling like shit the next morning, or not being really sure what had happened during a big chunk of his day. He called Nancy instead.

"Hey," she answered, "is this one of those I'm-going-to-be-late-tonight calls?"

"No, this is a how-'bout-I-fix-you-a-green-chili-cheese-burger call."

"Vincent, you know you can't cook."

"Wow, that really hurts. I've been watching YouTube, and I know everything there is to know about the world-famous super burger. Be nice, and I might make you one."

"Okay. It's a date. I should be home in about an hour or so. Is that too early?"

"Fine with me. See you then."

He clicked off. Now all he had to do was find a grocery store, buy what he needed, rush home, and find a YouTube video to tell him what to do.

"Cindy, you do realize this is not your wedding, and that Rick and Mariana get to make all the decisions?"

"Listen smarty-pants, they're young and in love. They don't have time to plan a wedding. They need my help." Cindy was smiling as she gently scolded her husband. She could have added "and I'm having fun," but didn't.

"I figured they'd be married in the church."

"Yeah, me, too. Apparently, that's created a little problem for Rick with his mom, but Mariana doesn't want a church wedding. I think maybe the religion issue is at the heart of her conflict with her mother. Anyway, she's adamant—no church wedding. Rick seemed not to care, so they're getting married here, in the back yard. The gazebo will be a perfect backdrop. There will only be a few guests, so it's not a big deal."

"When is this happening?" Jerry had been looking at their bookings. It seemed like they were close to full for the next few months.

"In about two weeks. Mariana's mom can't come, so it'll just be people from Santa Fe. For that and other reasons, they decided to have a whirlwind romance and schedule the wedding as soon as possible. Mary is upset again, though. She thinks they don't even know one another, and that getting married within weeks of meeting just isn't right. Hector told me, on the QT, that he and Mary were only engaged for three months, so maybe it's just how the Flores family does things. Even so, Mary's opposed."

"We're going to have a full house for the next few months. Are we going to need help, since Mary will be occupied? Plus, I guess Mariana will on her honeymoon."

"Maybe. I asked Nancy if she knew of anyone who might want to work for a few weeks to get us through. Mariana offered to delay her honeymoon until we have some down time, but I said no. We'll work something out."

"What's created all this demand? Is this your marketing in action?"

"A little bit me and whole lot of plain dumb luck. There are two conferences for writers coming up over the next month. They're scheduled back-to-back at the convention center. They anticipated a certain number to sign up, but it's come to double what they expected. So, the organizers of those events have been calling everyone, looking for rooms. Along with the guests we already had booked, we're full for more than a month. Hope you're well rested."

"I just hope Mary doesn't flake out on us—I can't handle that by myself."

"She won't. I've talked to her, and she'll be ready to handle her part."

"Guess I should call and see if Vincent might be available to drive the van. And maybe help serving drinks or something."

"Based on what I hear, he's pretty busy with his investigations."

"Yeah, could be. But I'll ask him, anyway."

"How did you figure out how to cook this?" Nancy asked between bites.

"Did you like it?" Vincent asked.

"Best damn burger I've ever had," she said, with her mouth full. "What was that sauce? Did you buy that or just make it up?"

"I got the recipe off the internet. It was actually really easy to make, but it does taste good, doesn't it? Maybe I should ask Jerry if I could do some cooking at the Inn. Could be a whole new career."

Nancy's smile said he'd better be kidding. "How many jobs do you need, anyway? I thought you were a big-time investigator."

Vincent chuckled. "Yeah, I'm the biggest. I've got one client, and that's Tucker. For whatever reason, I haven't been able to bond with Hill. I think he knows I think he's a jerk."

"You haven't said it to him, have you?"

"Well, no. But I've asked around. Tucker said he was a little on the edge in the past—but that's an understatement. His reputation is very much as a guy who cuts corners and doesn't worry about ethics."

"Sounds like your kind of guy."

"Yeah, he does in a way, but he's not. I've always been a

street guy. I can't really explain what that means, but there's a certain kind of behavior that's accepted on the street, and a whole other set of rules for these office guys. Jack Hill is the worst kind of office guy—right up there with politicians. People who basically have no rules—pretty much whatever you can get away with. I've had some pretty lowlife pals, but I trusted them. The trust came from the fact that we all understood what was okay and what wasn't. The Jack Hills of the world will change their definitions of right and wrong at the drop of a hat. You can't trust a man like that, because you never know what he'll do. And, yes, I know I should just shut up and ignore my ethics and take his money—he sure hasn't asked me to do anything that was out of line, But I'm not sure I can work for a jerk."

Nancy looked at Vincent for a long time before she spoke again. "Why would Tucker work for him?"

"That's different. Tucker does most of his work in a courtroom. The rules are clear there, not ambiguous. Plus, you have a judge to set you straight if you stray. Tucker is a guy who pushes those boundaries to their limits to benefit his client, but when you're in a courtroom, it's not like the real world—there are so many safeguards that, no matter how much you try to bend the rules, you'll never go too far. With me, the things they ask me to do can sometimes involve people getting hurt, or me getting hurt. And there are no judges going along to make sure everybody plays by the rules. Every asshole you meet now has a gun. That danger, that risk, is why the job has so much appeal. I know how to make the level of risk acceptable, but

I'm always on alert and on edge. I know this might sound silly, but if I'm going to do that, I need to know that the guy asking me to take that risk is a straight shooter, not a bullshitter who would risk me for some kind of personal gain. That's why I just don't trust him."

"Vincent, maybe I'd be a lot happier if you were the cook at the Inn."

Nancy started to cry, and Vincent suddenly realized that all of the nonsense he'd been spouting must have brought back memories of her husband being killed. "Nance, I know I made that sound bad, but I really am careful, and I know what I'm doing."

She smiled, but she didn't quite stop crying.

Me and my big mouth, blabbing on and on about risk and danger. Must have sounded like some kind of dumb death wish. Oh please, Nancy, let's make a nice life together while I go out and try to get myself killed on a regular basis. This isn't a bar scene with a bunch of brainless drunks who won't remember what you said, anyway. This is someone you love. Start acting like it, or go live by yourself.

27

Nobody Knows

"Vincent? Just got off the phone with Curtis Howard. I think we're close to an agreement regarding the security and money issues. While we were discussing those, he casually mentions that Francis told him that Anna made it clear to him she was going to leave the business to him in her will. Apparently, at least according to Francis, within the last six months, Anna was diagnosed with some kind of tumor. He says they have documentation that a lot of her travel to Amsterdam wasn't only to see Ilse, or to do anything else for the business, but also to be treated with some new drugs. She told Francis that even despite that, she didn't know whether she had long to live."

It annoyed Vincent that Tucker would call so early in the morning and immediately launch into a complicated conversation with no preamble at all. *Good morning to you too, you bastard.* He made a face. "I'm not sure I believe that. What was all the anxiety about money then, and keeping the gallery going? If you're dying, you have other things to worry about besides your business."

"Yeah, I asked the same thing. He says Francis thinks it was to raise the money to pay for some experimental operation

251

in The Netherlands. That she was desperate, and her behavior had changed because of the tumor."

"Was there an autopsy?"

"Should have been ordered by the police, given that it was a murder, but I don't know. I'll check." Tucker mumbled something to himself, probably about overlooking the obvious.

"Santa Fe PD is run by a pro, so I'm sure they ordered an autopsy," Vincent said. "But without any living relatives, they would have just kept that information to themselves. They sure as hell weren't going to volunteer it to us."

"Yep. Oversight on my part. Nobody's been charged, so there's no one that they have to disclose the autopsy results to. And we only represent Ilse in a civil matter, not a criminal one. So, we don't have a right to that information." Tucker paused. "If Francis is right, and they find a will naming him as the heir to the business, it would move his name to the top of the suspect list. Inheriting a multi-million-dollar business would be a strong motive. He finds out Anna's dying, and figures he's going to take over soon, and then she starts chasing after experimental treatments. What if she finds one that works?"

"Are we under any obligation to pass this along to the police?"

"Probably. We sure aren't covered by client-attorney privilege, and the attorney who is has already spilled the beans. You know it's going to screw up our negotiations if we go to the police and point them toward Francis."

"Should we meet with Howard and discuss this—or does that violate some ethical rule?"

"I think it is a very muddy area, but we should meet with Howard before contacting the police. We need access to the evidence he says they have about her travel to Amsterdam being for medical reasons. And if there's a will, where the hell is it? Maybe Howard or Francis have some idea."

"I'd put my money on the cops having it. They did an extensive search of her house. If she didn't leave it with an attorney, then my guess is it was at her house."

"Shit. That's probably right. If they charged someone, and if we represented that person, then we could demand that sort of thing, but right now we have zero standing for even asking about it. Would your buddy the chief give you a hush-hush update?"

"Nope. He's not really my buddy, but even if he was, he wouldn't tell me anything about an ongoing investigation."

"I'm going to call Howard back and see if we can meet in a couple of hours. I'll call you back."

Vincent sat back and thought about Anna. If she'd been told she was dying, then her behavior took on a whole new light. He wondered if Francis had made up the story, but he couldn't see any motivation for it. Even if Anna told him what he claimed, that the business was going to be left to him, that wasn't going to influence the probate court. Under certain circumstances, verbal statements can be used to help understand the intent of someone who's died—for instance, if their will is ambiguous—since you can't exactly ask them about it. But an unsubstantiated conversation, by itself, wasn't going to do Francis any good. And that meant what he'd told his attorney was probably true.

"Well, well. You look serious. Something in the paper?" Nancy had appeared quietly and was getting coffee.

"No. I just talked to Tucker." Vincent told her what he'd just learned.

"Poor Anna." She thought a moment. "If she was dying, why would she leave the business to Francis? And why would she tell him?"

"You should be an investigator, and I should run a bar. How 'bout a little role reversal?"

"No way in hell. I'll stick with bartending."

"I can only guess why she would leave the business to Francis, or why she'd tell him, but if it's true, then I bet she wanted something from him. Maybe he'd threatened to quit, and she wanted him to stay, or she wanted him to do something. She wanted leverage over Francis for something."

"You have a very suspicious mind."

"Yeah, I probably do."

The police arrived in full force at the tidy little stucco house with the blue flowers in the front courtyard. This was no casual visit. The chief was there, along with three teams, well-armed and prepared for the worst. They surrounded the house, and the chief rang the bell.

Francis answered the intercom. "Yes, who is it?"

"Mister Mitchell, this is Police Chief Stanton. I need

to talk to you about Anna Marks. Could you please open the door?" There was silence. He signaled to his men to stay in place. After what seemed way too long, but was only a few minutes, the outer door made the distinct sound of being unlocked. The chief opened the door and, with two of his men, walked through the garden to the red door. The chief raised his hand to knock, but the door opened.

Francis stood in the doorway. Everyone immediately went on alert. Not only was his appearance a little shocking, with his flowery housecoat, but again he was wearing the huge sidearm, and that ratcheted up the tension.

"Mister Mitchell, we're here to serve an arrest warrant. For the safety of everyone involved, I want you to very carefully remove your weapon and place it on the ground."

The chief had his hand on his service weapon. Francis looked at the gathered force. He made a small movement. It looked like his hand was moving toward his gun.

"Stop!"

Clive grabbed Francis' arm from behind and pulled it far from the holster. He gently removed the massive weapon and placed it on the ground.

"Please step forward," the chief said, "very slowly, and stay away from the gun."

Every officer remained primed. Francis and Clive stepped into the courtyard.

"I want you to lie down on the ground," the chief commanded.

Francis started to shake, and he looked at Clive as if to

ask, *can they make us do that?* Clive nodded, and lowered to the ground. Francis followed. The chief picked up the massive magnum and handed it to one of his men.

"Clive Walton, we have a warrant for your arrest for the murder of Anna Marks." The chief read Walton his rights and asked if he understood.

"No, I don't understand. I don't understand jack shit. I didn't kill her, you moron. I want an attorney, right now!"

Clive was being handcuffed by two policemen, while Francis looked on, just before curling up into a ball on the ground, mumbling to himself. "Fuck, fuck, fuck, fuck," Francis repeated.

The chief directed his men to escort Clive to the police van and take him to the station. Francis remained on the ground in the middle of all of it. He had gone quiet, and then, without saying anything more, he passed out.

"Call an ambulance, now." The chief wasn't sure what was wrong with Francis, but the whole scene reeked of the kind of chaos and danger he hated. And he damn well was going to do everything by the book until everything was calm again.

His phone vibrated—a sound he was beginning to dislike.

"Malone."

"I need a fuckin' attorney, right now. Can you get me one?"

"Clive?"

"Yeah. I've been charged with killing Anna. It's bullshit,

I didn't kill her. I have no idea who killed her. Look, I don't really know you, but you're a pain-in-the-butt kind of guy, and I want you on my side. Can you help me?"

"Clive, I'm not a practicing attorney any more. But as you know, I work for a law firm that's very good at this shit. If they don't have some kind of conflict of interest, they'll represent you. Where are you?"

"County jail. I was arrested by the Santa Fe police. Fuckin' police chief himself was there. I was in the back taking a nap, and Francis opened the door wearing his housecoat and the stupid gun. You know he has a permit for that damn gun. It's a miracle someone was not killed. Francis had some kind of panic attack or something; they took him to the hospital. Can you check on him?"

"That I can do. Give me a little time, but one way or another, I'll find you a good criminal lawyer." Vincent called Tucker.

"Well, shit. I don't see how I can represent him. I know Ilse's case is a civil matter, not a criminal one, but their interests are still at odds. Even if no literal conflict exists, the perception of it sure as hell does. If I ignore that, it could cause problems down the road, and Clive sure doesn't need that kind of complication if he's facing a murder charge. And that applies to the rest of my firm, too. In the old days, the rules were looser. We could have used one of our other lawyers and just put up a Chinese wall. But things have been tightened up, and that won't fly, these days. I've got a better idea, though. You know that group I started that's focusing on criminal justice reform?

I met someone through that who might be perfect."

Tucker sounded pissed. Vincent guessed that he wanted nothing more than to jump into the Clive's case with both feet. "Okay, what's his name?"

"*Her* name. Carol Moore. She's middle-aged, got her degree late in life, but definitely has a passion for justice. If I was charged with murder, I'd want someone like me, but if I couldn't get that, then I'd want someone like her. I'll give her a call. Any glitches and I'll call you back."

Vincent headed to Saint Anthony's hospital, the largest in the city, and the most likely destination for Francis. After that, he'd go to the county jail. The call from Clive was a surprise, but Vincent seldom turned down a genuine plea for help.

Francis had been placed in a semiprivate room. Vincent lied to the nurse on duty, saying he was a co-worker, and wondering how his friend was. She said he'd been involved in something with the police and apparently had an emotional breakdown. She shouldn't have given him the information with such ease, but Vincent had a kind face, or maybe she was just inexperienced. It was the kind of boundary Vincent had learned to push, long ago. Sometimes you'd get lucky, and if you didn't care what people thought of you, there wasn't really a downside. Francis had been given medication to calm him, and didn't seem to be in any immediate danger, the nurse said. He'd have a psychological evaluation the next day, and then, depending on the results, he could be released. Vincent took a quick look inside the room. Francis was obviously sedated and sleeping peacefully.

The county jail was a depressing place, and the officers manning the information windows seemed to have been chosen based on surliness. But after he mentioned by name everyone he knew with any authority, he was shown into a small room with a tiny table and four chairs. After an annoyingly long wait, Clive was brought in. He looked horrible. There was no reason to ask him how he was. It was obvious.

"Your lawyer will be here shortly. Her name's Carol Moore. She's going to tell you not to talk to anyone, including me. You should follow her advice. Peter Tucker recommended her because he has potential conflict of interest since he represents Ilse De Vries." He waited for a response, but none came, so he went on. "I went by Saint Anthony's, and saw Francis. He's been medicated and he was resting. He's going to have a psych evaluation tomorrow, and then he might be released."

"The way things are going, I'm sure they'll decide he's crazy and try to lock him up, too. Why the fuck do they think I killed her?"

"I don't know, Clive. Most likely they have some evidence that places you at the scene of the crime—maybe video, maybe forensics. Maybe even an eyewitness. More than likely, the police know about Anna's health problems and may have a copy of the will, which leaves the gallery to Francis. I want to emphasize, though—*I don't know why*. I'm just guessing. But I bet it's something circumstantial based on motive, which is the prospect of inheriting the gallery, and opportunity, which is evidence putting you at or near the crime scene. Why they moved forward right now, I have no idea."

"You know, it's funny. There were many times I wanted to kill her, but do you want to know why I didn't?"

"Sure."

"Aside from not being someone who goes around killing people, even though I may have said on a few occasions I hated her, truth is, I kinda liked her. We disagreed about almost everything when it came to art, but she wasn't a bad person. The whole fucked-up mess with her dad humiliating her for years, and then the fiasco about the forged paintings—it seemed like everything always turned against her. I liked her, and I felt sorry for her. But still, at times, I hated her. If I hadn't cared about her, Francis and I would have left a long time ago. Hell, I can make plenty of money in the art world. She needed me a lot more than I needed her. I was trying to help her, for god's sake, so why would I kill her?" His anger turned to tears—being charged with such a serious crime, and being in jail, had devastated him.

"We'll do everything we can to get you out of jail."

"Please, oh, please."

28

Masterminds We're Not

Vincent left the consultation room after the guards took Clive back to his cell. He was walking down the hallway to leave when he heard a woman's voice.

"What the hell are you doing talking to my client? Tucker said you'd help me, but instead, you're interfering. If you still had your fuckin' license, I'd do everything I could to get you disbarred."

She reminded Vincent of his second-grade teacher, whom he'd feared, just like every other kid in her class—big, loud, and scary. "Who the fuck are you?"

"Carol Moore, and Mister Walton is *my* client. These stupid jail people should never have let you talk to him."

Vincent stared at the woman, not quite sure what to say. "Look, I had no idea how long it would take for someone to see Clive. He called me for help. I was just assuring him that something was happening, and that hopefully he'd be out of jail soon."

"You had no right to do that. Do you understand that, mister?"

Vincent paused, looking at her blankly, letting her see

that her bluster didn't bother him. "You jump down my throat again and, woman or not, I'll bust your fuckin' nose."

Carol Moore flinched like she'd been slapped. "No wonder you're not a lawyer anymore." She turned in a huff and headed back to the front desk.

It looked like Vincent wouldn't be playing for the Moore team. He went outside and left Tucker a voice-mail message. "Just had an encounter with Carol Moore. It was ugly. She seemed pretty upset that I'd managed to get a meeting with Clive. Nobody jumps on my ass like that—man, woman, or dog—without me hitting back, so it looks like I won't be able to work with her. Sorry if that upsets your plans."

He disconnected. Now he was in a shitty mood. Everything seemed to be going in the wrong direction. Clive being charged with Anna's murder wasn't exactly a surprise. He'd shown real anger toward Anna. All that stuff about really liking her might have some truth to it, but people murdered people they *loved* all the time, let alone people they only liked. Clive's temper made him a prime suspect. And Anna probably knew what buttons to push to get him fired up. If they'd had any kind of confrontation that night, it could easily have escalated out of control. Still, seeing him jailed was unsettling. Vincent's phone vibrated. "Malone."

"She says you're the biggest fuckin' asshole she has ever met. Not sure what happened to get you both so excited, but you need to get over it. She was wrong to say what she did, and you were wrong to threaten her. My god, children, can we please just work together for a little while to help the cause of justice?"

Vincent chuckled. "Look, Tucker, I can work with almost anyone, but I'm not sure about this one. She didn't even introduce herself, just immediately starting yelling at me like I'm some kind of kid. Does she even know what she's doing?"

Long pause. "Okay, she probably overreacted because maybe she doesn't know what she's doing. Maybe I made a mistake." More dead air. "I was trying to set up something where I could direct her and keep control over this case, and I shouldn't have. The problem now is I'm not sure how to undo it."

"I thought you said she was good."

"Well, I guess I should have said I *think* she'll be good. She really knows her stuff, but she hasn't actually practiced for very long."

"So, let me see. You want to control this case on both sides, which is dead wrong. To do that, you recommended someone you figured you could control to represent a man charged with murder. The person you recommended has no real experience, although she made good grades in school. Are you out of your fuckin' mind? And *I'm* the one she wants disbarred. My god, Tucker."

"Yeah. I screwed up. Where are you?"

"In front of the jail."

"Stay there just a minute, okay?" He disconnected.

Vincent stared at his phone, shaking his head. He sat down on the steps, wondering if his friend had actually lost his mind. Carol Moore came out through the main jail doors and approached him. He didn't move.

"Sorry. I guess I, uh—I screwed up. Not sure why I yelled at you. I don't normally act like that, and I don't even know you. It's just that I was really nervous already, and the guard on duty was treating me like I was an idiot. Then he said that the guy's attorney was already meeting with him, and something snapped. But I was wrong. I'm really sorry. Plus, I don't want my nose busted. I'm going to call Tucker back and tell him I can't do this." She started to walk away.

"Hey, wait a minute. It's okay. You don't have to be nice to me. A large segment of the population isn't, so why should you be different? Plus, for the most part, I don't give a shit what people say about me or to me, and that includes you. And I shouldn't have threatened to bust your nose. I was on edge, too. Why don't we put it to one side and start over? My name's Vincent Malone." He extended his hand. She had to reach up, but she took it. "I thought you were coming from Albuquerque," he said, "and probably wouldn't be here until tomorrow. So, I wanted to settle him down and let him know someone would be here. Sorry I stepped on your toes. I should have called Tucker first to make sure that wouldn't be getting in the way."

Moore nodded and seemed to be thinking. "Tucker said you're an asshole—but a smart, brave asshole. And he should have told you I was with him, driving up for your meeting with Curtis Howard. So, this was my fault, your fault, and definitely also Tucker's fault. The bottom line is, I need your help. I know the law, but I don't know all the practical, real-world stuff, like how to deal with a jail clerk. Can you help me?"

Vincent smiled. "Yeah, I can help a little." Tucker owed him one for this, and he wasn't going to let the man forget it.

Curtis Howard came into the small conference room. Vincent and Tucker had been waiting longer than they'd expected to.

"Sorry about that. I called the police chief earlier, and just when you guys showed up, he called me back. Sure didn't mean for you to wait this long. But I did get some news."

"Yeah, well, we're getting used to waiting." There was an edge in Tucker's voice—he really was not a man accustomed to cooling his heels.

"The chief told me they found Anna Marks's will during their search of her house. I think the Albuquerque paper got an anonymous tip about it, and filed something in court to force the release of the document. Chief said they decided not to fight it, and it's going to be given to the paper later today—he called me as a courtesy. Anyway, apparently it does say that she leaves the business to Francis. The police think that gives Clive and Francis a motive to kill Anna."

"Did he say if they're going to charge Francis?" Tucker asked.

"He didn't say, but I'd bet they won't. This is just me reading between the lines, but I think the prosecutor is more comfortable with Clive as some kind of criminal mastermind manipulating poor Francis, while Francis didn't really know what was happening.

Vincent found the whole idea absurd. "Clive, a criminal mastermind? That's really what they're going with?"

Tucker jumped in. "I know Clive's defense and Francis's health have to be the priority issues, but we can't let this stalemate over the gallery and the paintings keep going. If we can get a copy of the will, then we can stipulate that Francis has authority to conduct the business. But we're still concerned about his ability to complete the contract, especially with Clive in jail. Might be in everyone's interest to divide what profits there are now, return the unsold paintings, and make a deal to wait six months to see what happens."

"Not sure about that, Tucker. Francis would be best served by completing the agreement that's in place. But we're concerned about Clive not being available, too. He's the one with the buyer contacts, and I have a feeling Francis wouldn't be very eager to move forward without his involvement. So, maybe there's a way we can go to our mutual corners and wait and see what happens. Let me talk to Francis, and then I'll get back to you."

Vincent was driving to the free clinic to see if Santa Claus was still working when he suddenly broke out laughing. Observed from afar, you might think he'd lost his mind, but he was actually just remembering the look on Moore's face when he said he would bust her nose. He couldn't stop laughing. *I really am a bad man.*

"Hey, Butch. Workin' a little late, aren't you?"

"Yeah. Couple of my bad kids got into a fight. Had to call the cops. I hate that, but I can't just let people kill each other. Shit, everybody will be mad at me for a few days because I called the cops. I don't know—there are days I really wonder if I'm doing any good or not."

"Well, you are, man. I don't know how you deal with this crap every day and then come back the next day and do it all over again. These assholes won't tell you thanks, but they know, and I know, and Nancy knows, and the damn police chief knows—a lot more people than you think, know."

"Thanks, Vincent. Hell, I never did this for the glory— it was always the money." Butch smiled, but still looked sad. "Hey, got some news for you. A semi-regular came in a few hours ago and said he saw someone get out of that car by the church. I know this guy, and when he's at least a little sober, he's reliable. Anyway, he said he saw this guy, and thought it was weird where he parked the car, and also where he went afterward. The guy headed down toward Canyon Road, and there's nothing open down that way that time of night."

"Could he describe the guy?"

"Said it was the drunk who slept on the cot the other night in the back room. The guy you brought in."

Trent Taylor! Gotcha!

"How 'bout a beer?" Nancy gave Vincent a broad smile as he

came in, obviously exhausted.

"That'd be wonderful. Sorry I'm so late. Lots going on today."

"I heard some of it on the news. They said the police found Anna's will, and that she left the art business to Francis Mitchell. He was her accountant, right? And they said Clive Walton has been arrested for Anna's murder. Does that mean the artist is in the clear now?"

"Probably. But arresting Clive is the easy part. Proving he did it will be hard, especially since I don't believe he killed her."

"Do you know who did?"

"Yep, think so."

One of the frustrations in practicing law, as well as in being an investigator, is that you can know something, but still find it damned difficult to prove. You may be sure in your gut, and every instinct you've got backs up that gut feeling, and even your experience joins in the chorus, but you still may not be able prove the thing you're so sure of—not beyond a reasonable doubt in court. That can be hard to live with.

29

Guilt

Francis was discharged from the hospital. The news that he had inherited the gallery seemed to have a positive effect on his mental state, along with being released back into the world. He went home, put on his dressing gown—without his enormous weapon this time, because the police had taken it away—and had a good cry. Clive was in jail, and it scared Francis to think what might be happening to him. He knew he had to do something, but the thought frightened him. He had a good idea who had killed Anna and why, and it was time he told someone. It was an odd choice, but in the end, the call he made was to the monster—Malone.

Vincent was taken aback to get a call from Francis inviting him to talk. Not only did he think the man was certifiably crazy, he was pretty sure Francis hated him. Still, he responded. Once more at the large wooden gate of the adobe house, he rang the bell. The outer door clicked, right away this time. As he entered the courtyard, he thought he could feel sadness shrouding the place—even the flowers looked forlorn. Of course, it was probably his imagination—maybe they just needed some watering. He was almost at the red front door when it opened, abruptly.

"Maybe we should just sit out here," Francis said. He looked very fragile, and Vincent wondered if he was still on some kind of medication. Francis waved them toward a pair of white Adirondack chairs in a shaded corner of the garden.

"How you doin'?" Vincent still wasn't sure why Francis had asked him to come. It was obvious the man was still not quite stable, but at least he wasn't brandishing his extremely large gun, this time.

"I've got to tell someone what I know. Clive didn't kill Anna, and they should release him from jail immediately. I know he's scared. Can you get him out?"

"He has a lawyer, and I'm sure she's working on that right now. What is it you know, Francis? Is this about Anna's death?"

"Yes, it's about Anna. I caused her death." He placed his head in his hands, gently swaying as he sobbed quietly.

Whatever Vincent had expected, it wasn't this. "You killed Anna?"

"No, no, of course not. I didn't kill her. But I should have stopped her once I found out what she was doing. Then she'd still be alive. I should never have agreed to keep quiet. But I wanted the business—not for me, but for Clive. I regretted it the minute I said I'd keep quiet. But I thought somehow it would all work out and nobody would be hurt." He moaned, and his gaze wandered off into the distance.

Vincent waited a bit, but Francis seemed in a trance, so he

tried to move things forward. "Tell me what happened. What was she doing that you found out about?"

"Selling forged paintings again." He laughed, glumly. "I couldn't believe it. After all the grief the last time, when she did it by mistake, and now she was doing it again. But this time, she knew. It was greed. She hadn't been fooled. She knew perfectly well they were forgeries. As part of my job I monitored the money as it related to total cash flow, but usually didn't look at all the details. One month I did. What caught my eye were payments to the Taylor Gallery in Las Cruces. It was a lot. I knew Trent had owned a gallery down that way, but I believed he'd closed it years ago. At first, I thought, well, maybe it's not the same Taylor. But I went online, and there it was. The place was filled with Trent's mother's paintings. He'd told me his mother was dead—he'd lied. Why on earth would Anna be buying paintings from Taylor Gallery? I started to track the sales. They were works by known artists. Not the *most* famous, of course, but well-known artists whose paintings sold for many thousands of dollars each. It didn't make sense."

"When was this?"

"Mostly over the last three years. But there had been hundreds of these paintings over the last year or two. It was a hell of a lot of money. Anna had paid Taylor Gallery over a hundred thousand dollars, and the paintings had resold for almost a million. Once I had the numbers, I knew something was wrong. So I confronted Anna. Of course, she just started yelling at me. Calling me names, saying I was a spy."

"When did you confront her?"

"About four months ago. That's when I should have stopped her. But after she yelled at me for what seemed like hours, she changed her approach. She told me no one had been hurt. After all, the buyers thought they'd gotten a bargain, and the forgeries were so damn good she didn't think anyone would ever know. She just needed time to complete this show with Ilse, and she would retire. That's when she said she'd leave the business to me. It's also when she told me about her health problems. She said she would write a will leaving everything to me. She indicated she didn't have any relatives and it would be what her father would have wanted. But if she didn't die, she'd sell me the galleries. Said we'd work out a plan to transfer the galleries to me if the treatment worked. I started to rational-ize everything. She needed the money to have an operation to save her life. And no one had been harmed. Plus, Clive and I deserved the business, since without Clive she would've lost everything, anyway. Right there, while she was still talking, I was already making plans about how we would do things, what we would change, and how we would turn the place into a real success. I agreed to keep quiet."

"Where was Trent getting those forgeries?"

"His mother painted them. Part of my agreement with Anna was that Trent would never know I'd discovered what was going on. She was worried that he'd do something rash if he ever found out she was leaving the gallery to me. She said she'd handle Trent, so I never talked to him about any of it. Anna told me Trent's mother had completely lost her mind, and that he could control her, and have her paint whatever he told her to. Apparently, she'd been a very talented artist at one time, and she still had the skills, so she could produce whatever you needed, if you gave her proper instructions. He would give her photos of paintings and, according to Anna, she would turn out these fantastic forgeries."

Vincent had to ask, "Do you think Trent killed Anna?"

"Yes."

"Why would he do that?"

"Anna had told me not long ago that Trent was pushing her to give him more money, that he was going to leave the country, and he needed cash. It was because of his half-sister. She'd found out that he'd been having his mother produce these paintings, and she'd threatened him. This is the same sister who went to jail for nearly killing him years ago, and he was really scared. Of course, Anna was absorbed in her own problems, with her health and with Ilse, and she told Trent she couldn't deal with him right now, and that she was done with the stupid forgeries."

"So, what happened then?"

"Then, on the day of the reception, he was making a big scene. I heard him clearly. He wanted money. She became angry, and told him she was sick of him, and that he was fired. And for some reason, she told him I was going to have the galleries after the show. She ordered him to leave. But he didn't. Anna was so distracted, I'm not even sure she realized he hadn't left. I think he killed her that night, either to get money, or just for revenge."

"Do you know where Trent is?"

"No. Can you get Clive out of jail?"

Francis was clearly having trouble staying connected to reality, but everything he'd said made sense. Trent had all kinds of motive, and now Vincent had a witness who'd seen him walking away from Anna's car at the park. That seemed enough to get him arrested. Francis's story was hearsay, so it wouldn't be allowed in court unless there was a way to fit it into one of the narrow exceptions to the rule—as a declaration against interest, for example—but that didn't matter at the moment. The goal right now, while the police were still investigating, was to persuade them that there was a more likely suspect than Clive or Ilse. There was no rule against the police using hearsay information— they did it all the time, and the rule only applied in court. If they followed it up, it might even lead them to evidence against Trent that *could* be used in court, making hearsay evidence unnecessary. Whatever else happened, there was certainly enough in what Francis was saying to focus the police attention on Trent as the likely killer, and that would be a step in the right direction.

"Francis, you're the one who can help get Clive out of jail. You have to tell the police chief the same thing you just told me. Can you do that?"

"Will he come here?"

"I think he'd probably agree to that."

"I'll tell him everything I know, if he'll come here. I'm not going to the police station."

"One more thing. Ilse said someone, a man, called her the night after the reception and told her one of her paintings had been damaged, and it was Clive's fault. Do you know anything about that?"

"Had to be Trent. Surprisingly, he was at the gallery when the paintings were brought back in. It was part of the security procedures he'd developed. He was supposed to inspect them in case there was any damage during transit. He got all excited and said one of the paintings was damaged, but Clive looked at it and said it was only the outer edge, and it was very slight, a minor ding that was easily repaired. At that point, he and Clive got into it. Trent was threatening Clive—said he was going to call Anna. Clive told him he should leave, or he was going to call the police. He told him he knew Anna had fired him, and what was he doing there, anyway? Trent kind of went crazy, yelling at Clive and calling him names. Then he just left. I don't know where he went, but when we locked up, we could not find him in the gallery."

Vincent called the chief and gave him all he had, including the homeless eyewitness and the new information regarding Taylor being at the gallery that night. He told him what Francis wanted. The chief showed up within the hour with a stenographer and recording equipment. They sat in the dining room, where Francis told his story again. The chief gently questioned him for a few extra details, and took some documents Francis had that accounted for the payments to Taylor Gallery.

Vincent, meanwhile, waited in the garden. The chief came out and took a chair.

"I called the station. Clive will be released in a matter

of a few hours. And, thank god. The jail people were about ready to kill his new attorney. Apparently, she's been raising hell all morning about Clive being held illegally. Is she a friend of yours?"

"Not exactly. Any leads on where Trent Taylor might be?"

"Well, we were already looking for him, to question him. We got a report from the Las Cruces police that someone matching his description had been seen there, so my guess is that he went home. The police over there will probably pick him up soon, if he's still in the area."

"Who gets charged now?"

"Good question. I've got good circumstantial evidence pointing to Taylor for the murder, but first we have to find him. And it's sure not an airtight case. Francis sure had a strong financial motive to want Anna dead, but there is no direct evidence. This forgery stuff is muddying the waters. It's a crime, but it's on Taylor and Anna Marks, at least so far as we know at the moment. Francis should have come forward and reported it weeks ago, but considering his mental state, I doubt the DA will do anything about it. Maybe Clive knew, and maybe he didn't, but at best that's obstruction, and that's not a priority right now. For all I know, Ilse could still have strangled Anna, but I don't have the evidence to hold her. And once she's back in the Netherlands, we won't have any way to realistically pursue it. Not very satisfying, but the only hope for some kind of justice is if we can find Taylor."

"I know your official position would be not to tell me the evidence you have against Taylor but we're the only ones here, and I have been cooperative." Vincent was curious and tried not to beg. He even smiled.

The chief paused and starred at Vincent. He chuckled and nodded. "We've got his phone records and video of him inside the gallery that night. He called Anna and then later called Iles. What Iles has given us about the call matches the time that Taylor called her number. About twenty minutes before that he had called Anna's number. What we don't have is any real proof of what happened. There's no 'smoking gun' video or conclusive forensics. Without a confession we might not be able to prove anything."

Vincent sighed. "Yep, crime fighting is a tough business."

"Why are you going to Las Cruces? You're not a cop." Nancy was frowning. It sounded to her like a lot of risk for no reason.

"I know. But this feels unfinished to me. I don't expect to bump into Taylor, but I need a bit more closure than just a shrug. And, who knows? Maybe his mother actually knows where he is. If she does she sure as hell isn't going to tell the cops, but maybe she'll tell me."

"Want me to tag along?"

"No, mom. I can handle this myself. I appreciate the offer, but this is a quick trip, and I'll be back before you know it. It would take you longer to make arrangements to be away than it will for me to go see if I can find anything out—which, more than likely, I can't.

She gave him a gentle kiss. "You gotta do what you gotta do."

It was late afternoon, and he was on the road. He knew making this run was a little nuts, but his instincts said to go. Of course, he could have waited and left early in the morning, but he wanted to end this case as soon as possible. If there had been a travel guide of America's most boring road trips, then the drive from Santa Fe to Las Cruces would have been featured prominently, but at least there was very little traffic.

He'd be surprised if he actually found Trent Taylor, but running into Joyce McGregor, the "Bad Ass Mama," was probably even money. With that in mind, he'd brought both of his handguns. He wasn't going to say it out loud, but the huge woman worried him.

As evening turned to night, Vincent spotted an exit that advertised accommodations at T or C. He found a no-name motel. There were a few cars in the lot, and a bunch of long-haul trucks, and Vincent found a spot between two of the big rigs. His room was small, and nearly bare apart from the bed, but that was fine. The anonymity of it gave him comfort, and he quickly dozed off.

30

Endings

Before getting on the highway the next morning, Vincent went to the McDonalds drive-thru for a sausage biscuit with egg and a coffee. Cheap and filling. The coffee was always too hot, which meant it lasted a long time as he headed to Las Cruces. *Damn it,* he thought, as he gingerly took a sip. *I may not be able to drink that until tomorrow, for cryin' out loud.*

He got into Las Cruces way too early to drop in at the gallery. He called Tucker.

"What the hell do you want?"

"Sorry to wake you. You know you're really rude, right?"

"You called me this early in the morning to tell me *I'm* rude?"

"Did Moore get Clive released?"

"Yeah, although she said it was really you who got him released. Father Malone heard Francis's confession, and suddenly Clive is a free man. Where the hell are you, anyway?"

"Headed to Las Cruces. It's just a hunch, but I thought I might be able to catch Taylor before he disappears, or his loving sister kills him."

"Not sure I understand all that, Vincent." Now Tucker

sounded concerned.

"I think Taylor's running. Pretty sure he killed Anna; I doubt anyone can prove it. He doesn't know that, so he took off. At least, that's what I think. He's from this part of the world, so if he wanted to disappear, I think his first thought would be Mexico, specifically, Juarez. That means he'd probably go through Las Cruces, which is home to him. I also think he might have money hidden out here—a getaway fund. Thought I'd just drop in and see if I got lucky."

"That is so fuckin' stupid. You're not the cops. You can't be doing this sort of thing—jeez, Vincent. You only risk personal harm for money, not some misplaced sense-of-justice bullshit. Haven't I taught you anything?"

"Yeah, yeah, I know. Look, Tucker, he might have killed Anna, but I don't think he's really dangerous. I know it's not my problem, but if I can talk to him, maybe I can help him understand he doesn't have to run, even if he did it, there are probably good defenses, including the fact that he is most likely nuts. I tried to call him, but his voice mail is full. And I thought it was worth a drive on the chance that he's here, and that I can help wrap this up." *Or maybe I think I'm an old west bounty hunter, and I have to track down the bad guy so everything is all tied up in a nice neat package, and I'm the hero?*

"Vincent, be careful." There was concern in his friend's voice, and the whole trip seemed suddenly absurd.

"I will. I'm just going by the gallery. If I don't find Taylor there, I'm headed back. Call you later."

He disconnected. During the drive to the gallery, he carefully considered the risks and the options that were open to him. Thankfully, he had his trusty weapons. He parked, and saw that the little sign in the window of the gallery said "closed." He tried the door, and it opened.

"Hello. Anyone here?" He waited, but there was no answer. "Hello." Again, no answer.

Vincent maneuvered through the cluttered showroom and made his way to the back room, pushing open the door. Someone was there, sitting in a chair at a battered old desk. It was Gloria Taylor. She'd been shot in the temple, and was very definitely dead. He looked around, but saw no one else. There was a small pistol on the floor next to Gloria. It might be a suicide, or a murder dressed up like one. He pulled out his phone to call 911.

"Put the phone up." Standing in the doorway was the very imposing Joyce McGregor, holding a large handgun. There were cuts on her face, and it appeared her arm was injured. "I remember you. Mister Question Man. Who are you, again?"

"I'm a PI, investigating a murder in Santa Fe of a gallery owner who was buying fake paintings from this gallery." Vincent wasn't sure of the best way to proceed, but he definitely wasn't going to make any quick moves. "I believe the forgeries were painted by your mother."

"Yeah. She painted them, the poor dear. She'd been crazy for a long time, but now she can rest."

"Did she kill herself?"

"She pulled the trigger, but it was her worthless shit of a son who killed her. Did my dumb fuck half-brother kill that person in Santa Fe?"

Vincent was having trouble reading what McGregor might do—kill him, or herself, or both. "I think so. I don't have all the details nailed down, but the gallery owner most likely met him that night at the gallery alone. Probably because he'd told her there was a problem with a very expensive painting. He might have demanded money from her so he could leave the country; she refused and maybe threatened to call the cops. He lost it, and strangled her. But all of that's just a guess. There's no video or eyewitness to the murder. He disappeared, and it seemed likely he'd try to hide out in Mexico. I thought he might come through here on the way—partly because it's on the route, and partly to get money." He watched Joyce very carefully. "Have you seen him?"

"Yeah, I saw him." She made an ugly sound deep in her throat. "My mother had called me some time back, and told me she might be doing something wrong. We weren't close, and I hadn't seen her in years—not since I almost killed Trent. She told me about the paintings. She was out of it most of the time. But she started to figure out it was wrong, and she was worried she'd done something bad. I called Trent right then, and told him that if I ever saw him, I'd kill him for sure, and that he should never come here again. Probably should've called the police, but that's just not how I do things. Plus, I wasn't sure what might happen with my mother if a bunch of cops came around."

"Was he here recently?"

"Yeah. I told you, I saw him. Last night. I came by to look

for my mother because she hadn't come home. When I walked in, he was here getting money out of one of the filing cabinets. I had no idea he'd stashed money here. My mother was here, but she seemed to be in some kind of trance. Of course, he and I got into an argument. I knocked him around some, hurt him. He pulled out a gun—that gun on the floor. We fought for it, and he dropped it. I was ready to give him a good beating when my mother picked it up and shot herself—fell right back into the chair she'd just stood up from. No warning, nothing. Just picked it up and shot herself in the head. We both stood there, stunned. Then I started to turn toward him. I was going to kill him, I'll tell you that for sure. When I turned, he hit me with a board, knocked me out cold. When I woke up, he was gone. I think he must have hit me with the board some more after I was out, or maybe kicked me, because I feel pretty busted up. It doesn't matter too much right now, but maybe you should call 911."

With that, the huge woman turned ashen and fell to the floor, blood seeping from her mouth.

"My name is Lieutenant Daniels, with Las Cruces Police."

It was a cop Vincent hadn't dealt with yet. He'd been waiting in the cramped interview room for a while now, and the plastic chair made his back hurt.

"Just got word on Joyce McGregor," Daniels continued. "Looks like she was hurt pretty bad by someone—internal injuries—but they think she'll make it okay. Could be a long recovery from that kind of damage, though. That was a hell of a story you told us, Mister Malone. And I have to admit, we weren't real sure about you. But we talked to the police chief in Santa Fe, and everything you said checks out. The gun that killed Gloria Taylor was registered to her son, Trent. Our people are saying that preliminary results indicate she shot herself, just like the daughter told you. There were powder burns on Gloria Taylor's hand. Anyway, at this point, we have nothing further we need from you—you're free to go."

Vincent left, feeling low. It seemed like suffering and death were following him everywhere. He felt a deep sadness and a need to be home in Santa Fe.

"My god, Vincent she could have killed you." Nancy wasn't at all pleased after he gave her the details.

"Maybe, but it was odd. It didn't feel risky. Old Trent will be deader than dead if he ever runs into his sister again. But I was pretty sure she wasn't going to hurt me."

"So, everything's settled?"

"I'm not sure. I think Ilse and Bobby are still at the Inn, but her mother and manager went home. In theory, Clive and Francis could have some problems with this forgery business, but I don't see that turning into much now. So, in some ways, I guess stuff is settled. Or maybe I've gotten tired of thinking about it. I'm just glad to be home."

"Cindy, everything is so beautiful." Nancy was almost in tears. The wedding was a touching ceremony, with two lovely young people making a lifelong commitment. The back yard and gazebo had been specially decorated, and looked like a photo shoot from a bridal magazine. Cindy really did have talent for event planning.

"I understand you almost got yourself killed by a female professional wrestler. That would have made one hell of a story, Vincent. Might have missed your big chance to become famous." Tucker's smile seemed to say he was kidding, but Vincent wasn't entirely sure.

Rick had asked Jerry to be his best man. It was a kind gesture, and seemed to have touched Jerry deeply. He and Cindy had turned their business venture into a warm and caring place for people to live or visit, and the goodness of their hearts was obvious to everyone.

The bride was absolutely gorgeous, and the groom could not stop smiling. Mary and Hector were beaming. Mary had cried for most of the day, but now that they were actually married, she seemed overjoyed. She kept hugging Mariana, saying how beautiful she was and how lucky her son was. Hector stood off some, observing, but clearly very proud of his newly expanded family.

The ugly grief that Vincent had been forced to see for so many days had never touched the lovers, who were in their own world, and their happiness filled the air. Vincent surprised himself by feeling jealous.

"Do you think you'll ever want to get married, Nancy?" He had no idea how the words had gotten out of his mouth.

"Is that some kind of weird proposal?" Nancy was smiling, but looked concerned, too.

"I don't know. Maybe. If it was, what would you say?"

"You can't propose that way. *Hey, if I asked you to marry me, what do ya think you might say?* Vincent you're a grown man, not some high school kid. You can do better than that."

"Nancy McAllen, would you do me the honor of being my wife?" Vincent actually knelt. He felt a little foolish with everyone watching, but he did it, anyway.

"Yes. I would love to be your wife."

Mary began to cry all over again, and this time Cindy joined her.

<h1 style="text-align:center">31</h1>

Chickens Come Home To Roost

Vincent really hated being roused by the phone at seven in the morning. He answered it, anyway.

"Malone."

"Sorry for the early call. This is Younger."

"No problem." *Yes, there is.* "What's up?"

"Ken Simpson's body was found in the mountains outside Durango. Shot once, execution-style. Cops contacted me because of the Flores case. Wanted to know if I knew anything. Which I don't. Asked about you and Tucker."

"Shit." *I knew it, things were going too well.* "Not sorry the bastard's dead, but that's going to land on my doorstep with a thud." Vincent paused to think about how it could cause problems. It wouldn't take long for the Durango cops to make a connection in Denver, and if they could be found, there would be several people willing to talk about his nose-busting visit. "Just as a precaution, I think I need to hire you. You have any inside information sources in the Durango police force?"

"Not really. I used to date a court clerk, but even when we were on good terms—which we aren't, right now—she was always tight-lipped regarding the police and the courts. Other than your not-so-friendly conversation, any reason for this to point to you?"

"I had a history with Simpson that wasn't pleasant. The Denver cops are going to be aware of that. And they'd be more than pleased to have a chance to cause me a little grief. On the plus side, I haven't been in Colorado since my trip to Denver to bust his nose, and he was alive and breathing when I left. I should be able to provide an alibi for whenever they determine he was killed."

Younger seemed to think about that a moment. "I'd bet my best dog this is directly tied to Max Franks Junior. My lowlife buddies tell me he thinks he's a mob boss. So, executing Simpson would fall right into his screwed-up world. The biggest problem with that is he apparently has some connections within the area's law enforcement, and possibly into the DA's office. He's one dangerous prick."

"Suggestions?"

"Number one, hire a good lawyer. You've done that. Number two, do nothing. This does not go away, but until we know how they're going to proceed, there's nothing to do. Just be aware there appears to be a shit-load of grief on your horizon."

"Yeah, you're right. Thanks. Check's in the mail for the retainer."

Fuck!

Fine time to have my life blow up, again! Marriage— what the hell was I thinking? Calm, happy, bliss-filled married life. No way, with all of the baggage I carry around. At this point, this will be my secret. Who knows? Maybe it will just go away.

Yeah, right!

Epilogue

Ilse De Vries

Once she'd signed a new financial agreement with the Howard Marks Gallery, Ilse received a substantial sum as her share of the sales. She agreed to let Clive and Francis handle the remaining shows as they'd originally planned, but made it clear that she would be reevaluating the relationship going forward. With plenty of money in the bank, Ilse gave herself a break. She spent a lot of time with Bobby in Denver, but eventually went home. She bought a new apartment in Amsterdam and made it clear to her mother that she wasn't welcome, not even for a visit. She became active in the thriving art scene in the capital city, and reconnected with several art professors from the University of Amsterdam. They enticed her into a lecture series about the role of contemporary art in the modern world, and she became something of an attraction. With this boost to her ego, she began painting again, and the rumor had it that she was producing some of her best work.

Bobby Hawkins

He was reluctant to make the ultimate commitment to Ilse. He knew he loved her, but just wasn't sure he wanted a life devoted to managing an artistic ego, unless it was his own. He was questioned by DEA and FBI officials about his relationship with a sex-and-drug club operating in New York City and LA. While he admitted he'd joined the club years ago, and may have used some drugs in the past, he claimed he hadn't known the "social club" itself was illegal. The feds didn't believe him, but didn't have evidence to charge him with anything, either. Bobby knew he'd dodged a bullet, and swore to himself he'd be a better—and more careful—person. With his business thriving, he became one of the richest men in Colorado, and then took things in an unexpected direction by buying a minority interest in the Colorado Rockies Major League Baseball team. Even people who knew him hadn't expected it. No one had even known he was a baseball fan. He soon became the public face of a very popular team, and rumors began to circulate that he might run for mayor.

Trent Taylor

He never resurfaced. Most people connected with the murder case were convinced he was the killer, but since he was never found, and therefore never charged, the investigation remained officially open. There were multiple sightings of Taylor in Mexico, Canada, Texas, and various South American countries. Santa Fe PD investigated some of the reports, but as time passed, they began to ignore them. The Santa Fe police chief told several people he thought Taylor was dead. When pressed on why he would think so, he said he had his sources, but never elaborated.

Joyce McGregor

Joyce's recovery time was long, and her internal injuries healed slowly. She lost a lot of weight, so that when she was released, the nickname of "Bad Ass Mama" could have been amended to "Bad Ass Babe." With a new image, she returned to wrestling, and soon became a sex symbol with an entirely new fan base. She accepted several engagements in Mexico and became a star in the very active professional wrestling world south of the border. Lesser known was the fact that she spent a great deal of time and money on research and investigators trying to locate her half-brother. No one knows if she found him, or what happened if she did, but rumors persist among her fan base that she was successful, and ended his misery—permanently.

Clive Walton

Clive and Francis talked about marriage, but Francis always seemed to want to wait, and would never commit to a date. Clive suspected it had something to do with Francis's new found wealth. Clive managed the final shows for the De Vries paintings, and sales exceeded expectations—the controversy around Anna's death hadn't hurt prices any, and the paintings sold for record sums. Based on that success, Clive was offered a senior management position at a large art dealer in New York City. He talked to Francis about it, and he told Clive that he shouldn't pass up the opportunity. Clive's final words to Francis were, "Fuck you!"

Francis Mitchell

Francis went through several emotional breakdowns in a single year. He knew he'd been close to losing his mind, but inheriting and then running the gallery had given him focus and brought him back to earth. He'd never felt so empowered and important, and began to make his own decisions about the business. He knew Clive had been much of the driving force behind the gallery's success, but he was ready to step up and take more responsibility. Some of it had to do with Francis finding out about an affair Clive had had with a very attractive up-and-coming new artist. It crushed him at first, but he knew Clive was just being Clive, and if he wanted something else, he'd have to move on. It helped that, with his new financial status, some very attractive young men had begun flirting with him. Clive had opened a door in Francis's world, and now he was ready to walk through it.

Bente Smit

Ilse made it clear she wanted her mother out of her life. Bente cried for days, but cheered up after she discovered her daughter had deposited a substantial sum into her bank account. She called Ilse several times to thank her, but never got further than voice mail. She was on her own. Even with a fat bank account, it was scary. She asked Dirk to marry her, and let him know she had money. He said it wasn't enough—he was fed up with her and her daughter. He left. She cried.

Almost everyone else will return in the next Vincent Malone novel: Fiction No More, available now. Visit TedClifton.com for details.

About the Author

Ted Clifton has written mystery novels which feature the settings of New Mexico and Oklahoma, places where Ted spent considerable time. One of his books, *The Bootlegger's Legacy*, won the IBPA Benjamin Franklin award and the CIPA EVVY award. Today Ted and his wife reside in Denver, Colorado, after many years living in the New Mexico desert.

Keep in touch

Once a month, I send my readers a newsletter with a little of everything in it: southwest US culture, be it art, recipes, or local sights; my thoughts on writing and reading; book recommendations; updates on my current writing project; and from time-to-time a short story.

To sign up, visit **TedClifton.com** and either wait for the pop-up window, or scroll to the bottom of the page. Everybody who signs up receives a mystery gift, with my compliments.

You can also learn more about me and my latest books by visiting **TedClifton.com** or emailing me at **ask@tedclifton.com**.

Books by Ted Clifton

The Bootlegger's Legacy

(Prequel to the Pacheco & Chino mystery series.)

When an old-time bootlegger dies and leaves his son Mike a cryptic letter hinting at millions in hidden cash, Mike and his friend Joe embark on a journey that takes them through three states and 50 years of history. What they find goes beyond money and transforms them both.

This is an action-packed adventure story that partially takes place in the early 1950s. It all starts with a key, embossed with the letters CB, and a cryptic reference to Deep Deuce, a neighborhood once filled with hot jazz and gangs of bootleggers. Out of those threads is woven a tapestry of history, romance, drama, and mystery; connecting two generations and two families in the adventure of a lifetime.

Winner of the IBPA Benjamin Frankling Digital Awards (2016 Silver Honoree).

"The Bootlegger's Legacy takes the reader on a wild ride through Oklahoma's bootlegging history. It makes for a wonderful escape into a fascinating, dangerous, and strange world filled with characters your mother warned

Dog Gone Lies

(Pacheco & Chino Mysteries Book 1)

Sheriff Ray Pacheco returns from his introduction in The Bootlegger's Legacy to start a new chapter as a private investigator, along with his partners: Tyee Chino, often-drunk Apache fishing guide, and Big Jack, bait shop owner and philosopher.

The trio are pulled into a mystery immediately when an abandoned show dog appears at Ray's cabin and the dog's owner is reported missing. Ray and his team pursue leads that bring them into confrontations with the local sheriff, the mayor, and the FBI, while in the meantime two bodies are found—neither of which is the missing woman.

Sky High Stakes

(Pacheco & Chino Mysteries Book 2)

Tired of spending his days fishing, Ray Pacheco takes on his second assignment with his partner Tyee Chino when the state Attorney General asks them to find out just what the hell is going on in Ruidoso, New Mexico. With the town's sheriff in the hospital with a mysterious illness, acting sheriff Martin Marino is running rough-shod over everyone around him.

What seems like a simple assignment becomes more complicated when Marino is found dead, shot at close range while sitting in his patrol car on Main Street. The suspects include most of the town, from Dick Franklin, manager of Ruidoso Downs racetrack, to bar owner Tito Annoya, to members of the local law enforcement.

At the same time, Ray has an uneasy feeling that the AG is withholding critical details about what exactly is going on in Ruidoso—and why the state was so slow to respond.

It all comes to a surprising conclusion with the involvement of a Spanish princess, a drug lord gone mad, and a few other lowlifes . . . and leaves Ray wondering if maybe fishing wasn't so boring after all.

Murder So Wrong

(Muckraker Mystery #1, with Stanley Nelson)

After his first day as a political reporter in 1960s Oklahoma, Tommy Jacks finds himself investigating the murder of a competing reporter at the state capitol. The mystery becomes a story of intrigue, love and tragedy, involving a would-be mentor, a gorgeous lover, a jailed father, an adopted mom, and shocking violence.

Murder So Strange

(Muckraker Mystery #2, with Stanley Nelson)

In an exclusive residential neighborhood, a U.S. Senator's wife has died. Tommy Jacks and his fellow journalists don't believe the police chief's story blaming it on natural causes. It has the smell of a crime. So begins a new journey set in the 1960s involving numerous dead bodies, high-tension political intrigue, police corruption, the drug underworld and unsavory hidden pasts. Tommy has a lot to write about in his My View political column.

Only in his second year as a political columnist, he finds new romance and emotional healing among a chaotic mixture of characters, from his new mother and his recently out-of-jail father to his acerbic journalistic mentor and antagonist and a foul-mouthed lawyer of questionable ethics, all wrapped inside the saga of two competing daily newspapers still at war.

Lurking in the shadows is the powerful and corrupt police chief, who seems to think it might be best if Mister Jacks, even so young, was dead.

Murder So Strange continues the 1960s saga of Tommy Jacks: Muckraker.

And More...

To keep up-to-date on all of Ted's newest books, visit www.tedclifton.com.